NYMPHS OF
DIONYSUS

NYMPHS OF DIONYSUS

Susan Tinoff

This book is a work of fiction.
In real life, make sure you practise safe sex.

First published in 1997 by
Nexus
332 Ladbroke Grove
London W10 5AH

Copyright © Susan Tinoff 1997

Typeset by TW Typesetting, Plymouth, Devon

Printed and bound by
BPC Paperbacks Ltd, Aylesbury, Bucks

ISBN 0 352 33150 X

For J

One

Chryseis lay face down on the bench, her arms stretched back along her sides, her head resting on a pillow filled with sweet-smelling herbs. She felt languid and relaxed after a cool bath. It had been another hot day, and the evening breeze which came through the unshuttered window still carried the smell of baked earth from the vineyards surrounding the villa. The slight movement of air caressed her body, drying the last few droplets of water from her naked skin.

The dry, dusty smell from outside contrasted with the citrus tang of the oil her slave was preparing for her massage. Chryseis smiled in lazy anticipation and watched the uneven light from the terracotta oil-lamp play across the room's murals. The flickering glow made it seem as if the beasts and birds moved with irregular life, chasing each other along the sinuous painted river.

Palmeda came and stood beside her, rubbing the scented oil between the palms of her hands. Chryseis rose for a moment to take a mouthful of wine from the goblet on the table beside her, then lowered herself back down comfortably. Palmeda waited till she was settled before starting to massage her neck, probing the muscles with inquisitive fingertips then soothing them again with sensitive strokes. Gradually, Chryseis let her mind drift into drowsiness.

Palmeda worked Chryseis' back in silence for some time before clearing her throat and hesitating, as if

1

about to say something then changing her mind. She repeated the sound several times until Chryseis' stupor was broken and she began to get impatient with the slave. The unvoiced comments hung heavily in the air, disturbing the placid pleasure of her massage. Had it been any of the other household slaves who annoyed her in this way, she would have had them whipped. Eventually, she could stand it no longer and twisted round on the bench to break the silence herself.

'For Metis' sake, Palmeda, what is it you want to say?'

Palmeda looked down at the floor. 'Tomorrow ... I'm scared, mistress. I've never travelled by sea before. I've heard tales of strange beasts that devour ships whole.'

Chryseis laughed at her slave's simplicity, though it echoed her own fears. 'There are no monsters in these waters,' she reassured her. 'My uncle's trading often takes him across the Aegean, and he has never seen any. Anyway, we have no choice if I am to go to Chalcis and marry Timon.'

She lay down again, but on her back this time, and gestured for Palmeda to continue.

'Do you know what this Timon is like?' asked Palmeda, as she rubbed the oil into Chryseis' shoulders, digging for the muscles beneath the soft skin.

Chryseis sighed, knowing that now she had given the girl permission to speak only a direct order would shut her up. Then she would sulk and perform her job faultlessly but unimaginatively. 'Old,' she replied briefly, not wanting to dwell on it.

'Wouldn't you prefer someone younger? A virile young man who could give you everything you desire?' Palmeda probed.

Chryseis avoided inspecting her feelings too closely. Some things were predestined and fighting them would only bring unwarranted grief. 'My uncle chose him.

2

He's rich, I'll have a good life. Comfortable at least. And anyway, I'm sure I'll find a way to have a few lovers.'

Palmeda's hands circled down from Chryseis' shoulders to the upper slopes of her breasts. 'Timon's slaves will be loyal to him. They will know everything you do. If they refuse to aid you . . .'

Chryseis smiled as Palmeda's sure touch tingled against her skin. 'That is why I'm taking you as my personal maid, to make sure I don't suffer from too much neglect.'

Palmeda giggled and took the time to massage each nipple in turn, spiralling in from the circumference of Chryseis' areola to the hard nubs of flesh in their centres. 'You may not have noticed, mistress, but I lack certain . . . capabilities.'

Chryseis' laugh was mixed with a groan of pleasure. 'Not many. You cover your deficiencies well.' She caught her breath as Palmeda tweaked a little harder. 'You are right though, I should take advantage of every opportunity I can before the wedding. Fatten up my memories in case there are lean times ahead.'

'A wise course of action. Do you want to begin now? Shall I get one of the house slaves for you? Phaon perhaps? It is said he has no deficiencies at all. Or perhaps you would prefer a couple of labourers from the fields?'

'Mmmm, perhaps.' Chryseis teased, squirming in anticipation as Palmeda began to work her way down her belly. 'But since you are here, you may as well continue for the moment. We can always call them in later if your energies flag.'

'I don't expect they will. I am feeling particularly energetic today.' Palmeda's fingers passed over Chryseis' black triangle, moving on to knead the tops of her thighs. Chryseis held back a cry of complaint and let Palmeda continue at her own pace. The slave loved to

3

orment her, but the build-up was always worthwhile. Soon, the supple hands had completed the journey to her feet and were working their way back again.

Chryseis let her legs fall open and Palmeda began to stroke the soft skin of her inner thighs. Each pass of the slave's hands brushed the dark forest that lay between Chryseis' legs, sending signals to the core of her body, awakening it for action.

Chryseis felt herself moisten and open to the cool air as Palmeda's hands slowed and their touch became lighter. Now, they circled the small area of most responsive skin at the very tops of her thighs, the edge of her hand nudging insistently at the cleft of her sex.

Chryseis licked her lips and swallowed. The delicate sensations had her fully aroused now, and her need for relief was urgent. She opened her legs wider. 'Now,' she ordered in a whisper.

Palmeda slipped one finger into the wetness, then another, working them in and out, letting her thumb rub across the pearl of her sensitivity. Chryseis felt the heat spread from its core between her legs and wash all over her. It pulsed upwards in intensity till it was the only feeling she was aware of and the rest of the universe faded away. It was her favourite moment, on the absolute brink of orgasm when the joyous sensation was at its peak. She tried to hold back, to prolong it, but too soon she lost her balance and tipped over the edge into the brief spasms of relief.

Afterwards, Chryseis lay back with a faint feeling of regret that the experience was once again over. It was so fleeting, so ephemeral, that once it was past she would wonder where the hunger and need had come from. She brushed off Palmeda's hands that still gently caressed and stroked her body and stood up.

Palmeda rose also. 'Did I please you, mistress?' she asked, with her eyes downcast.

Chryseis hadn't the heart to blame the slave for her

4

own jaded mood. 'You did fine,' she said. 'I'm glad you are coming with me. You will make the sojourn less lonely.' She forced a laugh. 'And you are also to help me stockpile some memories, remember?'

'Certainly, mistress.'

With quickening interest, Chryseis added, 'My uncle has decided that we need a bodyguard for our journey. I hear that he intends to hire a mercenary for the job.'

Palmeda smiled as she caught Chryseis' meaning. 'And you have heard that mercenaries have a certain reputation as lovers?'

'Exactly. My uncle may be providing more cover for me than he had anticipated. I certainly hope so. We shall make this bodyguard my first diversion.'

Acantha lay on the bed in her lodging above the taverna, one hand behind her head, the other drowsily stroking Alexis' back. The serving lad had kept her company all afternoon and now curled against her with his cheek on her breast, his dark-lashed eyes closed. It was dusk now and he would have to go soon to help with the evening's influx of customers. Acantha wondered if she could afford to persuade him to return later.

Not that Alexis had demanded payment. Acantha flattered herself that she was still a good-looking woman and that he had taken as much pleasure from her as she had from him. But she was too experienced to ever again mistake such interest for love. She had ached for the smooth skin and graceful lines of many such youths. And in return she had learned to sweeten their interest with generous gifts which fell just short of outright payment.

Now, her funds were almost gone and it was time to earn some money again. As she grew older, however, her self-confidence waned and she felt the need to lavish even more upon the youths she desired while work itself was harder to come by. She sometimes felt the chilly mantle of age creep over her, and to throw it off she rolled over and began to kiss the sleeping lad's face.

Alexis woke with a start and for a moment Acantha could see into his unguarded eyes. She saw nothing there of what she feared, only sleepy pleasure, but even so she immediately mistrusted it, choosing to believe that the lad was a more proficient actor than she had given him credit for. To hide her confusion, she turned away to lift the amphora of wine from the floor and pass it to him.

Alexis hoisted it straight to his lips, gulping down several mouthfuls but letting much of the red liquid pour over his chin and run down his chest and belly. He looked down at himself, watching as the last drops trickled into the black hairs around his groin. 'I seem to have spilt some,' he said, as if in surprise, then grinned.

Acantha relaxed. 'That's a terrible waste,' she scolded.

'It is,' agreed Alexis, putting on a crestfallen expression. 'I would lick it off, but . . .' he curled his body in demonstration, '. . . I cannot reach.'

'I suppose I had better do it for you,' sighed Acantha. She leant forward and began to lick his face. The cheap wine was usually slightly sour but it improved greatly when lapped from warm flesh and Acantha let herself become immersed in the task. She cleaned his mouth and chin then nuzzled and licked the skin along his jaw and down his neck.

Alexis stirred and reached for her breasts, but she grasped his wrist and pushed him back on to the bed. The wine was already drying into long purple streaks as she followed the trail down his smooth chest. She cleaned him carefully, counting his ribs with her saliva-slick tongue, relishing the feel of hard bone under lean flesh. He squirmed and laughed when she probed too hard, tickling him, but she held him firm.

His stomach was softer, the muscles relaxed, and she

rubbed her cheek against its velvet smoothness. A small pool of wine had collected in his navel. She sucked it up with a kiss, lapping the indentation clean with her tongue.

Alexis groaned softly and she felt him brush her cheek. She turned her head at the touch and smiled at the sight of his erection straining towards her. She kissed its tip, then held it aside with her fingers as she followed the purple trail into the dark hairs surrounding its root. The smells of their earlier love-making were still sharp and clear. The scent of his semen and her own sweet juice mingled with the aroma of wine as she nuzzled his groin.

A hair caught in her mouth, trapping itself between her teeth. She fell back, laughing, as she worked it free.

Alexis used her moment of distraction to roll over and switch their roles. Now he pinned her arms down as he nipped at each breast in turn before rising up to examine her body with unhurried arrogance.

Acantha let him pretend for a moment that he owned her, but the inspection awoke once more her sense of uncertainty. Her body was no longer young and she wondered what was really going through Alexis' mind as his gaze flickered over the fine tracery of old wounds that marked her skin. He paused at the larger scar on her left shoulder and traced the hardened tissue with a finger.

Eventually his finger drifted, as she knew it would, towards the talisman that hung at her throat. It was a hand-span in size and she never took it off.

'You must be rich to afford such treasure,' Alexis said, then added as an afterthought, 'What kind of bird is it?'

Acantha laughed without mirth. How predictable the lad was. She shouldn't blame him, she supposed; he was only looking out for his interests. 'It's a phoenix, and it's the only treasure I have. It isn't for sale; it brings me luck.'

7

He stroked the heavy gold, as if counting the rubies set into the flames. Acantha watched with cynical detachment.

'I took it off the first man I killed,' she said casually and laughed again, harder, when Alexis quickly drew his hand away. 'I'd never been in a battle before and I thought I was going to die. Instead, it was someone else's turn, and I lived.'

'The bird wasn't so lucky for him then.'

'I don't know; maybe it was. He was an old soldier, a rare thing, and when he died it was from a single blow. Surely that's as much luck as any warrior can ask for in this world.' She stretched over the side of the bed and picked up the bronze sword which, as always, lay within easy reach. 'Look,' she said, holding it up. 'When I had this made, I had a matching design cast into the hilt. I have the same device painted on my shield. It's my good luck.'

'And when you lose it, you will die?'

'No. I'm not that superstitious. But if I ever lose it, things will be going badly wrong.' She stroked the outline of the bird delicately, then replaced the sword by the bed. The only weapon she needed now belonged to Alexis. She was just about to arrange for it to be sheathed when there was a knock at the door.

'Mistress? Are you in?' It was Cronan, the owner of the taverna, his voice wheezing from the effort of hoisting his fat body up the stairs.

'Yes. What do you want?' Acantha called, irritated because he probably wanted Alexis to return to his duties in the kitchen. Or he was looking for the rent, which was worse.

'There's a man downstairs. He wishes to speak to you.'

'Who?' She asked, immediately suspicious. She didn't have friends who made social calls.

There was a pause. 'It's difficult to talk ... If I may come in?'

'If he sees me, he'll drag me back downstairs,' warned Alexis in a whisper.

'That would ruin my plans for you. No, I need you here. I know ...' Acantha sat up and leaned back against the wall, then pulled the blanket up to cover him completely, leaving herself exposed from the waist up. 'We'll pretend you're not there,' she declared brazenly, looking at the large hump he made.

'It is terribly dark under here,' Alexis protested with a laugh as he squirmed about. 'I can't see where I am going ... Oh, what is this I've bumped into? All warm and covered in hair. It's a little animal to keep me company in my cave.'

'Don't you dare –'

'Mistress?' Cronan called again from outside the door.

'All right, all right. You'd better come in,' Acantha shouted, slapping at Alexis' head.

The door scraped across the floor as it opened and Cronan sidled in. Acantha wrinkled her nose at the sight. He was a sweaty ball of lard, and his tunic was spattered with food from the kitchens. His eyes opened wide at the sight of her naked breasts, and he licked his lips nervously.

His stare annoyed her. She didn't mind a little honest lechery, but there was something furtive about him that she found faintly repellent. It made her want to cover herself up, but she'd be damned before she allowed the likes of him make her hide herself. Instead, she lifted her chest defiantly and let him look a little longer before demanding, 'Well? I thought you were going to tell me who was asking for me. Who is it?'

Cronan looked up at her face with a guilty start. 'He refused to say, but I know him anyway.' He smiled beseechingly, like a puppy seeking a reward.

Beneath the blankets, Alexis stirred. Acantha could feel his fingers tracing the soft skin of her inner thighs

9

as he turned his head in her lap. Cronan saw the motion and swallowed convulsively.

Acantha laughed silently to herself, and let Alexis nudge her thighs further apart. 'And?' she demanded, as if totally unaware of any activity under the blanket.

'And?' repeated Cronan, looking blank for a moment. 'Oh, yes. His name is Pythias, a local landowner. He is looking for a bodyguard, he said. He insisted that only a woman would do.'

Acantha nodded thoughtfully. Several times in the past she had met men who enjoyed being dominated. They seemed to find strong women exciting, especially when they were dressed as warriors in hardened leather armour. Acantha had even responded to a few of the more pleasing ones, and considered the experiences intriguing, if not especially to her own tastes. Certainly, in her current financial circumstances, she was not in a position to be fussy about her next job.

Alexis' fingers delicately stroked along the lips of her vulva, carefully easing them open.

'Send him up,' she said. 'I'll see him here.'

Cronan paused. 'I think it would be better if you came down,' he suggested.

Acantha shook her head and restrained a small start as Alexis' fingers began to probe deeper. If this Pythias really enjoyed being dominated, his first taste of humiliation would be having to stand by and watch Alexis make love to her while they discussed business. It would add a little zest to their bargaining and put up her price. 'If he wants to see me, he can come up here,' she replied breathlessly as she let the twin peaks of her blanket-covered knees move further apart.

Cronan wrung his hands in agitation, and Acantha was sure she could see the front hem of his tunic lift slightly from the pressure below. 'Go on, tell him,' she ordered again, and after a moment's hesitation, the man shuffled away.

10

Alexis' head emerged from underneath the blanket. 'Can I come out now?' he laughed. 'Is it safe?'

'No, I don't think so. I think you'd better hide again, just in case he comes back.' Acantha grinned as she put her hand on his head and pushed him back beneath the cover. 'Your little friend will get lonely otherwise.'

'I think I am getting hungry and may have to eat her. Do you think –'

There was a sharp knock at the door and, without pausing, a heavy-set man strode in. His himation, the toga-like sheet worn by the Greeks, was of fine wool and draped in elegant pleats over his left shoulder, then fastened beneath his right arm with an expensive-looking silver pin. He had a thick, well-shaped beard and he took in the scene with a single glance of distaste from beneath glowering eyebrows. 'You are the mercenary?' he demanded.

Acantha slapped Alexis away and stood up, ignoring her nakedness to confront the intruder. She had misinterpreted what this man wanted, that was for sure, and now she was keyed up and alert. 'Yes, I'm Acantha. And you are Pythias, a local landowner.' She repeated Cronan's snippet of information casually, as if it were the least part of her knowledge. 'What can I do for you?'

'My niece and I are travelling to Chalcis on the island of Euboea, where she is to be married. I am her guardian and I require a bodyguard to look after her.'

'I heard you were especially looking for a female bodyguard. Why?'

Pythias snorted in derision. 'I thought that would have been obvious, even to you. It will be a long journey. I wish for a female bodyguard so as to avoid any possible last-minute temptations to my ward. Her husband-to-be demands that his bride be chaste.'

Acantha held back her anger at the overbearing little man. She could put up with a lot, if the payment was right. 'I want two drachmas a day.'

11

'Two? What makes you think I still want to employ you after this lewd display?'

'You're paying for my skills as a fighter, not my morals. Those are my own business.'

'You would still be a bad example to my ward. She is still an innocent. For your ability as a bodyguard ...' He looked her up and down, as if buying a slave.

Acantha endured the inspection without embarrassment; her body might be scarred, but it was still trim enough. She had not gone flabby.

'I see you are from the northern regions,' Pythias said, commenting on her fair skin and light red hair. 'They have a reputation as fighters. Three obols.'

'Three obols?' She genuinely felt slighted; the offer was only a quarter of her suggestion. 'For that you'd barely get an old veteran who'd lost both legs. Eight obols, or nothing.'

Pythias glowered at her, his thin lips twitching within the nest of his beard. 'Eight, then,' he spat with ill grace. 'Meet us at the docks in the morning. We sail with the noon tide.' Without waiting for a reply he strode from the room, leaving the door hanging open.

Alexis' head popped into view again. 'Has he gone?' he asked, looking around.

Acantha grinned at the lad. 'Yes. I'm glad I wasn't relying on you for protection,' she teased.

'Hey, I'm no bodyguard.' He winked. 'Except of the most intimate kind. But you're not going to work for him, are you? He's a nasty piece of work.'

'I've worked for far worse. Pythias is just a pompous old wind-bag who has no authority other than what he buys.' She shrugged. 'And just now, I need the cash.'

'If you go, I'll miss you,' Alexis said, mournfully.

'All you'll miss is my money, and I've just told you I don't have any more.'

Alexis shook his head. 'So brave, yet so little confidence. I care nothing for your money.'

'Really?' Acantha snorted. 'And would you have been so eager to please me if I hadn't been so generous?'

Alexis smiled easily. 'Why don't you close the door and find out?' he drawled in a low voice. 'Tonight will be just for the fun of it. Something to remember during the long dark nights of the journey, when you only have your cloak to keep you warm.'

Acantha turned and laughed in the face of one of the taverna's patrons who was staring at them from the hallway, then slammed the door shut and returned to the bed. 'So where did we leave off?' she asked.

Alexis lifted himself on one elbow and pushed her gently on to her back. Then he leaned over her and traced a fingertip round the pale circle of her left areola, so gently she could feel only the lightest of touches. 'About here, I think.' He sounded very serious. 'I was just inspecting your breasts.'

Acantha looked down at herself. 'They're a bit small, aren't they?'

'Mmmm,' he considered. 'They are not as large as some, but that is different from being too small. They are a nice size and well shaped.' He cupped her breast where it spilled over the side of her ribs, lifting it to his lips. He brushed her nipple with a kiss, sending a sweet ripple of sensation down to her belly, then drew his head back to examine it again.

They both watched as her nipple hardened and seemed to grow slightly.

'Kiss it again,' Acantha whispered.

Alexis obediently dipped down and put his mouth to the little nub of flesh. He moved his head slightly from side to side, so that she could feel his soft lips rub across the very tip of her nipple, sending shivers of anticipation through her body. Occasionally, he moved his head further, so that he rubbed her with the silky skin of his cheek, or the faint stubble of his chin. Each change of texture produced a new sensation, kept her interest

13

alive, though as yet he had not strayed from that one tiny area of her flesh.

His tongue emerged, wet with saliva, and circled the tiny peak, enveloping it in slick warmth. Her nipple stood up fully now, refusing to bend under the pressure of his insistent examination. Acantha put her hand up behind his head, digging through his wiry hair so that she could feel it tickling the softer skin between her fingers, then pulled his head firmly against her.

Alexis responded hungrily, sucking hard on her breast so that the nipple, areola and surrounding flesh were drawn into his mouth. Acantha gasped at the intensity of the sensation and arched her back in pleasure, pushing herself harder against his warm, wet mouth.

Alexis continued to suck on her breast, kneading the pliant flesh with his lips and tongue, drawing it in between his sharp teeth. Her skin sang with the vibrancy of the feeling that spread out from her breast to her belly and down to her groin, where it lingered, unsatisfied and wanting more.

Acantha slipped her hand between her thighs, feeling how her labia were swollen and wet. She slipped two fingers inside herself, juddering with nearly painful pleasure as her work-roughened fingers scraped that most delicate of flesh. She rubbed herself gently, resisting the urge to let her body take control and to bring herself rapidly to orgasm. There was no hurry. Instead, she drew her slick fingers out from within her and smeared her juices across her breast, beside Alexis' mouth.

The rich, musky smell seemed to fill the air. Alexis moved his attention from her nipple to lick up the glistening fluid, then he lifted his head as if seeking more. Acantha slipped her fingers between his lips, sliding them in and out as he sucked them clean, dancing with his tongue in the darkness of his mouth.

She withdrew her fingers, dipped them again into the

14

nectar forming between her thighs, and fed it to him again. This time, when he had lapped her fingers clean, he drew back himself and, with a small smile, slid down her body so he could drink from the source directly.

He wasted no time in gentle circling, there was no need for further preliminaries. He placed his hands at the soft spot at the top of each thigh and pushed them back and apart so that her sex was fully exposed to his gaze. Then he kissed her lightly, once, on her engorged labia, before hungrily nuzzling into her, simultaneously seeming to probe her with his tongue, nose and lips as if he wanted to bury himself entirely within her.

She could feel his nose pressing against her clitoris as his tongue strained to delve deeply within her. He twisted his head from side to side, perhaps trying to reach further inside her, trying to fuck her completely with his tongue, perhaps intentionally rubbing his nose against her little pearl. His hunger for her, the desperate need he seemed to have for her body, stimulated her as much as the physical sensations. She could feel her skin tingle as her breath grew shorter and the world shrank till it consisted of little more than the sensation of his mouth on her genitals.

She grabbed his head and held him tight as she rocked her hips in unison with his writhing, flickering tongue. She moved faster, the blood pounding in her head. She could hear her own voice gasping and groaning, getting louder and louder. There was hot pleasure in her loins, spreading out, filling her. And then, for a brief moment it filled the whole world and she bucked wildly and uncontrollably as she screamed out in release.

Alexis gave her no time to recover. He swivelled round rapidly, reversing the position of his mouth on her vulva and presenting his engorged penis for her attention, rubbing it against her face. She grasped it by its root and drew it to her mouth. The purple head was shining with moisture and she could smell the tang of

15

his arousal. She wet her tongue and ran it over the smooth, tight skin, delighting in the way his organ twitched in response. The taste was slightly salty, one she had come to know and love over the years, and despite her recent orgasm she felt her interest quicken again.

She probed the tiny eye-hole at the tip of his organ with her tongue, then kissed it lightly. Gradually, the kiss became hungrier and she opened her mouth wider till Alexis' shining helmet slid between her lips. He tried to push further within her, but she held him back for a moment. Instead she opened her legs wider, clasping him with her thighs in an invitation for him to resume his attentions. She felt his breath on her sex, tickling it, then his tongue probing for her clitoris. She drew his penis further within her mouth in reply, massaging it with her tongue and lips. Alexis' tongue trembled against the focus of her pleasure, awakening it to life as she bobbed her head back and forth over his erection.

Her breath quickened once more as she pictured the circle of their love-making, her mouth over his sex, his over hers, in an unending loop. His hips moved more hurriedly now and she could feel him tightening, ready for release. The knowledge excited her, made her suck harder upon his manhood, eagerly trying to draw the semen from within him. His tongue darted ever more swiftly in return, her excitement feeding his, his feeding hers.

Alexis' penis seemed to swell even more than before, as if ready to burst, then it pulsed and jerked, filling her mouth with thick salty fluid. He drew back slightly, so that semen splashed across her face, filling her nostrils with its faintly pungent aroma. The smell and taste filled her senses and, once more, she tipped over into orgasm, gentler this time, a quieter finish to their love-making.

Gradually, she regained her breath and her heart slowed to a mere pounding beat. Alexis was also gasping for breath and she realised wryly that in her passion she had clamped her thighs around his head, nearly suffocating the poor lad. His face was flushed and shone with both his sweat and her juices, but he grinned contentedly at her as he bestowed feather-light kisses to her still sensitive labia.

Acantha responded in kind, gently lapping the spilt semen from the head of his subsiding erection, stroking his buttocks and thighs. Alexis turned, so that his face was level with hers, and licked the last of his seed from her cheek and lips. Then he lay down beside her and closed his eyes.

Her last thought before she drifted into sleep was that she was glad her parting love-making with Alexis had been so satisfying. If Pythias had his way, it would no doubt be the last sex she had for some while.

Two

To pass the time while waiting for Pythias, Acantha made herself comfortable on a pile of old fishing nets and watched lines of men load the ship they were to travel on.

It was a medium-sized merchant galley, big enough for about fifteen oars down each side. A third of the way from the high, curving prow was a single mast on which a square sail could be hoisted when the wind blew exactly right. The rest of the time the crew would work in shifts, rowing non-stop to keep the ship moving.

A cabin was perched on the deck like an afterthought, its only fixed part being the roof. The walls were merely matting screens which were currently tied up around the edge of the roof, ready to be let down when required. Presumably, when there were no passengers, the cabin was used by the crew. This trip they would have to sleep with the cargo, either on deck where Acantha had watched them lashing down bales of wool, or in the low cramped hold where they had stowed a hundred or more large amphorae of wine.

'I hope you're more alert than you look,' snapped Pythias behind her.

Acantha looked up from her comfortable spot and quelled her flare of anger at his tone; she had been well aware of his approach. Still, Pythias employed her now; she should remember her place. She got to her feet in a single, easy motion. 'Of course, sir,' she said equably, offering no further explanation.

18

Pythias' dark eyes glittered beneath his heavy brows. Eventually, however, he gestured behind him, in the direction of the two women who accompanied them. 'My niece, Chryseis,' he said, by way of introduction. His gesture was vague but there was no doubt as to which of the two he was referring. Although the women were both young and presentable, one was dressed in the simple sleeveless dress called a peplos, while the other wore the more fashionable linen chiton, which originated from this region of Ionia. It was made from a single sheet of the material, folded in half, so that the crease formed the seam between front and back that ran down the left side. The two halves were then pinned over the arms with a series of silver clasps, and held around the waist by a finely embroidered girdle. The front and back were not held together down the right side of the garment, and occasionally parted sufficiently to reveal the warm flesh within. Obviously, the latter was Pythias' ward, while the first woman was no more than a slave, of no account in his reckoning.

Acantha bowed courteously to each in turn. 'M'lady. I hope I can serve you well,' she said politely.

To her surprise, Chryseis merely glared at her, for some reason more annoyed with Acantha than her uncle had been. As Acantha wondered what she had done, Chryseis brushed past her and clambered unsteadily up the narrow gangplank, her maid scurrying nervously behind her.

Acantha studied the retreating figure with disparaging care. The young woman looked soft and self-indulgent. Her body was shapely enough, but the curves came from easy living and in a few years she would be a fat old matron wheezing from the excess weight she carried. Her face promised no future delight either. It was marred by unhappiness so that her mouth turned down at the corners and her eyelids drooped in contempt at all she saw.

Despite this, Chryseis exuded a heavy sensuality which proclaimed her love of pleasure to any with the eyes to see it. If Pythias really believed there was any hope of preserving her chastity, then he was a gullible old fool. Unless Acantha had seriously misread her, it was long gone.

'Hurry up,' snapped Pythias as he turned on his heel. 'I'm not paying you to day-dream.'

Acantha sighed, picked up her small bag of belongings, her sword and her shield and followed.

When she dropped her possessions under the roof of their cabin, Chryseis looked up from where she was already settled on a small rush mat. 'What's she doing here?' she snapped at Pythias.

'Acantha's your bodyguard. She's here to protect you.' He stated it bluntly, as if not caring whether Chryseis approved or not.

Chryseis folded her arms. 'I don't need protecting.'

'You do not realise how dangerous the world is outside the safety of my estate, Chryseis. I want to be sure that no one molests you.'

Acantha kept quiet. It was going to be pretty cramped in here anyway, but if she volunteered to sleep on deck Pythias would probably force her to stay, just in order to assert his authority.

Chryseis looked Acantha up and down. 'If I'm going to be molested by anyone, it's probably by her. Real women can never be soldiers.'

Pythias gave Acantha a heavy look. 'I don't think you need worry about that,' he said dryly. 'I would not have hired her had I thought her tastes unnatural. However . . .' He gestured with his hand, dismissing Acantha as if she were no more than a fly.

With relief the mercenary went to seek out a quiet corner for herself amongst the cargo. Despite the over-riding petulance, she had seen the speculative way in which the young woman had examined her body and

20

the small *moue* of disappointment when she had been told that Acantha wouldn't be interested in her. Acantha just wished it were true. Instead she had a feeling, mostly a familiar flutter in the pit of her stomach when she was near Chryseis, that this job was going to become more complicated. Chryseis was going to bring her nothing but grief; she was sure of it.

Chryseis scowled at Acantha's back as she left the cabin. It wasn't the warrior's fault that she was a woman, but Chryseis had hoped for the company of a man to pass the idle moments of the journey with. Even so, the mercenary's masculine leanness had its own appeal, as had the exotic red tinge to her hair. The leather tunic she wore instead of a normal woman's dress left the light skin of her arms and legs bare, showing them to be firm and supple yet without a man's heaviness. Had Pythias not indicated that her tastes lay elsewhere it would have been interesting to bed her and explore that intriguing mix of male and female qualities in one body.

Chryseis leant back against Palmeda and let her imagination roam freely as the slave brushed her hair. In her mind she saw the warrior woman totally subservient to her, forced to obey every command without question. She would make her regret her insolent ways; she would make her crawl across the floor and kiss her feet, licking them clean, sucking each toe in turn. From there, Chryseis would permit her to clean her ankles, shins, knees and then onward. Acantha would resist then, balking from the sweet softness of Chryseis' inner thighs, but Chryseis would insist and the proud mercenary would have to obey. Maybe Chryseis would have to punish Acantha; the thought made her smile. A chain around the warrior's neck, a whip to lash that fine body and bend it to her will. One way or another she would make that aloof woman bow her head to Chryseis' aching sex and lap it like a fawning pet.

21

Chryseis wriggled in sensuous delight at the picture and Palmeda, dear Palmeda who always anticipated her every command, stroked her neck with shivering delicacy as she continued to brush Chryseis' hair. Chryseis wriggled back some more so that her shoulders pressed against the soft pillows of Palmeda's breasts.

Perhaps Chryseis should require Acantha to attend on Palmeda as well; it would be interesting to watch her slaves pleasure each other, their heads dipped between each other's legs. Or better, both working together for Chryseis' sole delight, one hot mouth on each nipple while their fingers danced together in the slick tunnel of her vagina, courting the hard nub of her clitoris, fighting over the honour of gratifying her.

As her breath grew shorter at the vision behind her closed eyes, Chryseis felt herself moisten and open, and wished she could satisfy the desire swelling within her. It was difficult under the open cabin, with Pythias only a few feet away, absorbed in his scrolls of accounts, and with the crew working around them. Even so, Palmeda grew more bold, sliding her hand through the loose opening at the side of Chryseis' chiton, stroking the subtle mound of her stomach and the heavy globes of her breasts. Her agile fingers found Chryseis' already erect nipples and rubbed them gently, arousing them even further and making Chryseis' sex tingle with impossible desire.

Hovering between pleasure and frustration, Chryseis leant back against her slave and surveyed the crew through half-closed eyes. Perhaps she could arrange something with one of them later. She had heard that sailors sometimes picked up interesting tricks on their travels and Chryseis was an avid student of all strange customs relating to sex. In the meantime, she could only watch the sailors' firm bodies as they went about their work.

They were getting ready to depart. Illaris, the ship's

master, shouted orders and men scurried to obey. Ropes were cast off and, while several men used long poles to push the ship away from the quay, others settled at the rowing benches and readied the oars. Illaris gave a long, drawn-out shout and raised one arm. The rowers made ready and as Illaris cut the cry off and jerked his arm down they dipped their oars into the water on each side of the craft and pulled back. Chryseis could feel the ship jerk forward with the force of the stroke. There was a moment's pause, then Illaris shouted again. There was another stroke, then another and the initial uneven motion as they built up speed settled into a regular rhythm.

The ship headed west, past the protecting quay and started to rise and fall in the swell of the open Aegean Sea. The white, flat-roofed buildings of Ephesus receded behind them and as they moved further out to sea, Chryseis could see further along the coast of Ionia to where Pythias' estate clung to the hillside. It had been her home for almost fifteen years, ever since her parents had died, and she felt uneasy at leaving it. She would have felt frightened had she allowed herself to, but there wasn't any point in it. Her fate was not within her control. She was a piece in Pythias' schemes to form a trading alliance between his family and Timon's. It was as much as she could expect from life.

She rubbed a hand over her face as if to erase the thought. The movement caught Pythias' eye and he put down the scroll he had been studying to come over and speak to them. 'How are you feeling?' he asked Chryseis, not noticing Palmeda's hand as it slithered out from inside her dress. 'The ship's motion doesn't trouble you?'

'Only slightly,' Chryseis replied, touched for a moment by his concern. She didn't add that the only bother was that the undulating movement added to her horniness and she couldn't see any way of relieving the problem.

'Good. It's a long trip and we don't want you looking sickly when we arrive at Chalcis. Timon is expecting a healthy bride and I am relying upon you to fulfil your duty.'

'Certainly, uncle.' Chryseis bowed her head to hide her disappointed anger. She might have known his concern was not for her. 'I will not let you down.'

'Good, good. It might do you good to walk around a bit though. You are looking somewhat flushed.'

Chryseis stood obediently. 'Come on, Palmeda. You can keep me company,' she said and hurried out from under the low roof of the cabin.

Outside, Illaris was shouting more instructions. The rowers unshipped their oars and ran to hoist the white square sail, heaving on the ropes as the great sheet rose to the top of the mast. As she walked past the men she was very aware of their eyes following her. She could feel them inspecting her body, from oiled hair to sandalled feet, lingering over the soft ache of her breasts, the tingling curve of her buttocks. She could smell the fresh sweat as their muscled bodies bunched and relaxed, pulling in unison on the ropes. She could hear them grunting with effort as their sinews cracked. Her nostrils flared at the aroma of their masculinity; her mouth grew dry and her belly fluttered in excitement. She couldn't remember having felt this horny ever before.

They reached the prow and Chryseis leant back against the bulwark, watching the crew work. 'All these men, and no way to get at them,' she grumbled.

Palmeda glanced back at the figure of their bodyguard, Acantha, sprawled out on top of some wool bales, laughing and joking with the crew. 'She doesn't seem the sort to spoil another's fun,' she observed.

'Then why did my uncle hire her?' Chryseis demanded. 'I only ask for a little excitement before I'm incarcerated in Timon's private estate.'

The last ropes were tied and the crew settled down for

a rest as the sail filled out and sped them through the rising sea. A couple of the men came forward and leant over the rail nearby.

'You like watching the dolphins?' the younger one asked.

Chryseis hadn't noticed them but briefly turned to look at a pair of the sleek creatures sporting in the clear waters by the bow. Then she turned back and let her gaze linger over the sailor's tanned skin. 'They are beautiful,' she agreed. 'They look so smooth, like polished stone.'

'But they don't sink like one, eh?' the other sailor said. The joke was feeble but his laugh was a deep rumble, just what might be expected to emerge from his bull-like chest. Soon the four of them were chatting and laughing easily and Chryseis learnt that the younger sailor was called Eldo, his larger companion Leonidas. Both were fine-looking men, though in completely different ways. Eldo was younger, slimmer, with smooth unblemished skin and only the first wisps of a beard. Leonidas was a giant of a man, covered in hair from head to foot.

They stood at the bow talking for some time. The men boasted of their travels and the far-away places they had seen; the women exclaimed in surprised awe and showed how impressed they were. Soon their home was no more than a thin line on the horizon behind them, and as they sailed further out on to the ocean the waves increased in size and the ship's motion became more vigorous. A particularly unexpected movement threw Chryseis against Leonidas. The man supported her with an arm like a small tree trunk, taking her weight with ease. 'Careful, m'lady,' he said laughing. 'The seas are getting up. We wouldn't want to lose you.'

'I've heard that the dolphins save people from drowning,' Chryseis said, not moving back from his hold, her hand resting against his bare chest, ruffling the dark

25

hairs. 'Wouldn't I be safe?' The question had nothing to do with dolphins.

Leonidas' laugh rumbled in his throat as his hand casually drifted down to her buttock, curving underneath it so the tips of his fingers approached her most sensitive places. 'Maybe, but I wouldn't try it just now though. Our friends are leaving us; they don't hang around once the weather begins to turn.' He pointed to where the creatures were disappearing into the distance. As Leonidas had said, dark clouds were accumulating in the sky and the sea looked cold and murky.

'I'd have to rely on you then, wouldn't –'

'What are you doing? Get your hands off my niece. Now! Immediately, do you hear me?' Pythias bustled up, his face red with fury. The ship's master, Illaris, followed close behind, looking worried.

Leonidas backed away and Chryseis felt a pang of disappointment. Even this great bull of a man wouldn't stand up to Pythias. He would get his way again, as he always did.

'Didn't you see this?' Pythias shouted at the mercenary woman who was sitting up and watching them. 'Didn't you see this animal mauling my niece?'

'It looked to me as if she slipped and he –'

'Don't argue with me! I know your sort. I expect you to do your job, not flirt with the crew.'

Humiliated and embarrassed, Chryseis hurried away without listening to the rest of the tirade that followed and for the rest of the afternoon she stayed under their shelter, with Pythias watching her sharply. All she had to occupy herself was to keep a surreptitious eye on the crew and watch the storm clouds gradually fill the sky. It wasn't long before the first drops of rain spattered around them and Palmeda was instructed to unroll the matting walls to their shelter. Then they huddled inside, listening to the wind and rain lash their frail cabin.

At dusk, while Chryseis and Palmeda ate figs and

26

oranges, Pythias hung back, avoiding the sight of food. Soon they heard him retching over the side of the ship. Chryseis giggled at the sound and helped herself to another fig, tearing it in half with her thumbs and sucking out the seed-filled flesh. The wild motion of the ship excited her and made her feel alive, and even the simplest acts seemed more vivid than normal.

'I think I'll get some fresh air,' she said.

Palmeda gave her a knowing look. 'I'll stay,' she said. She clutched her stomach. 'I don't think I can . . .' She closed her eyes and swallowed visibly.

'Oh, well. All the more for me,' Chryseis declared and slipped out through a gap in the mat walls and on to the rain-swept deck. She made her way forward, clutching at the cargo lashings for support. In the gathering dusk she could not, at first, see anyone. Then she made out a lone figure standing at the prow. From his huge silhouette she could tell it was Leonidas, wrapped in a cloak of oiled leather. 'Where is everyone?' she called over the wind.

He wiped the rain from his face and grinned at her. 'Below, in the hold.'

'Why aren't you with them?' She leant with the deck as it tilted from side to side and held his arm for support.

'I'm the lookout. Someone has to make sure we don't run aground, though what I'm supposed to see out here, the gods alone know.' He slipped his arm around her waist and drew her close, enveloping her within his cloak. 'Are you going to keep me company?'

'You got into trouble for that before,' she warned, but didn't pull away. Beneath the cloak he wore only the short working kilt common to the sailors. In the cold rain she could feel the heat radiating from him, alerting her whole body to his proximity.

Leonidas' laugh was rich and full. 'That's why I'm here. Our captain, Illaris, thought I should pull an extra

27

shift for having dared to touch you.' He nodded towards the ship's stern. 'Eldo's been made steersman.'

Chryseis had to lean back to look up into his face. His black beard hid most of it, but even in the darkness she could make out the amused glint in his eyes. 'How unfair,' she said, 'having to pay the penalty without having reaped any of the benefits.'

'And do you believe in fairness?' He raised an eyebrow quizzically.

'Oh, absolutely. I shall go to Illaris and protest. Make him reduce your punishment.' She patted his big chest reassuringly. 'After all, you hardly touched me.'

'He won't listen.' Leonidas heaved a great sigh of regret. 'He is not a reasonable man.'

'No? Well, since it seems you must endure the punishment, I can only make sure you get the appropriate benefits, can't I?' Chryseis let her fingers wander through the hairs of his chest, seeking out a nipple and pinching it gently.

'It seems the only course,' agreed Leonidas seriously. 'I think we were in about this position before,' he said, placing his huge hand on her buttock.

'Perhaps more over this way,' she said, adjusting the position slightly so that he could feel the cleft of her behind more clearly. She rested her head against his barrel-like chest, letting the warmth of his body seep into her. 'There. That's better. I don't see what all the fuss was about. Do you?'

She closed her eyes a moment, savouring the sensations of the moment: the tossing of the ship and Leonidas' restraining embrace, the crash of the waves and the tang on her lips of the salt spray, the cold rain trickling down her head and dripping from her hair while the rest of her remained snug under the cloak. It was a wild moment and she revelled in it, treasuring it in her mind as a moment to remember.

Leonidas bent his head to hers, nuzzling her wet skin.

With surprising gentleness for such a giant, he licked the rainwater from her eyes, brushed her lips with his.

She responded eagerly, flickering her tongue against his in a slick dance. He pulled her closer, belly to belly, his soaked beard cold against her face, his chest pressing her breasts flat. She felt his erection nudge at her hip and squirmed against him, enhancing the sensation of touch along the length of her body, rubbing her legs against his and wishing she could feel him with every small bit of her skin at once. His hands moved restlessly in reply, walking down her vertebrae one by one, stroking her body through the linen of her dress.

He drew away slightly, then tried to undo the girdle which kept her chiton clasped around her waist. His big fingers fumbled at the laces and she slapped them away. For a moment he looked hurt, until he saw her undo the knots herself. She pulled the garment over her head, not bothering with unfastening the clasps along each sleeve, then hesitated a moment with the bunched material clasped to her chest, revelling in the little-boy look of anticipation on Leonidas' face and the broad smile of delight when she let it drop.

Chryseis had worn nothing beneath the dress and, though Leonidas could have seen little in the twilight gloom, she stepped back from his enveloping cloak so that he could examine her bare body. The rain and wind ran icy fingers across her skin, puckering her nipples and running with insolent familiarity between her legs. She had not been naked to the elements since she was a child and she stood with her arms and legs wide, like a giant star, laughing with joy at the sense of freedom as air and water caressed her skin.

Leonidas laughed with her, sharing her delight. He slipped the cloak from his shoulders, then undid the broad belt that secured his kilt. In a moment he was as naked as she and, although she had seen the rest of his body while he had been working, she now had a chance to examine his manhood. She was pleased to see that it was in proportion to the rest of him and that it rose up eagerly in front of him, as if searching her out, swaying as the ship rocked on the turbulent ocean.

A fire seemed to ignite in her belly at the sight. She moved back against the opposite bulwark, the rough timber vivid against her rain-softened skin, then leant back on her elbows and with feet spread thrust her hips forward.

Leonidas stepped closer but paused just short of her so that the head of his bobbing erection brushed lightly through the short hairs of her mound. She laughed at the teasing, then pushed her hips further towards him, catching his penis in the crease that led between her thighs, one spot of warmth in the cold night. They smiled into each other's eyes in mutual agreement, then Chryseis lifted one leg, hooking it around Leonidas' waist, opening her sex in welcome to his.

Leonidas nudged forward, the length of his penis stroking between her legs, exciting her even further till she thought her juices were sufficient to wash away even the rain. She could have sworn she felt every single vein, every ridge and hollow along the length of his member as it caressed her labia, inviting them to open even further in readiness. Only then did he let the tip of his penis seek out her entrance. It slid unhindered between her open lips in a single thrust. Despite her arousal, Chryseis drew a long breath as his hard flesh pushed its way into the welcoming softness of her vagina. It stretched the delicate walls apart, forcing its way up inside her belly till his pubic bone bumped against hers, filling her with heat.

Still they kept the rest of their bodies apart, letting the wind and lashing rain stimulate their skins with feral fingers. Apart from Leonidas' hand supporting her leg around his waist, there was no other contact between them. He did not even move himself within her, letting

30

the rolling motion of the ship do the work for him, sliding him gently in and out of her in time with the waves. Her clitoris was sandwiched exquisitely by the motion while the tip of his manhood nudged at her cervix. It was like the elements themselves were making love to her and she laughed in delight as the rain trickled in cold rivulets over her upturned face and the sea broke against the side of the ship. Only the heat of his flesh reminded her that he was human and not some spirit of nature.

Lightning flashed, letting her glimpse his eyes and wide, panting mouth. He seemed as possessed by the experience as she and when the crash of thunder rolled over them seconds later, he lifted his head and roared in exultation. Then, as if it had been a signal he began to move his hips, driving his member within her, grasping her now with his other hand and pulling her on to him. She felt impaled, felt him harden and grow with every stroke, stretching her even further.

Now she wanted to feel nothing but his body, to envelop every part of him and draw it into her. She hooked her other leg up around his waist also, trapping him within her by the strength of her thighs, and when he shifted his hands beneath her buttocks she levered herself up to clasp her arms around his neck. He supported her fully now, his great hands lifting her up and down upon his hard length.

Her clitoris rubbed hard against his pubic bone and she rocked her hips back and forth to increase the pressure. Harder and harder she pressed as if truly seeking to create fire, but the heat was all within her, flooding up from her groin to suffuse her breasts, throat and face in a warm flush. Suddenly she was there, on that plateau of pure sensation. She slowed abruptly, trying to prolong the moment, but it was too late and her body bucked and heaved as she cried with mingled pleasure and loss.

Leonidas continued to move, lifting her up and down upon his member. His breath was shallow and he made small whimpering sounds deep in his throat as he approached his own climax. She wanted to delay him, prevent him from coming so that he would continue to pleasure her, but abruptly she felt him pulse within her, explode with his seed as the sky filled once more with lightning.

Chryseis clung to Leonidas' great body like a limpet, forcing her mouth upon his, sucking on his tongue, drawing it into her mouth, wanting the pleasure to go on and on. Leonidas tried, flickering his tongue in response to hers, but his moment of passion was spent. She could feel him subside within her and knew it would take time for him to work up to such a frenzy again.

Just as disappointment washed over her she felt another pair of hands caress her body, their cold, wet fingers running over her ribs and back. She twisted round, still hanging in Leonidas' grasp, and saw Eldo behind her, grinning madly.

Leonidas gave one of his deep booming laughs, totally unabashed to be found naked in the rain with a young woman impaled upon his cock. 'Well, old friend. What brings you from your post?'

'I saw you in the lightning,' replied Eldo, 'so I came to investigate.' His voice quavered, perhaps from the shivering cold, perhaps for other reasons.

'Well timed. I have been trying to please the lady here, but I think she is still hungry.' By way of explanation, he added to Chryseis, 'Eldo has a certain reputation with the ladies ...' He let the comment linger, its implications unstated.

'A reputation is nothing,' Chryseis commented as she slipped from Leonidas' arms and turned to face the smaller man, 'unless a man can prove himself when the need arises.'

Eldo undid his cloak, letting it fall to the deck, then

32

did the same with his kilt. His erection sprang up in front of him and Chryseis smiled at the sight. For all his size the man was magnificently endowed and she grasped it in her hand, marvelling at its thickness and length. Her fingers could not fully encircle him and as she rubbed her hand up and down he seemed to grow even more.

Despite her preoccupation, a thought came to her. 'I thought you were steering the boat,' she said. 'Who is looking after it while you are here?'

'It's all right,' muttered Eldo. 'I lashed the steering oar in place. It's perfectly safe.'

'Good,' Chryseis responded. 'I'd hate for you to be distracted at the crucial moment. Now lie down,' she commanded, using her hold on his turgid member to force him to the deck. 'I am going to ride you.'

33

Three

Acantha relaxed back on a spare sail kept in the hold and tried to doze. It was a habit of hers, picked up from many years of campaigns, to always make herself as comfortable as possible. You couldn't break off in the middle of a fight and ask for a siesta so it made sense to grab any sleep while you could.

The hold was dark. The ship was pitching too violently to risk using the small clay lamps in case the burning oil spilled everywhere. She was aware, however, of one of the sailors moving beside her; she could feel his weight tilting the bundled sail and hear his hoarse breath above the wind.

He touched her arm. She felt him grope a moment, identifying which bit of her flesh he had made contact with. His calloused hands were rough but he was very gentle and she was intrigued. She could have taken offence at the anonymous exploration, but the whispering touch was more an invitation than a demand and she decided to let him continue a while longer. So she lay silent and unmoving, inhaling his odour of fresh sweat and masculinity.

The unseen sailor followed her arm up to her shoulder and along the line of her collarbone so gently she could barely feel it. He moved up her neck to the line of her jaw, then stroked her cheek with the back of his hand, the soft hairs tickling her as lightly as feathers. He found her lips and traced their outline with fingertips which smelt of the things he had been touching: wood, tar and salt. Acantha parted her mouth invitingly and the anonymous finger probed between them. She bit it delicately, grasping it between her teeth and running her tongue across it, savouring the various flavours. She closed her lips about the finger and sucked on it as the unknown man slid it in and out, the motion easing as his flesh became slippery with her saliva.

The sailor shifted position; she could feel his breath on her face, soft and spicy, then his finger withdrew as his lips closed on hers. His kiss was as light as his touch and it was she who first slid her tongue out to meet his. Back and forth they went, tasting each other, sharing each other.

The total anonymity excited her. In the noisy, stifling darkness there was just this one point of warm, soft contact. She put her arms around him and pulled him on top of her, needing to feel his weight pressing into her. His knees wedged between hers, and she embraced him with her legs as well as her arms, wrapping herself around him. His hips ground into her and she responded in kind, urging him on. She could feel his hardness through the thin layers of cloth that separated them, but wanted to feel it standing naked and proud, wanted to feel it twitch and grow within her. She pushed him up slightly, so that she could worm a hand between them, lifting the hem of his brief kilt to reach the naked flesh beneath.

She grasped his long, slender penis in her fist. Its inner core was rigid under the thin layer of skin, and she let her hand glide along its length, noting its elegant shape and the distinctive way it curved slightly to one side. This was a delicate instrument, one to probe her with precision. She squeezed it approvingly, delighting in the responding twitch.

The man's hands were also busy, and she felt his fingers explore the opening to her sex, sliding in and out as his tongue moved within her mouth. She pulled his erection down towards her entrance, guiding it into place. The round, smooth head nudged at her vulva and she stroked it up and down the length of her cleft, feeling herself open even more, eager to engulf him.

The unknown man pushed insistently forward with his hips, and Acantha yielded to him, changing her hold so as to pull him within her. He slid into her opening, stretching her gently till he could go no deeper though she lifted her knees and grasped him to herself as hard as she could.

He pulled back, slowly, tantalisingly, till only the very tip of his cock was still within her, then slid fully home again, filling her once more. Again and again he repeated the procedure, each time, thrusting forward with greater vigour.

Acantha could feel the heat spread from her groin up through her navel to her breasts. Her face felt hot and flushed and she was so short of breath she stopped kissing her faceless lover in order to gasp for air. Instead she clung to him, their heads side by side, listening to his breathing become sharper and sharper as his strokes increased in speed.

Then he thrust forward one last time, as if trying to pierce through her. His cock pulsed and twitched, and she could feel his climax within her. She hung on to him tightly, lifting her hips to grind her pubis against him, harder and harder till her own release washed over her and she cried out in pleasure.

There was laughter from around them and ribald comments. She had forgotten they were not alone and that they would be overheard if not actually watched, not that it would have stopped her.

Her anonymous lover kissed her briefly in the darkness and she stroked his hair, wondering who he had been or whether she had even noticed him before amongst the crew, or would recognise him again. The only thing she was sure she would know once more was his gently curving cock, should she ever meet it again in the dark ship's hold.

On the rain-soaked deck, Chryseis knelt over Eldo's rampant manhood, kissing it and savouring its flavour. She slid her mouth further over it, feeling the smooth skin of his glans against her tongue and palate, while her hand continued to grasp his root, controlling him. She drew back slightly, allowing her tongue room to roam across the head of his penis, exploring the curved rim of his helmet, twirling round the tiny hole at its tip. It tasted salty, though not from the sea; it was thicker, richer, and she sucked hard to draw up the first drops of his excitement into her mouth.

She was ready for him now and planned to straddle him and lower herself on top of his hard meat when the ship lurched unevenly, sending her sprawling to the deck.

'Is it just me,' she said laughing unsteadily, 'or is the sea rougher?'

But the men weren't laughing. 'The steering oar,' gasped Eldo. 'It's broken free.' He stumbled to his feet, attempting to head back to the ship's stern, but a sudden wave twisted the ship sideways then broke over it, sluicing cold water over the deck. The whole craft rolled to one side and screams rose from the hold below. Eldo clutched at the lashings that secured the cargo, but they snapped, sending bales of wool skittering about. He screamed once, piercingly, then disappeared over the side and into the dark waters.

Terrified, Chryseis clung to the bulwark as another wall of water smashed against the ship, which was now broadside to the waves. The sea poured over her, filling her mouth and nose with cold, salty water. She coughed and retched, and through streaming eyes saw Leonidas stretch out his hand to clutch her by the wrist. She hung

37

on, scrabbling with her free hand for any available purchase.

In the hold, Acantha was just about to ask the sailor his name when the ship suddenly keeled to one side. In the darkness the motion was terrifyingly violent and irregular. Men cried out in alarm and Illaris screamed instructions for the crew to return on deck. In the darkness she lost contact with her lover of moments before; all passion was forgotten.

Someone threw the hatch open with a bang and dismal light, no more than a faint change in the darkness, filtered down into the hold. Acantha was one of the closest and she wasted no time darting up the crude ladder, and on to the deck, battling through the cold water that cascaded over her as she escaped.

As Acantha coughed brine from her lungs, lightning speared down to the raging sea and she had a momentary glimpse of the ship. Men were cutting the sail loose, to bring it down as swiftly as possible, while the remainder struggled to get their oars into position. Meanwhile, the deck cargo had broken loose and slid about freely, causing havoc. The cabin at the rear of the ship had been smashed flat. Acantha was about to struggle towards it when she heard a woman's scream. She turned and glimpsed Chryseis hanging over the side of the ship, the giant sailor, Leonidas, clutching her hand. Then he lost his grip and Chryseis tumble backward into the sea.

The girl was no more than a lighter smudge in the waves, receding fast, when Acantha dived in after her.

Black, cold water closed over her. For a moment she tumbled, lost, in the heaving sea. Her head broke the surface and she gulped air, then she sank again, dragged down by the weight of her shield strapped to her back and the sword at her waist. Real fear clutched her heart. There were no choices; she unbuckled the shield, dropped the sword and struggled back to the surface.

This time she stayed afloat and heard Chryseis' piercing scream off to her left. She shouted back, something incoherent choked off by a mouthful of sea, but Chryseis responded. Acantha swam towards the sound, trying to guess its direction as the wind tore it apart. Lightning again, and a brief glimpse of pale flesh right beside her. Three strokes and Acantha caught Chryseis' arm. The woman shrieked in terror at the touch, flailing her arms and legs till the water frothed.

'Stop it, you stupid girl,' yelled Acantha.

With a whimpering cry, Chryseis switched from terror to relief and flung herself at her saviour. She wrapped herself totally around the mercenary, pinning her arms and legs so that she couldn't move. They sank again immediately and Acantha had to lever the woman's grip from her by brute force. By luck, a bale of wool from the ship swept by and, though waterlogged, it provided some support. Acantha was able to transfer Chryseis' grip to the sodden bundle, then look around for the ship.

When she finally saw it, it was no more than a ghostly outline low to the water, fading invisibly into the distance.

It was a long, lonely night. Chryseis had screeched for help until her voice cracked into hoarse croaks while Acantha fought her own terror and saved her strength. Even if the ship came back to look for them, there was no way it could find them in the dark, heaving sea. They were on their own, and they could only hope that they would get their bearings once the new day dawned. The waters around here abounded with islands. With luck, they would find one that was inhabited.

Gradually, the storm faded away and the clouds broke up to reveal the waxing moon on a field of stars. The silver light glittered off the broken surface of the waves and Acantha was sure it would have been pretty if only she had been in the mood to appreciate it.

Instead, she had to put up with Chryseis' moaning in a perpetual undertone of self-pity. Bit by bit, she had pieced together what had happened and thought that Chryseis might have been fortunate to be washed overboard. It was nothing compared to what Illaris would have wanted to do to her for distracting his men.

When dawn finally lit the sky, Acantha was at first unsure whether she was imagining it. Imperceptibly, however, the new day arrived and with relief she was able to make out the rough outline of hills against the western sky, their tips reflecting the first rays of the morning sun. They were within sight of land and by alternately cajoling Chryseis and threatening to leave her behind, Acantha persuaded the woman to assist in kicking their makeshift raft shoreward. By the time the sun had lifted clear of the horizon, they had ground the raft on to the shingle and could stand upright.

Chryseis managed no more than six tottering steps up the beach before collapsing in a self-indulgent heap. Acantha looked down at her in disgust. If the silly girl hadn't screwed the lookout they'd still be aboard ship. Now, however, they were cast up on some unknown shore, without food, weapons or, in Chryseis' case, even any clothes. For a moment, the temptation to leave the blubbering Chryseis behind proved almost too much, but Acantha reminded herself that there was no point in having dived into the sea to save her if she then abandoned her on some beach.

Also, and more importantly, Acantha now needed the payment for this job in order to replace her sword and other kit. It was imperative that she delivered Chryseis to her future husband, Timon, and be paid in full.

Something in the air caught her attention. She lifted her head and sniffed carefully: woodsmoke and cooking – there was hope yet.

Chryseis sat on the damp sand with her knees huddled to her chest and let the sun slowly soak life back into

40

her frozen limbs. Her hair hung in heavy, lank strands down her back and over her face, still dripping cold water. Her mouth stung from the brine she had swallowed, and she desperately wanted a drink of cool, fresh water to remove the taste. But most of all she was weary, bone weary, from lack of sleep and the effort of clinging to the bale of wool all night. She was, undoubtedly, more cold, tired, hungry and miserable than she had ever been before.

Instead of doing something about it, however, the barbarian woman just stood with her head up sniffing the wind. Chryseis stared at her furiously, resenting the woman's indifference to both their situation and herself. When she could take it no longer, Chryseis spat out, 'Well? Are you just going to stand there all day? I need some clothes and I'm hungry.'

The woman looked down impassively and seemed to consider before replying. 'There's someone up the coast a bit.' She pointed to where a small headland marked the end of the beach they'd landed on. 'It's not too far. It won't take long for us to get there.'

If the woman had been Palmeda, Chryseis would have ordered her to go by herself and fetch food and clothes. This woman, however, might not bother returning. Chryseis rose stiffly to her feet. 'Okay, I'll come with you. You'd better give me your tunic.'

The barbarian blinked. 'My tunic?'

'I'm naked. I can't walk around like this.' Surely the idiot could see that.

The barbarian gave half a laugh of surprise. 'Why? What about me?'

'You're a servant; it doesn't matter if you are naked. Don't you know anything?'

The barbarian grinned with malicious humour. 'I know I wasn't fucking the lookout when the ship foundered. And I know enough not to let my clothes get washed away by the sea.' She turned on her heel and walked off.

Furious, Chryseis looked around for someone else to help her. The beach was deserted. There was no sign anywhere that another human had ever visited it. The only person was Acantha, striding away without a glance over her shoulder. Blinking back hot tears, Chryseis trudged behind her, barely catching up by the time Acantha had clambered over the rocks that spilt out into the waves from the small promontory.

Beyond the headland was another small cove, only this one was inhabited. A small fishing boat with a large blue and white eye painted near its prow was pulled well up on the beach and behind it lines of nets hung drying from poles. Further back from the water, clear of the sand and surf, stood a group of three small huts. Two looked deserted, but a thin line of smoke rose from the third.

The door to the last hut opened. Two men emerged and began to walk down the shingle towards the boat. They were busy talking and did not see the women immediately. Then one of them looked up and stopped dead, his mouth open. His companion looked around to see what the fuss was, then did the same. Chryseis could feel their eyes on her and started to hide behind Acantha, then thought better of it. It wasn't her fault she was naked, and in any case her breeding should show from her bearing and her manner, not merely her clothes. She ignored her thirst and hunger to put on her haughtiest demeanour and wait with Acantha for the two men to approach and greet them.

The older man, who had introduced himself as Odic, stroked his greying beard with a weathered hand as he listened to Acantha explain how they had arrived there, his eyes never leaving Chryseis' breasts. 'You were lucky to survive,' he said when she had finished. 'You'd better come to our hut, to eat and warm yourselves. We don't have much, but you are welcome.'

He and his younger companion, a youth called

Philemon, led the women back to their home. It was low and primitive, with just two crude beds in opposite corners, an uneven table and a cooking fire that filled the room with pungent smoke. After a night in the sea, however, it seemed like paradise and Chryseis sank gratefully on to the nearest cot.

Philemon solicitously pulled the thin blanket around her shoulders. Then he served her a bowl of fish stew from the pot by the fire, a hunk of bread and as much fresh water as she could drink to wash away the taste of salt. He did the same for Acantha, then stood back with Odic and watched as the women ate and drank.

Finally, the stew was finished and Chryseis used the last piece of bread to wipe around the bowl, making sure none was wasted. It was as crude a meal as she had ever eaten, but undoubtedly the most satisfying, and she leant back against the wall with a sigh.

It seemed only moments later when she opened her eyes, but outside the open door the sky was dark once more. She sat up and found that her muscles had stiffened and cramped while she slept. She gave a small groan of pain. Acantha and the two men looked up from where they had been talking in low voices on the other side of the room.

'I've found out where we are,' said Acantha. 'By luck, we've struck Euboea itself, but we are near the south end of the island and on the opposite side from Chalcis.'

Chryseis couldn't picture what that meant. 'How do we get back? Is there another ship?'

'No. Nothing like that. Our best means of getting to Chalcis and meeting your uncle again – assuming the ship didn't actually sink – is to travel diagonally across the island, north-west, till we reach the opposite coast.'

'By horse?'

Acantha laughed. 'These are fishermen. They no more have a horse to sell than you have the money to buy one. We'll have to go by foot.' She turned to the men

43

again. 'Have you any spare clothes or weapons you can let us have for our journey?'

Odic sucked his breath in between his teeth and shook his head. 'Well,' he said, 'it's not that easy, you know. Of course we want to help, but we can't afford much.'

'I'm afraid we don't have anything to pay you with.' Acantha held her empty hands palmward and shrugged. 'We lost it all in the storm.'

'You haven't anything?'

'Not an obol,' Acantha said.

Odic pursed his lips and tutted sympathetically but said, 'I'm afraid there is little I can do without some payment.'

Chryseis panicked; how was she going to manage without even a rag to cover herself? And food, what about food? 'Your necklace,' she blurted at Acantha. 'Offer them your necklace. It must be worth something, even if it is a fake.'

Acantha glared at her. 'It's not for sale.'

'Really?' exploded Chryseis, her own anger igniting in response. 'Well, I am naked, barefoot and once more hungry. If these men will take your precious little bauble in exchange for some clothes and provisions, then I think you should give it to them.'

'Please, please.' Odic held up his hands between them. 'That isn't what I had in mind. Perhaps . . .' he paused suggestively, 'some other arrangement could be made?'

His meaning was obvious and Chryseis curled her lip in scorn. Neither man suited her, Odic being slightly too old and Philemon seeming a bit dull. While she was free enough with her favours when it pleased her, she had never yet had sex for anything other than her own pleasure and had no intention of starting.

Acantha it seemed, had no such qualms. 'What are you offering?' she asked bluntly.

Odic shrugged. 'Some food for your journey. A blanket or two. We don't have much.'

44

'What about me?' interrupted Chryseis. 'I need clothes.'

Acantha glanced over at her. 'You can make your own arrangements,' she said briefly, then turned to Odic with a smile. 'It's a deal. How would you like your payment?'

Despite the wrinkles in his weathered face, Odic's grin looked boyish as he leant forward to whisper in Acantha's ear. Whatever he said, Acantha's laugh sounded genuine as he loosened the belt around her waist, then helped her out of her leather tunic. Acantha responded by easing him out of his own clothes and in moments both of them were naked, her skin pale against his.

In spite of her disdain, Chryseis felt a flicker of interest as she watched Odic place his mouth over Acantha's breast while his hand stroked the tawny triangle of her pubic hair. The man's body looked wiry and strong, not weak with age, and he appeared to know how to please a woman, if Acantha's smile was anything to go by. Acantha looked good too. She was as hard and lean as Chryseis had anticipated, and though her breasts and hips were not as rounded as her own, they were well shaped.

Chryseis glanced at Philemon, who was standing beside her, obviously unsure of himself and undecided what to do. He kept wetting his lips nervously while looking back and forth between herself and the other two, who by now had fallen to the bed. Chryseis found his indecision unappealing. She pulled the blanket tighter around herself and ignored him.

Acantha laughed from beneath Odic's body. 'Forget her, lad. She's not as good as she thinks.' Then Odic rolled off her slightly and she held out a free arm, welcoming him. Philemon needed no further encouragement. In moments he had stripped off to reveal a firm, well-muscled body, and joined the other two.

Even though she had rejected him first, Chryseis felt a surge of anger; did he have to be so eager to join the others? She watched sullenly as the three of them murmured to each other while exploring their bodies.

There was no room in the narrow bed for all three of them at once. Acantha lay between the two men, with Odic propped up on his elbow on one side of her, and Philemon kneeling on the floor on the other. From what Chryseis could see, Acantha was enjoying herself as both men worked along her body. Odic's deft fingers explored the dark cleft between her legs while Philemon seemed content to suck on her breast, occasionally rubbing his face across it in sensuous delight.

Acantha was not idle either. She grasped both erections in her fists: Odic's wiry and thin like his body, Philemon's thick and fat and rubbed them in unison, coaxing them to full hardness. When both were ready, she then used the cocks like handles to tug the men into new positions, making them kneel before her, their erections lined up in front of her mouth. Acantha wet her lips seductively as she smiled up into their eager faces, pulled each foreskin fully back to expose the purple head beneath, then bent to kiss each shining helmet in turn. She ran her tongue over them, first Odic's then Philemon's, leaving each gleaming with her saliva and the thin drops of moisture emerging from the tiny orifices at their tips.

The men worked together side by side, drawing Acantha in towards them as they must haul in a laden net. Acantha pushed their cocks together so that they rubbed against each other, then kissed and licked both at the same time, gradually engulfing both within her mouth at the same time.

As she watched, Chryseis could feel the heat in her own belly, the ache in her breasts. She stroked the pouting lips of her vulva, feeling the slick wetness before sliding one finger inside herself, then another. She lifted

46

the glistening fingers to her mouth to taste her own rich juices. The smell and flavour of her own arousal excited her even more and as she sucked she put her other hand back between her legs, taking her time in seeking out her own pleasure. First, she used her nails to stroke the sensitive skin on the inside of her thighs, that delicate place where the lightest of touches sent shivers of anticipation through her body. She let her fingers wander, tracing the length of her sex without entering it, then stretching further back till her fingertip circled the tight ring of her anus. She pushed against it, feeling the dry resistance. She took her fingers from her mouth, slick with her saliva, and slid them beside the others, making the hidden entrance wet and slippery before pushing in. The sensation skewered up into her belly, primitive but exciting and she worked her finger in and out of her rectum slowly as she watched the action on the other side of the room.

Acantha took the men's cocks from her mouth and kissed each in turn, then she got Odic to lie back as she squatted over him, the head of his slender knob rubbing along the notch of her sex. Odic strained up with his hips, trying to penetrate her, but she held him firmly, preventing him from reaching her. 'Now,' she said with a smile, 'I think I've paid you both for an old blanket. Is there anything else you could let me have as well?'

Odic gave a strangled gurgle and tried once more to lift himself into her. Acantha laughed and rose with him. 'Come on, I'm sure you could let me have something else. A good knife perhaps if nothing else.' She rubbed his cock enticingly along her wet slit. 'Think about how grateful I'd be.' She looked over her shoulder at Philemon. 'And I'd need something extra for looking after you as well.'

Odic groaned. 'All right, all right. I've an old sword you can have.'

'That sounds good.' Acantha lowered herself a

fraction, then changed her mind and rose up again. 'But I'd better see it.'

Odic glowered up at her then snorted in dry amusement. He groped one-handedly under the bed and removed an ancient weapon in a broken leather scabbard. 'It's good bronze,' he said as he passed it to her. 'Not that cheap iron that people use nowadays. I'll expect to be paid well for it.'

Acantha drew the blade free and inspected it carefully. She felt the edge, then held her thumb up to display the fine red line running across it. 'Dangerous weapons,' she murmured, 'should always be kept sheathed.' As if to demonstrate her point she began to slide the scabbard back over the blade while simultaneously lowering herself on to Odic's upstanding penis.

'See how well they fit together?' she said, as both weapons were fully sheathed. 'It is their proper place, don't you think?' She rocked her hips back and forth, forcing herself as far over Odic as she could possibly go.

With each thrust, Chryseis pushed her finger within her anus, finger-fucking herself in time to his movements. She used her other hand to stroke her breasts and stomach, teasing the hairs of her mound then retreating, resisting the temptation. That was too easy, too obvious. She tweaked her nipples, twisting them till they hurt to make them stand up, then caressing them gently. All the while, she kept her finger working in and out between her cheeks and her eyes on the trio across from her.

Now she saw Acantha lean forward along the length of Odic's body while Philemon rubbed himself against her bottom, his erection thick and straining for release. Acantha reached back to grab his penis, and Philemon looked down to watch as she carefully guided it between her buttocks. Philemon pushed slowly with his hips, easing himself into place. Then it seemed he had gained entrance, for Acantha took her hand away and with a single thrust his erection disappeared inside her. Acantha closed her eyes with a gasp, arching back at the double coupling.

Chryseis couldn't resist any longer. She slid her hand down from her breasts, across her flat stomach and into the dark bush between her thighs. Her sex was more swollen and wetter than she had ever felt it before. Her fingers slid in without resistance, first one then two, three and four while her thumb pressed hard against her clitoris. She could feel the juice oozing between her fingers and paused to lick more of it from her hand. Then she concentrated on the sensation of her fingers meeting within her, and wondered how it would feel with two cocks in her instead.

The men began to move in unison, sliding in and out of Acantha together while she groaned and grunted in time with them. She lifted up on her arms so that her body was clear of Odic's, and each thrust made her breasts swing back and forth. The rhythm grew stronger, Acantha's cries became sharper as her face and chest flushed red.

Chryseis felt her own pleasure mount with theirs. Now her disdain was forgotten and she wished that she were participating.

Suddenly, Philemon grunted and thrust, quivering, against Acantha's round buttocks. His orgasm must have triggered Odic's, for he too gasped out while Acantha, sandwiched between them screamed in an ecstasy of release. Then the three collapsed in an untidy pile, laughing unsteadily and catching their breath before disengaging from each other.

It was Odic who noticed Chryseis first, and drew the others' attention to what she was doing. For a moment she thought they would mock her for her previous aloofness. Instead, Odic gestured for her to continue while Philemon grinned in lazy satisfaction. Only Acantha seemed uninterested in the show.

At Odic's encouragement, Chryseis opened her legs and lifted one foot up on to the bed, exposing herself even more to the men's inspection. Their eyes stroked her skin like fire and inflamed her even more. 'I'm so horny,' she whispered. 'I need someone to satisfy me.'

'I'm not sure we can afford it,' Odic commented dryly, one arm still around Acantha, his hand supporting the shape of her breast as it hung down.

'I don't want payment,' Chryseis begged. Her fingers had taken her to the very brink of orgasm but it would be so much nicer to have someone to help. 'Please.'

Philemon laughed easily and got off the bed, walking towards her unhurriedly. His limp penis glistened as it swayed, still moist from Acantha's body. 'I always like to help a traveller in distress,' he said as he knelt before her and leant forward to kiss the entrance to her sex.

Chryseis took her hands away, so he could reach her more easily, and quivered in delight as his tongue flickered lightly along the length of her vulva. He missed nothing, travelling from the start of the crease hidden within her pubic hair, along between her thighs, then beyond, to gently circle her anus before returning. Finally, he pressed his mouth firmly to her opening, his tongue questing within her for the little bead of pleasure. She cried out as he sucked on it, drawing it into his mouth, teasing it between his teeth.

In moments, the heat of orgasm flushed once more through her body. This time she let it build up, higher and higher, till she exploded and her hips bucked of their own accord against Philemon's face, covering it in her juices as she ground out her lust against him.

Afterwards, when her heart had stopped pounding, she clutched Philemon's solid body against hers, stroking his soft skin as she drifted into sleep. It was a light slumber from which she was awoken twice during the night for more love-making. And if one of those times, in the darkness, she thought her lover was more slender and wiry than before, she did not complain. She enjoyed herself and was content with the promise that, in the morning, when she and Acantha set out on the next stage of their journey, she would have an old blanket to make into a tunic.

Four

Acantha looked back at Chryseis who was struggling up the hill after her. The storm was long passed and in the renewed summer heat the young woman was finding the trek hard. Only Acantha's threat to leave her behind had prevented her from resting under every shady tree they had passed.

While she waited, Acantha studied their surroundings, planning out their route. The sea was barely visible now behind them, between the peaks of the intervening hills but, even so, their progress was much slower than Acantha would have liked. She would have preferred to keep to the most direct route to Chalcis and head straight north-west. Unfortunately, a large forest spread across their path and they had been forced east, where the hills thrust far up above the tree line. Here, there was only brown, wiry grass and thorny bushes too tough to sustain even the hungriest of goats.

Chryseis panted up beside Acantha, then flopped to the ground. 'I'm thirsty,' she said, holding out her hand. 'Give me some water.'

Acantha hesitated, bridling at the tone. Then she took great satisfaction in tossing the water-skin at Chryseis' feet, and watching the girl discover that it was already empty. 'You had the last of it ages ago,' Acantha said with amusement as she picked the bag up again. 'You'll have to wait till we find some more.'

'But I'm thirsty now,' Chryseis whined.

52

Acantha shrugged. 'So am I, but complaining won't help.' She had just turned away when a stray eddy of breeze brought the chime of bells to her. She lifted her head at the sound, seeking its direction. A moment later, she had it. 'Come on,' she urged, with renewed vigour. 'There's water over the hill.'

Chryseis didn't even bother turning her head. 'I don't believe you,' she sighed wearily. 'I'm too old for that trick.'

Acantha gritted her teeth and thought of the promised fee for Chryseis' safe delivery. 'I can hear goats,' she explained with strained patience. 'They won't stray far from water.'

Chryseis exhaled heavily and Acantha relented enough to put her hand under the young woman's elbow and help her on to her feet. 'Come on. All that soft living isn't good for you. It's time you got some exercise.'

'I was managing just fine without it,' replied Chryseis dryly, but at least she quit moaning.

On the other side of the hill, they found a small group of stunted trees huddled round the pool of water which filled a small depression in the terrain. A dozen or so goats milled about, nibbling the occasional blade of green grass or ripping leaf-buds from the bushes. Acantha scanned the area for a goatherd or any other human, but couldn't see anyone. It was quite possible that the animals had been left to fend for themselves. In the bleak highlands, away from predators, it was not uncommon. Even so, something undefinable niggled at her and as Chryseis dashed towards the water, Acantha hung back, looking around uneasily.

The pool where the goats drank was muddy and fouled, but just above it was a second pool, which Chryseis made for with a cry of delight. Its steep, rocky sides made it less accessible to the animals, and its undisturbed water was crystal clear. Chryseis lay across one of the boulders at the water's edge, lowered her face to the sparkling liquid and drank greedily.

Acantha sighed impatiently and hauled the woman back by the material of her makeshift tunic. 'A little at a time,' she warned irritably. 'Drink cold water too fast and you'll give yourself cramps. Don't you know anything?'

Chryseis sullenly wiped her mouth with the back of her hand and said nothing.

'Oh, please yourself,' Acantha muttered in disgust, and bent to quench her own thirst. The icy liquid leeched the heat from her belly, and she resisted the temptation to take any more than a few small mouthfuls.

Chryseis set her mouth, her bottom lip sticking out petulantly, but at least she stopped gulping down the water. 'You have no objections to me taking a swim, I suppose?' she asked with acid politeness.

'None. Just let me fill the water-skin before you stir up the mud.' When she was finished, she nodded to Chryseis. 'Carry on. I'll keep watch.'

Chryseis laughed. 'Here?' she asked scornfully. 'It must be the most isolated spot in the whole world.'

'You're probably right,' Acantha replied easily. 'It's just good practice.' She didn't mention the uneasy itch at the back of her neck; the last thing she needed was the silly girl's imagination running away with her.

Chryseis pulled a dismissive face, then undid the rough rope she had used to girdle her makeshift chiton, and pulled the garment over her head. She wore nothing underneath, and though Acantha was still looking around for the source of her disquiet, she was very aware of Chryseis stretching herself in the sunlight. The young woman's skin gleamed where the sun caught it, making the shadows dark and mysterious by comparison. Acantha noted the hollow of Chryseis' back, the curve of her hips and the dark cleft between her but-

tocks. She followed the lines with her e̶
round to where they led into the sec̶
legs.

Cautiously, Chryseis stepped dow̶
crystal surface glittered as it parted to e̶
hugging her shins and calves then working̶
a silver bracelet up her thighs. Chryseis' rib̶
with a long, gasping breath as she slowly lowered ̶
further into the chill liquid. The water-line reached ̶
hips, curling into the shaded crannies that had aroused
Acantha's interest moments before. The mercenary lay
back and watched dreamily, imagining the private places that icy sheath touched, imagining her fingers
caressing the youthful figure as intimately. Then, when
the water reached her waist, Chryseis took a final breath
and plunged forward, the image of her body dissolving
in a sparkling trail of bubbles.

Acantha tore her gaze away from Chryseis to scan
their surroundings again. She still felt uneasy, but she
saw nothing suspicious, and her attention kept returning
to the young woman. Chryseis was now washing as best
she could with the plain water. Through the rippled
surface, Acantha watched the young woman's hands
playing across her body, and observed with interest how
the water buoyed up her breasts, and made the brown
nipples erect.

The sight and sound of the cool water aggravated
Acantha's own discomfort from the heat. She had
ignored it all morning, but now her skin prickled unpleasantly and her short hair clung in damp threads to
the nape of her neck. Maybe that was all her sense of
foreboding had been, drying sweat. She certainly
couldn't see any other cause for it, and the goats were
grazing placidly without a care in the world.

Chryseis scrubbed her face, the sound of splashing
water irresistibly enticing. It was more than Acantha
could bear. She stripped slowly, knowing that Chryseis

..ching, then leapt straight into the pool. Her
escaped in a shriek as the icy water closed over
...nd she shot back to the surface and smoothed the
back from her face as she regained her composure.
Didn't you realise it was cold?' Chryseis called, and
...r once her laugh didn't sound malicious.

'Not like this,' Acantha gasped. She submerged herself again, gradually acclimatising to the chill. It was a
pleasant change from the scorching heat of the day, but
she wouldn't want to spend too long in it.

As Acantha sluiced the day's grime from her body,
she glimpsed Chryseis watching her intently. She pre-
tended not to have noticed and when she managed
another surreptitious peek, Chryseis still hadn't looked
away. Acantha hid a smile; it appeared the young
woman's tastes matched her own after all.

The bodyguard slowed her movements, giving her
charge plenty of time to admire her. She could almost
feel the other woman's eyes as she made a show of
cleaning her breasts, caressing her hands over the subtle
curves. Her entire areola, not just the nipple, seemed to
swell outwards and she tweaked the pink peaks, encouraging them into even greater prominence. She
pressed the pliant flesh with the palms of her hands,
massaging it, squeezing it, making it ache with a desire
which spread out through her body. Chryseis' eyes
burned on her as she slid her hand between her legs,
running stiff fingers through the tawny tangle of hair,
feeling her own heat as she cleaned each crevice and fold
of her body.

The water surged as Chryseis sidled closer, and
Acantha anticipated the warm touch of the young body.
But if she succumbed to Chryseis now she would have
no control over her for the remainder of their journey.
Acantha had been a soldier for too long not to understand the need for discipline, and Chryseis couldn't be
allowed to stop for a rest whenever she felt like it. There

56

was no harm in a little mutual fun, however, so long as their roles were clearly defined.

Acantha looked over her shoulder at Chryseis, who was watching her with lust-filled eyes. 'Wash my back,' she ordered, rolling her shoulders. It was an invitation, but on her terms.

Chryseis understood those terms exactly. Her face changed, desire dissolving into anger, and she turned away without a word.

Acantha cursed her own stupidity; Chryseis was bound to have rejected the offer. And, no doubt, at some time in the future she would seek retribution for the insult.

A flicker of movement caught her eye. A stone rolled down the bank and splashed into the water.

Acantha scanned the hillside above them, her heart pounding. She saw nothing significant, but she wanted the comfort of her sword in her hand. The weapon lay with her clothes on the bank behind her. She turned towards it, but the weight of the water dragged at her legs, slowing her down.

'Just leave it where it is.' A man's voice, curt and flat.

Acantha looked back and saw a figure silhouetted against the sun, the slender line of a javelin in one hand, two more held in the other. She had no choice but to obey. Inwardly furious, she schooled herself to wait calmly. There was no point in demanding explanations; the stranger would tell them what he wanted in his own good time. In the meantime, she didn't argue as Chryseis sidled behind her, seeking protection. It was, after all, what she was paid for.

The man stepped aside, so that he was no longer outlined against the sky, and Acantha could see him properly. The first thing she noticed was that he was surprisingly good-looking and young, perhaps only a few years older than Chryseis. Unusually, he was also clean-shaven and had fair, tightly curled hair. He wore a short cloak over a plain tunic and, more importantly, a sword in his belt as well as carrying the javelins that Acantha had already noted. He rested the butt of one javelin on the ground and leant on it as he studied them with an impudent grin.

Acantha was furiously aware of his interest in the way that the cold had puckered her nipples till they stood out like thumbs. 'What do you want?' she demanded curtly.

The man shrugged innocently. 'I only stopped for a drink of water,' he said. 'Then I heard you arriving.'

'And scurried into hiding,' she snorted.

'Of course. You never know who you might meet in these hills.'

'Well, if you haven't had a drink already, take one now,' she said. 'Then leave. We wouldn't want to detain you.'

'Wait.' Chryseis pushed forward with her hands on her hips and her chest out. 'There's no hurry.'

Acantha grasped her arm. 'Now, just wait a –'

'What's your name?' Chryseis continued blithely, shaking off the hold. 'What are you doing here?'

'This isn't a social –'

'My name is Eucrates,' the man said, inspecting Chryseis with a widening smile. 'I'm the son of a merchant, travelling in search of new markets. And you?'

'I am Chryseis, niece to Pythias of Ephesus. This –' she gestured in Acantha's direction without actually looking at her '– is my bodyguard.'

Acantha dragged Chryseis back, forcing her to listen. 'Don't you realise that this brigand might just want to slit our throats?'

'Of course he won't,' Chryseis said disdainfully. 'He's a respectable merchant; he wouldn't.'

The comment was too stupid to bother with. Acantha turned to the man, 'I might only be her bodyguard, but what I say goes. Take your drink and leave.'

'And if not, I suppose you'll make me?' Eucrates suggested, with amusement.

'That's right,' Acantha agreed grimly.

Eucrates raised his eyebrows. 'Considering you are a woman, and are stuck in the middle of a pool, you have a high opinion of your chances,' he mused with a speculative look.

'It's easy to be confident when you have all the weapons,' Acantha replied, her voice cool.

Eucrates nodded slowly, then laid his sword and javelins to one side and stood back with a mocking bow.

Acantha clambered up on to a large, flat boulder, then stood bent over with her hands on her knees, letting the water stream from her naked body, filling time as she considered her strategy. Finally, when she was ready, she stood up and approached him on the open ground he had chosen for their contest.

They circled each other in a wary crouch, though Eucrates' smile suggested that he could hardly be bothered trying. He was careless, leering at her instead of watching for her move. When it came, he was totally off-guard. She surged in, feinted high, kicked low, striking the thigh just above his knee.

Eucrates staggered back, cursing, then lumbered forward, arms wide to crush her in a bear-hug. She ducked aside but turned her ankle on a rock. His arms wrapped around her as she stumbled, one hand cupping a breast. He could have hurt her badly, but instead seemed more intent on groping her. Well, that was his concern. She elbowed him in the stomach then, as he released her, spun round with a high kick at his head. His eyes widened at the unobstructed view of her vulva just before her foot smacked against his ear, sending him sprawling.

Now, finally, he faced her with due respect and it was Acantha's turn to grin. 'I don't like being under-estimated,' she said, and struck towards his face.

His hands rose automatically and she darted in, snatched a feel of his balls, then retreated out of range. He looked startled at the treatment, and she winked at him. 'I'd be careful, if I were you,' she warned. 'You have plenty there for me to grab on to.'

Eucrates' jaw tightened and he lunged forward.

Acantha side-stepped, but he had anticipated the move. He hurled her to the ground then dived after her. She threw herself back to avoid him and in her haste tumbled down the hillside. Goats scattered, bleating madly, and Acantha splashed face-down into the mud by the lower pool.

The glutinous slurry oozed over her pale skin, completely covering the front of her body. Eucrates laughed and whooped with delight as she tried to stand then slipped back into the mire. The cold mud insinuated itself into every sensitive crevice of her body, making her so angry she could barely think. It took three attempts before she succeeded in slithering her way to firm ground and shaking the worst of the mud from her hands.

Eucrates bounded easily down the slope, grinning at her misfortune. 'Had enough?' he asked with patronising smugness.

Acantha set her teeth in cold rage and began cleaning the muck from her torso. She scraped the mud from one breast, revealing the smudged and dirty nipple, then, with a shriek of pent-up fury, splattered it into his eyes. Eucrates staggered back with a wordless cry, clawing the sticky mass from his face.

She kicked his legs from under him, knocking him backward, then slipped once more and fell on top of him. He grabbed her and they rolled through the sludge, neither gaining the advantage. Somewhere, though, the mood of the fight had changed and become less vicious. As they slithered over and under each other, Acantha was very aware of Eucrates' sleek frame and the way her own body responded to it.

When she finally hooked her legs around his neck and clamped him in a lock, the position provided each with a good view of the other's groin, and Acantha couldn't help but notice that Eucrates had a sizeable erection. She ran her hand over it, assessing its hardness. Eucrates thrashed slightly, but didn't seem to be making a serious attempt to break free; the fight had definitely evolved into a different kind of rough and tumble. Acantha was not sure she should succumb to temptation though; Eucrates was still an unknown factor and she didn't trust him.

On the other hand, that didn't mean they couldn't have some fun. She was just about to investigate the possibility more thoroughly when Chryseis appeared.

'Oh, leave him alone,' she demanded, still naked and looking like some wayward water nymph. 'Can't you see he's had enough?'

Acantha blinked in astonishment, so surprised she relaxed her hold, allowing Eucrates to roll free, his face flushed red.

'That's right,' he wheezed to Chryseis. 'I think she's really hurt me.' He groaned dramatically and massaged his throat.

'Oh, you poor thing,' Chryseis said. She intervened between them, virtually pushing Acantha out of the way, and stroked his forehead. 'She's so uncouth. Where does it hurt?'

'There. Lower, lower . . . ahh . . .'

Livid with fury, Acantha snatched up her clothes and stalked off upstream in search of somewhere to bathe for a second time. In the meantime, if the silly little slut got her throat slit, that was her own problem.

Chryseis watched Acantha retreat with a self-satisfied glow. Just when the bitch was all hot and ready, she had literally taken the man from right between her legs. 'The dried up old shrew thought you fancied her,' she laughed.

Eucrates propped himself up on his elbows and watched the mercenary retreating up the hill. 'Mmmm. Well I had thought . . .' Then he glanced at Chryseis, and changed what he was about to say. 'But she's not as beautiful as you, of course.'

'Not in the same class, at all,' Chryseis emphasised, determined to leave no doubt about her superiority. 'Like you, I'm also from a merchant family; my uncle trades widely across the Aegean. Acantha is merely a servant, another body for hire.'

Eucrates raised his eyebrows. 'It makes a difference?'

'Of course,' Chryseis responded, surprised he should ask. She ran her fingers over the symmetrical contours of his face. 'I can tell you come from good stock; breeding always shows.'

His laugh held a note of derision. 'Like a horse? Thank you.'

'You know what I mean.' She ran a hand over his groin, assessing with pleasure the extent of his interest in her. 'Though in your case a horse may be correct.'

He grasped her hand, stilling it. 'So you think it's beneath you to consort with mere servants?'

'Oh, they're all right for one's occasional amusement, but that's a different matter. For something more refined, however, . . .' She leant forward and kissed him lightly, making sure she didn't get covered in mud herself. He tried to grab her and she drew back, laughing. 'I've already bathed and you are filthy. Go on, clean yourself up. I'll wait.'

She sat on the bank, letting the hot sun dry the moisture from her body as she watched Eucrates strip off. He seemed almost shy, standing half-turned away from her as he pulled off his tunic, though he had no apparent cause to be. His body was well shaped, the powerful muscles sheathed in smooth skin. She particularly liked his hands; they were large, all sinew and bone, with a sprinkling of fine hairs which shone golden

62

in the sun. They looked strong and capable and she shivered in anticipation of their touch.

As Chryseis watched, Eucrates bent over to sluice his muddy garments in the icy water, exposing his tightly muscled buttocks to her gaze. So unlike a woman's: there was no hint of softness to them and, as he leant further over, she could see between his legs to his softly swaying scrotum and penis.

Enthralled by the sight, Chryseis let her fingers stray between her thighs, teasing herself into readiness for what was to come. This man was different; she could sense it, and her skin tingled expectantly.

Eucrates spread his tunic over a bush, then lowered himself into the pool, dipping his head under the water then throwing it back so that his wet hair flipped a sparkling arc of droplets into the air. He rinsed the rest of his body quickly, then pulled himself out of the water and shook himself like a dog.

Chryseis giggled at the sight of his penis, shrunk by the cold to a mere fraction of its normal glory. 'Come here and let me warm it for you,' she said, surprising herself with the huskiness of her voice. He walked slowly over and knelt beside her. She reached out to touch him, marvelling at the soft fragility of his dormant organ. It hardly seemed capable of piercing her, of filling her to capacity. She squeezed its base lightly as she kissed it, her other hand cradling his balls. His penis twitched in her hand and she kissed it again, this time enveloping it with her mouth, rolling the malleable flesh about with her tongue. The blood pulsed through the soft tissue and with each beat it swelled, stiffened, lengthened, until she could no longer contain it. Reluctantly, she allowed much of it to escape her mouth, contenting herself with the taste and feel of his smooth glans, slippery with her saliva and the first drops of his excitement. She bobbed her head over the upright penis, scraping her teeth across the sensitive ridge of the helmet and smiling to herself at the gasp of pleasure she evoked.

His scrotum tightened, the testes drawing up expectantly. His breath shortened and he dug his fingers into her hair, encouraging her to stay with him, though not forcing her. He was close now and she knew he would soon fill her mouth with his seed. She imagined the thick, salty come spurting over her tongue and down her throat and moaned with the urgency of her desire.

Eucrates must have heard and taken the moan for one of discomfort because he tried to pull back. She wouldn't let him though; she knew what she wanted and had every intention of getting it. She slipped her hand between his legs, pulling him towards her as she sought out the tight ring of his anus. The puckered orifice felt tiny beneath her fingertip and she circled it lightly before attempting entrance. Eucrates yielded to her slowly and she had to push her way in gradually, pumping gently until her finger found the inner softness and was fully within him.

He groaned heavily and bent forward to kiss the top of her head, then released himself to the urgency of his need for her. His hips rocked harder, pushing his cock deep within her mouth while his anus gripped her finger and seemed to draw it further within his rectum. His speed increased, grew sharper, till suddenly he cried out and she felt him spurt within her.

The semen was thick, rich and smooth, the texture of albumen. It had a distinctive taste: faintly bitter, like almonds, but with a musky undertone that aroused her senses. She savoured the jissom as she would a fine wine, rolling it around her palate to extract every nuance of its flavour, and sucked on him till she had extracted every drop.

She let the viscous liquid slide down her throat, then began to lick him clean, running her tongue over the smooth skin of his knob and probing at the tiny hole in its end. Now he was spent, his glans was over-sensitive to her touch and she giggled in delight and satisfaction as his breath caught with overloaded pleasure.

Now it was Eucrates' turn to please her, and she lay back on the rough turf, her aroused skin sensitive to every small stone and each wiry blade of grass beneath her. She was ready for him now, needed him immediately, and he knew it. He wasted no time before dipping his head to kiss the soft mouse-pelt below her belly, nuzzling his way between her legs till he could kiss her swollen labia.

Chryseis raised her knees and tilted herself up to meet his subtle mouth. Eucrates kissed her more firmly, his tongue running up and down along her cleft, but not yet hard enough or deep enough to please her. She hooked her arms around her knees and pulled them up to her breasts, exposing herself completely to his ministrations. He drew back a moment to contemplate her body, tracing the line of her vulva with a fingertip then grinning up at her before bending again to his task.

This time there was nothing tentative about his approach. He put his hands beneath her buttocks, lifting her further upward, then applied his mouth to her pudenda as if to suck the juice from a succulent peach. He kissed her labia, scoring his tongue backward along her cleft till he crossed her perineum and circled her anus, his tongue flitting across the tight hole. He moved swiftly on, returning to delve within her vulva, exploring its inner secrets and lapping her nectar with as much gusto as she had drunk his. He rubbed his face across her quim, seeming to revel in the flavour and scent of her sex. He pressed his mouth tight against her, flickering his tongue in and out of her vagina as if he sought to reach all the way to her womb.

She squirmed impatiently, eager to gain her own orgasm, and finally, he focused his attention on her clitoris, that diminutive source of so much pleasure.

He lashed it mercilessly with his tongue and Chryseis felt her whole body ignite in response, the rosy warmth spreading up from that single spark to kindle fires in her stomach and breasts. It was as if she were burning inside, and she basked in the glow of her inner sun.

The fiery coruscation built to a climax and there was a long drawn-out cry that she barely recognised as her own as her body bucked and heaved in an explosive orgasm. Waves of dark pleasure obscured the outer world again and again, before subsiding back into undulating ripples of pleasure.

Gasping for breath, her heart pounding, Chryseis lay on the rough grass and stroked Eucrates' head as he bestowed some last lingering kisses to her tender vulva. A handful of small clouds drifted across the sky and she watched them with drowsy pleasure, feeling relaxed and at ease with herself, the world, and especially this new lover. She knotted her fingers in his hair and tenderly drew him up to kiss his mouth, sharing the taste of her own nectar on his lips as he must taste the lingering flavour of his own.

She heard Acantha return from her fit of ill humour, but didn't bother covering herself. Let the bitch see them and know what she had missed.

Instead of being jealous, however, Acantha burst into mocking laughter. 'Well,' she said. 'It seems you ended up with someone of your own worth after all.'

Chryseis rolled over, puzzled, then saw what Acantha was pointing at. High on Eucrates' shoulder was the dull purple weal of an old scar. It formed the shape of three links in a chain: the brand mark of a slave. She felt anger and the sharp pang of betrayal; he was nothing more than another worthless slave after all, and probably a runaway at that.

Eucrates stared back, his eyes unreadable below half-closed lids, but with his mouth tight. She turned away, her face burning.

Eucrates snorted and answered her silent thoughts, his voice bitter. 'Oh, yes. It's a slave brand. But what have you got to be so high and mighty for? You might have been a fine lady once, but from your clothes – had you been wearing them – I would have said you'd fallen on hard times, too. You're no better than I am.'

Chryseis turned on him, but before she could find the words to express her hurt, Acantha suddenly hissed, 'Someone's coming,' and ducked down.

'Who?' asked Chryseis. Maybe it was someone who would help them. She tried to stand, but Acantha pulled her down again with such a vicious glare that she daren't argue. She listened carefully and heard a rumble that could have been the sound of distant thunder, except it was getting louder. It was the pounding of approaching horses.

Eucrates raised himself cautiously, then crouched down again swiftly. 'Bandits,' he whispered. 'I recognise them.'

Acantha threw Chryseis her clothes. 'Get dressed,' she ordered.

'Wait a minute,' Chryseis interjected hotly. 'Why are you taking this slave's word for it? I think we should wait and see who they are.'

Acantha rubbed her hands over her face with strained patience, then turned to Eucrates. 'Well?' she asked. 'Any chance of talking with them?'

'None,' Eucrates replied, hurrying to pull on his tunic. 'The best you could hope for is that they'd kill you straight away.'

Acantha looked grim, but unsurprised. 'And the worst?'

'They're the sort to rob you, rape you, then sell you into slavery.'

'You see,' she explained to Chryseis with a bleak smile, 'the question is not whether I believe him, but whether I'm prepared to bet my life on his being a liar. How about you?'

Chryseis swallowed and shook her head.

'Good. Because I wasn't going to carry you if you'd decided to stay.'

'They'll be heading here to water their mounts,' said Eucrates. 'We'd better get a move on.'

'In that case, our only hope is the forest,' said Acantha, dragging Chryseis to her feet before she was even dressed. 'Come on.'

They ran as hard as they could and had almost reached the crest of the hill when a faint cry informed them they had been seen.

Five

Acantha heard the tempo of the hoof beats increase as the bandits urged their mounts in pursuit. She risked a fleeting look over her shoulder, assessing their chance of escaping into the forest before the riders caught them. Fortunately, the terrain was too uneven for the horses to stretch out into a full gallop. Most of the bandits were carefully picking their way down the hillside; only three pursued them with reckless haste.

The forest itself was still a couple of stades away, its boundary a spreading belt of bushes and saplings which offered no concealment or protection. It would hamper the fugitives, forcing them to veer amongst the undergrowth, while the heavier horses crashed straight after them.

They weren't going to make it.

Chryseis stumbled and would have fallen if Acantha hadn't seized her elbow and hauled her upright. The girl was still naked, her bare feet slowing her down and her ripe buttocks doubtless an additional incentive to the pursuers. Eucrates grasped Chryseis' other arm and helped pull her forward. They ran on.

They had reached the first saplings by the time the thud of hooves and jingle of harness sounded loud at their backs; the foremost horseman was on top of them, laughing. He probably thought this was going to be easy. Acantha spun round, sliced him from his saddle with her sword, and ignored the spray of blood.

Anger darkened the second rider's face. He tilted his spear and urged his mount forward. Acantha ducked under the lethal point, then stabbed upward into the horse's belly. The beast screamed horribly and fell in a tangle of legs and harness, smothering the bandit beneath it.

She had lost sight of the third rider. She looked around frantically and realised too late that he was charging at her from the side, the point of his spear level with her chest. Time slowed but she couldn't move fast enough to escape. She saw her own death coming for her, then the slender needle of a javelin pierced the rider's throat. He jerked back, his spear flying wide, then tumbled over his mount's rump.

Time snapped back into normality. To one side, Eucrates was recovering his balance from the throw that had saved her life, but there was no time for thanks. She chased after Chryseis who at least had had the sense not to stop running. Eucrates followed close behind.

They dodged bushes and ducked under lashing branches, with the main band of horsemen still charging after them. The trees became sturdier and the undergrowth more impenetrable, hindering their progress. The horsemen were closing the gap.

Then all sound of pursuit ceased.

Acantha glanced over her shoulder, then staggered to a halt to look again. The remaining riders, about fifteen or so, had pulled up. One stood in his stirrups to shout and shake his fist, but apparently they had abandoned the chase. Eucrates and Chryseis returned to stand beside her, their breath rasping.

'I'm not complaining,' said Eucrates, his chest heaving, 'but why?'

'I've no idea,' Acantha wheezed painfully, 'but we'd better push on before they change their minds.'

They took the chance, however, to catch their breath and let Chryseis dress, watching all the time to make

70

sure there was no trick. The riders stared back, but came no closer.

The bandits' reluctance to follow them amongst the gloomy trees left Acantha with an ominous feeling in her belly. She had disliked the look of the forest since the first time she had seen it, and had originally planned to skirt round it. Now, she heard the riders' mocking laughter and she shivered apprehensively.

Her unease grew as they penetrated deeper within the forest. It was very still under the shaded canopy; whatever winds blew in the unseen sky above, not even the faintest zephyr stirred down here. The motionless air was thick with the aromas of bark and moss and the warm, moist smell of fallen leaves. A lone woodpecker hammered in the distance, then fell silent. The hairs on the back of Acantha's neck prickled as she looked warily around.

Trailing moss and dirty cobwebs covered the ancient trees. Dark-leaved bushes with pallid blossoms crowded the spaces between the trunks forcing the three of them to twist and turn one way then another. Initially they followed the lie of the land, travelling downhill, deeper into the forest. After a while, however, the slope levelled off and there were no clues by which to determine their direction.

Acantha slowed to a halt and looked around at the enclosing trees.

Chryseis sniffed miserably as she bent to massage her feet. 'Where are we?'

'I don't know,' Acantha replied. Every direction looked identical.

Chryseis snorted. 'You mean we're lost!'

Acantha didn't need the obvious pointed out to her. 'Stop whining,' she snapped. 'If it hadn't been for you, we'd still be safely aboard the ship.'

Chryseis blinked and drew back. 'Don't speak to me like that!' she stammered.

71

'I'll speak to you any way I like, you little slut,' Acantha responded tightly and turned away without waiting for a reply.

'She doesn't deserve that,' commented Eucrates.

'No? And who asked you for your opinion? In fact, while I'm thinking about it, who exactly are you and what are you doing here with us?'

'I told you –'

'Did you? I wonder if that were the truth.' Acantha leant forward to peer into his eyes. 'Perhaps those weren't bandits after all. Maybe they were just honest citizens trying to recapture a runaway slave.'

Now it was Eucrates' face which darkened with anger and his voice rose. 'If you don't like –'

Undergrowth rustled. Bushes swayed, although there was no wind.

'Not animals,' whispered Acantha, easing her sword in its scabbard, but not yet drawing it. 'Our voices would have frightened them away.'

Eucrates reached for his weapon, then halted and gestured with his eyes to something behind her. She whirled around and saw strange faces peering out from the enclosing foliage. The first things she noticed were the stubby horns curling from the tops of their heads, and when the bushes parted and the figures emerged into full view she stepped back in alarm. From the waist down they were covered in wiry brown hair, while their enormous genitals stood proudly erect in a display of perpetual priapism.

'Satyrs!' squeaked Chryseis, rapidly sidling into the gap between Acantha and Eucrates.

Acantha had not been raised on such legends and was more sceptical. For a moment she wondered if she were dreaming. Then she looked more closely.

'Those horns are tied on,' she said quietly, so only her companions could hear.

'And those are leggings, not their own hair,' agreed Eucrates with relief.

'And those aren't real erections, just carved wood,' pointed out Chryseis wistfully.

Acantha counted ten of the newcomers. They were armed with bows and arrows and two carried a pole with a small deer slung from it. They had obviously been hunting and didn't seem especially hostile, merely inquisitive, walking round the trio and inspecting them. Chryseis remained between Acantha and Eucrates, who kept their hands cautiously upon their swords although they didn't draw them.

Eventually, one of the men addressed Eucrates. 'I bid you welcome to our forest, human. May you travel in peace,' he said formally, with a bow.

'Thank you,' Acantha replied, not trusting Eucrates to speak for her. 'It is a beautiful place. The trees are . . .' She skirted her true feelings about the claustrophobic greenery and weakly settled on, '. . . beautiful.'

The satyr studied her curiously. 'So long as you don't get lost,' he commented dryly.

'True,' Acantha acknowledged, suspecting he was toying with her. 'We are heading north-west to Chalcis.'

The satyr laughed. 'Then you must let us guide you. You have strayed far from your path.'

Acantha forced a smile. 'That is kind, but there is no need. If you would just point us in the right direction, I'm sure we could manage.'

'No, I insist. But tonight, you must come back to our village. We are having a feast.'

'That would be delightful,' Acantha said prevaricating, 'but our journey is urgent and we must hurry.'

'Our village is directly on your path,' insisted the satyr. 'In any case, it will be night soon and impossible to travel anyway. You will enjoy the revels; they are in honour of Dionysus, our god of wine and pleasure, and it is fitting that we share them with visitors.'

'I'm sure, but –'

'My subjects and I would make you most welcome.'

'Your subjects?' queried Chryseis, picking up the phrase with sudden interest.

'Yes.' The satyr gave a small bow. 'I am Seba, king of this forest.'

'How fortunate,' Chryseis cooed, 'to meet someone who can look after us so well. Of course we would be delighted to come with you.' She linked arms with Seba and walked off with him, chatting gaily, leaving Acantha and Eucrates to exchange disgruntled looks and tag along behind.

Chryseis' main reason for striking up a conversation with Seba had been to escape her companions. Acantha constantly looked down at her, and Eucrates' deception still rankled. However, to her surprise, she found Seba enthralling company. He identified the different trees and plants along their route and described the creatures that lived amongst them, from the highest branches to the meanest burrow amongst the roots. He was, indeed, lord of his domain, and she found herself attracted to his confident mastery.

It was late afternoon when the party eventually reached the satyrs' village, though she had not even realised it was there till Seba pointed it out to her. True to their adopted way of life, the satyrs had woven their homes and shelters out of the boughs of living trees. They were an integral part of the forest, invisible amongst the dense foliage until the travellers walked directly up to them.

The whole village, it seemed, turned out to inspect the newcomers. Youngsters peered from behind tree trunks and dangled from branches, as much at home in the forest as the beings they emulated.

The women appeared a few moments later. They, like their men, went in the guise of the mythical creatures associated with their god, Dionysus. In the women's case it meant taking on the appearance of nymphs, the

74

female counterparts to the satyrs. Nymphs and satyrs, with their love of wine and wild dancing, had been amongst the first followers of the hedonistic god. Now it seemed a cult had grown up to honour those early worshippers. What Chryseis couldn't say, however, was that the women dressed for the part. Nymphs wore nothing, and the women had depilated their bodies completely to reveal the cleft mounds of their pudenda and their labia. It was a display of sexuality as blatant as the phalluses adorning the men, and Chryseis felt a flutter of awakening interest.

The nymphs laughed at the newcomers, plucking in amusement at their clothes and chattering amongst themselves. However, they were as capricious as the beings they emulated, and their interest soon waned.

Within moments, two youths had hurried off with the deer carcass, followed by the jubilant children and the women who slipped their arms around the returning hunters and led them off. Soon there were only the three travellers and King Seba left.

He urged them towards a shelter built, like the others, from living boughs. 'You can rest here until it is time for the feast,' he said. 'I have business to attend to.'

'It must be hard work, being a ruler,' sympathised Chryseis, laying a hand on his arm. She felt Acantha's disapproval like a chill breeze at her back, but it didn't stop her running her fingers over Seba's well-formed biceps.

'Sometimes,' agreed Seba. 'However, it is mostly very stimulating and exciting.' He grinned at her and added, 'Just like a new lover.'

Chryseis felt a frisson of anticipation run down her spine. Seba's magnetism stirred her senses and she wondered how his own erection compared to the wooden phallus strapped around his waist. She was also curious to discover which of the two he used to please his women. 'And have you many lovers?' she asked.

'I always have room for another,' Seba replied.

'So long as they remember that I am his queen,' an icy voice added.

Another nymph had approached while they talked, perhaps the most beautiful Chryseis had seen so far. She strode towards them with lithe grace, her sensual features failing to conceal the hard glint in her eyes. Chryseis knew her attentions to Seba had not gone unmarked.

Seba smiled with ingenuous warmth, while carefully disengaging Chryseis' hand from his arm. 'Carme, come and meet our guests,' he said and, after introducing them all, obediently allowed Carme to lead him away. To her chagrin, Chryseis was left alone again with the others.

Acantha wasted no time before trying to bully Chryseis and order her around again. As soon as Seba and Carme were out of sight, she confronted Chryseis, prodding aggressively at the girl's chest. 'I want a word with you,' she hissed through clenched teeth. 'What do you think you're doing?'

'What's it to you?' Chryseis demanded furiously. 'Do you see your payment for my safe delivery slipping from your grasp? Well, too bad; that's your problem.'

'And do you think you belong here?' Acantha's voice was taut and low as she glanced around. 'These people are mad, you know, pretending to be what they are not. Eucrates has been telling me about a cult of Dionysus' worshippers called the Maenads, which is what these seem to be. They are unpredictable and very dangerous. We don't need you aggravating things by messing around with Seba.'

'Maybe I'm simply helping to establish friendly relations and secure our passage out of here. Had you thought of that?'

'That wasn't how Carme saw it.'

'Seba is king here. He can do what he likes,' Chryseis

said, then turned and walked away. She knew Acantha wouldn't make a scene by publicly dragging her back.

Chryseis walked through the village until she came to a large clearing where the evening's festivities were being prepared. By now, only the highest tree tops were splashed with sunlight; the villagers had lit lamps hung from low branches while in the centre of the clearing a large fire crackled into life. The deer caught by the hunters was already turning on a spit over the growing flames, adding the aroma of cooking meat to those of bread, fruit and cheese from the platters laid out on the grass. The most pervasive smell, however, was the sweet fragrance from the garlands of flowers that decorated the trees and hung around the villagers' necks.

Gradually, the bustle of preparation changed to an expectant murmur. Everyone gathered around the fire and a group of nymphs and satyrs with musical instruments appeared. A hush fell, then a drum spoke, a slow pulse at first on a single instrument, welcoming the dusk. Soon, other drums joined in, swelling the tattoo to a throbbing beat, while the pipes and lyres threaded a melody through the rhythm.

Satyrs and nymphs began dancing, twirling and gyrating across the hard-stamped ground. A young satyr, his wooden phallus canted up before him, took Chryseis by the hands and dragged her up to join in. Giggling at the sight of his wildly bobbing erection, she tried to follow his prancing steps. Other hands took her by the waist and spun her round, passing her from satyr to nymph to satyr. Somewhere along the way fingers caught at her chiton, the one she had made from Odic's old blanket, and ripped it free from one shoulder clasp. The cloth flapped around her as she whirled in time to the music, exposing her so completely that there was no point in maintaining any semblance of modesty. She tore off the last shreds of material and flung them high into the air to a chorus of cheers and calls.

Someone thrust an amphora of wine into her hands and Chryseis stopped to lift the jug and pour the red liquid down her throat. A grinning satyr took the chance to run his hands over her body, his fingers darting towards the narrow cleft between her legs. She laughed in delight then passed the amphora back to him, and spun away once more, awash with excitement.

The drum beat pulsed in time with the blood pounding in her ears, and though she knew her legs were already weary from the day's travels they felt capable of dancing forever. Flames and sparks from the central fire shot skyward, seeming to move with the music. They warmed her bare skin as she pranced in a complicated pattern of intersecting paths with the other dancers. There were many collisions, each an opportunity for inquisitive exploration. She ran her fingers across the bare pudenda of the nymphs, marvelling at the softness of their skin, in return accepting curious fingers exploring her own dark triangle and moist recesses.

A dancing couple parted to make way for her, then came together again as she twirled between them, sandwiching her between their bodies, the satyr in front, the nymph behind. The satyr kissed her greedily, his tongue searching her mouth. She reached up curiously to touch his horns and was surprised at the shudder of mock ecstasy that went through his body as he stroked his wooden phallus up and down her belly in lascivious delight.

The nymph rubbed her breasts against Chryseis' back, the soft mounds punctuated by the hard points of her nipples. She nuzzled the nape of Chryseis' neck and ran her hands over her rib-cage. Then one hand slipped down, insinuating itself between Chryseis' legs, brushing her anus and stroking the entrance to her sex before curling up between her body and the satyr's. Chryseis saw the nymph's hand grasp the great phallus and pull it down so that its bulb nudged between Chryseis' legs, answering her question as to whether it was purely decorative. She shifted position, giving the couple better access, and felt the nymph guide the carved glans between the eager lips of her vulva.

She didn't know whether she could take all of the enormous dildo within her; it was fatter and longer than any real cock, and she feared what would happen if the satyr should plunge the full length inside her. Still, she persevered. She wanted to be impaled, wanted to feel herself stretched over the mighty shape, wanted to pant and grunt in wanton abandonment as the enormous phallus pounded into her to the rhythm of the drums.

Gradually, she felt her vagina stretch to accommodate the unreal helmet. She bit her lip and ground down, working with the nymph to feed him into her. Around them, the other villagers continued dancing, too involved in their own pleasures to spare more than a passing glance for what she was doing. The head of the dildo finally eased its way into her and the rest of the rigid weapon slid home. The satyr's face was alive with excitement, his yellow eyes burning as he stared at her while thrusting himself into her in time to the ever present drums. She moved in response, continuing their dance, prevented from unbalancing and falling over by the nymph's supporting arms. Chryseis abandoned herself to the music, the beat, the pulse and felt the heat of her excitement spread upwards from the pivotal point deep within her belly. Her breath quickened and her vision closed in until she was swept up into a long, delicious orgasm.

The satyr pulled free, the end of his phallus gleaming with her moisture. The nymph darted round, took his hands in hers and twirled away without a backward glance. Chryseis had barely blinked at the abruptness of their departure when she felt feather-light caresses round her hips and groin. She looked down to see another nymph kneeling in front of her, kissing her pubic mound and licking at the secretions running down the inside of her legs. In moments the nymph's hot tongue was probing at the crevice of Chryseis' sex, flickering across the small pearl of pleasure and bringing Chryseis to a second orgasm. Chryseis staggered weakly back, her knees trembling from the paroxysms of her second climax. The nymph stood up with a satisfied smile, her face still wet with the juices she had been lapping, bestowed a brief kiss on Chryseis' mouth and departed as rapidly as she had arrived.

Chryseis felt a small laugh bubbling up from deep within her as she looked at the orgy around her. She had never seen anything so outrageous in her life, and thought it was wonderful. All around her, satyrs and nymphs were melded in previously unimagined permutations and combinations while still keeping time with the incessant beat of the drums. She saw one nymph perched on a satyr's shoulders, but facing backward so that her groin was in his face, while both continued to wave their arms to the music. Another nymph was on her hands and knees, impaled fore and aft by a pair of young satyrs who seemed intent upon meeting each other in the middle of her body. A further satyr was barely visible as he lay on the ground beneath a pile of pale nymphs, the smallest of whom was even gratifying herself upon one of his horns.

She saw Acantha with a goblet of wine in one hand, a satyr's wooden phallus in the other, seemingly undecided which to sample first. Eucrates rose and fell upon a nymph who had her legs wrapped around his waist and was moaning ecstatically. Chryseis felt a disconcerting pang at the sight which she immediately ignored. Instead, feeling hungry all of a sudden, she picked her way among the writhing bodies in search of something to eat.

The deer was cooked by now and she tore off a strip of pink meat with her bare hands. It burnt her fingers

and she let it cool by juggling it fr[...]
other.

'Here, use this,' offered Seba, h[...]
platter, which Chryseis accepted [...]
you enjoying our festivities?' he c[...]

'They're fun. But what's the oc[...]

'Occasion?' Seba laughed. 'We [...]
moon is waxing and, most important, it is a who[...]
since our last revels. What other reasons do we need?'

'You do this every night?' She wondered how they
could keep up the pace – as well as everything else.

'Why not? It is, as you say, fun, and what other
purpose is there in life but the pursuit of pleasure. That,
after all, is what Dionysus taught us.'

'Some people, my uncle for one, say that we should
aspire to loftier values.' She tore at the hot meat with
her teeth, letting the bloody juice run down her chin.

'And do you agree with him? The very words betray
the belief that pleasure is not in itself a worthy aspir-
ation.' Seba cupped one of Chryseis' breasts in his hand
and ran his thumb across her nipple, stirring it into life.
'Why should we deny ourselves the simplest and most
basic of delights? The gods gifted us with bodies which
are capable of providing us with all the pleasure we
need. Wouldn't we be thwarting their grand purpose if
we denied it?'

'I suppose, therefore, that this is really a form of
worship,' agreed Chryseis, licking the juice from her
fingers one by one.

'Of the most pious kind,' grinned Seba, his eyes
locked on hers as his thumb continued to tease her.

Chryseis felt desire stir in her again as the tingle in her
breast spread throughout her body. But she thought to
ask, 'What of Carme?'

Seba glanced over his shoulder. 'What about her?' he
asked, dropping his hand from her breast.

'She seemed to think she had some rights over you.'

d, noting his discomfort. She stroked his
added, 'But if you're king here, I suppose you
whatever you like.'
a's laugh sounded forced, but Chryseis didn't
'Exactly,' he said. 'And, in any case, do you think
could be so enthusiastic if we remained with only one
partner? No, there is no exclusivity here. All can make
love with whomever they choose, just as freely as they
speak to them.'

Chryseis took his hand in hers and replaced it on her
breast. 'You're speaking to me.'

'So I am,' Seba smiled. He put his arm around her
and led her to the other side of the fire where he eased
her down on to the thick animal skins which had been
spread across the ground. The fur soothed her skin,
lightly caressing her naked body like a thousand gentle
lovers. Seba sat beside her and ran his hands over her,
from her feet to her shoulders, along her arms then back
again. He was in no hurry and wanted to inspect every
crack and crevice as intimately as possible. He lifted one
foot and studied it minutely before kissing it, first lightly
then harder, sucking on her toes and licking between
them. The act was oddly arousing, perhaps because no
one else had ever bothered before. Chryseis lifted herself
on to her elbows to watch the satyr nibble, taste and
explore each toe in turn as if it were the sole object of
his desires, before progressing to the next. Then, when
all had received their due, he moved up to her ankles
and investigated them with the same thoroughness.
Slowly, he progressed up her body. He remarked on the
faded scar on her shin, the mole on her right calf. He
discovered how the backs of her knees were especially
sensitive, and she would squirm and giggle at the
lightest touch. And he chuckled softly at the way her
breath caught when his wet tongue left a cooling trail
across the fragile skin of her inner thigh.

Now she could reach him with her hands. She stroked

his head, running her fingers through his hair and feeling the points of his horns. She found the ribbon holding the strange adornment in place and tugged it loose. Seba's breath shortened as his caresses became more urgent. He burrowed his head between her thighs, savouring the dried streaks that marked her earlier encounters. Then, finally, he delved into the crevice of her sex, his tongue twirling around the hub of her passion, following the folds of her labia, plunging within her vagina. Chryseis arched back in a spasm of pleasure and placed her feet on Seba's shoulders to present herself better to him. The satyr responded eagerly: eating, kissing and devouring her until her orgasm washed over her and she cried out as if wounded.

As she gasped and caught her breath, Seba knelt over her, offering his wooden phallus to her lips. Chryseis turned away, refusing it. She wanted the real man, not the false satyr. She grasped the massive dildo and ripped it from him, and saw for the first time his own erection. It made her wonder why Seba, at least, felt it necessary to embellish the truth. His own phallus was long and thick and rose upwards like a young tree trunk from the dense undergrowth of his pubic hairs. Chryseis dipped her head to smother the organ with her mouth, sliding her tongue around the gleaming dome, sipping the satyr's lust as it seeped from the tip. It tasted musky and dark, the essence of man. Seba pushed harder at her mouth, wanting to penetrate her further. Chryseis tried to accept him but couldn't. Even in reality, he was too big for her mouth and, as she let him slide free, he almost whimpered with the urgency of his need.

Chryseis turned, kneeling on the animal skins on her hands and knees, presenting him with her rump. Seba barely paused before propelling himself within her, violently stretching her to capacity. Her cry was pain and pleasure mingled in equal portions and she did not understand how she could feel both in the same moment. She grunted and yelped as Seba pounded against her womb, pushing back as best she could. She lowered her head till it touched the ground and looked back beneath her body at him. Her breasts hung down, quivering in time with his thrusts, swaying in front of her view of his legs and balls as they slapped against her elevated vulva. She reached back, letting her fingernails scratch lightly at his scrotum as it jerked back and forth. Seba responded by bellowing his need for her and lay across her back, reaching round to grasp her breasts and maul them with abandoned passion.

Chryseis' breath sobbed in uneven pants as she bore the brunt of his lust. In this position, she could do little except submit to his needs. Seba's movements grew shorter and sharper, then he thrust deep inside her one last time and ejaculated, releasing his sperm. His cock pulsed within her, triggering her own orgasm, so her moans of satisfaction echoed his own cries.

For a moment they remained locked together, savouring the last moments of their union, then slowly disentangled themselves and rolled over on to the bed of animal skins. They rested, entwined, basking in the glow of their satiated lust and the leaping flames of the fire.

Around them, the revels continued. No one paid them the slightest bit of attention; all were too busy with their own pleasures. Satyrs and nymphs ate and drank, laughed and danced, and, most of all, they copulated, fucked and made love. Chryseis could see couples and groups entangled with each other at various points around the fire, merging one into the other so that the chain of people pleasuring one another formed a never-ending circle.

Only one person was watching them. She stared at them from the other side of the fire, the flames glittering in her eyes. It took Chryseis a moment to recognise Carme, the nymph's face was so twisted with hate. The look made Chryseis uneasy, but she turned away, ignoring it. Seba was king here, and in any case, she had better things to do than worry about a jealous rival. She rolled over and began fondling Seba's soft testicles and penis, marvelling at the speed with which his erection revived. Carme had no reason to be possessive; Seba obviously had the capacity to please them both. Chryseis bent her head to kiss the tip of Seba's phallus, still moist with their love-making. There was no point in wasting such a bounteous harvest.

Pain tore at her scalp as her hair was yanked back. She glimpsed Carme's face, dark with fury, as her clawed fingers struck towards Chryseis' eyes.

Chryseis ducked and Carme's nails slashed her cheek, tumbling her sideways. Carme kicked her ribs, her breasts, her stomach, driving Chryseis back to the fire. 'Get away from him,' she screeched. 'We don't want your sort here. You're disgusting.'

'But – but –' Chryseis babbled while desperately looking round for help. She was close to the fire now, the crackling wood only a body-length away.

'Go on, burn,' Carme screamed, pushing her backward. 'Let the world be rid of you.'

Sparks stung Chryseis' naked skin, the heat scorched her flesh. She began to panic.

Seba wrapped his arms around Carme from behind and lifted her aside, kicking and thrashing, so that Chryseis could step clear. 'That is enough!' he barked.

Even as she stood shaking from shock, Chryseis noted that the drums had stopped, the lyres and pipes fallen silent. Everyone began gathering around, watching her, their eyes accusing. It was a relief when Eucrates appeared beside her, naked and clutching a sword. Acantha arrived moments later.

'Outsiders,' Carme hissed at Seba. 'How can you bear to have that filth touch you?'

'You were jealous!' Seba exclaimed. He managed to look both guilty and also slightly pleased with himself.

'But why? You've never minded others ...,' he said gesturing around at the other nymphs.

Carme stamped her foot in frustration. 'They are different; they're my sisters and cousins. They know you are mine and I know they are only having some fun.' She turned and glared at Chryseis. 'But this one. I saw the way she took you. She meant to keep you for herself; she wanted to possess you.'

A disapproving whisper rippled through the watching villagers. Chryseis thought that Carme was the one being possessive, but before she could even the score Acantha spoke up.

'We are sorry to have offended your hospitality,' she said with formal politeness. 'We will leave immediately.'

'Do you think that is enough?' screeched Carme. 'Do you think you can walk away as if nothing happened? I saw her.' She stabbed a finger at Chryseis as if it were a knife. 'She took Seba's seed, not the satyr's gift, but Seba's own, human, seed. He is mine, and mine alone.' Her face contorted with fury and the spectators muttered angrily.

Seba cut in hurriedly. 'Yes. It is probably best that you leave. But,' he added, looking around to see who would challenge him, 'the morning is soon enough.' A whisper ran round the watchers. 'The morning,' emphasised Seba, holding up his hand for silence. 'Then we will lead you to the edge of the forest. The route is quite direct from there, so long as you don't get lost again.'

'Perhaps you should hope that you do, though,' commented Carme venomously. 'Because, if I ever find you, I swear I'll get my revenge.'

Six

Acantha's resentment drove her to set a gruelling pace throughout the next day. The disgrace of the previous night still burnt and, to make matters worse, she had not managed to get rid of Eucrates, whom she still distrusted. When she had suggested that he leave them and go his own way, Chryseis had said that she needed another servant to look after her, and handed him her pack to carry. Surprisingly, Eucrates seemed quite happy with the arrangement and Acantha suspected that he had a soft spot for the Chryseis. Whatever, it had been obvious that he had no intention of leaving and Acantha had been forced to back down, a further source of humiliation.

She had little sympathy, therefore, for the young woman who stumbled along behind, whingeing about her lack of sleep and the state of her feet. There was nothing in these highlands which ran the length of Euboea except sparse grass and rocky outcrops, and she wanted to reach more hospitable lands as soon as possible. Even so, they were still crossing wide, bleak moorland when the sun dipped towards the horizon, casting long shadows across the ground. They needed to find shelter for the night. Acantha stopped and studied the surrounding area as she waited for the others to catch up with her.

'See anything?' Eucrates asked.

Acantha gestured to their left, to where a dip in the

...id all but the very tops of some trees. 'Maybe
...e. If nothing else, there should be wood for a fire.'
Eucrates nodded and extended a hand to help Chryseis
back to her feet. The young woman had already slumped
to the ground in exhaustion and she groaned painfully as
she was pulled upright. The sight almost moved Acantha
to pity her a little, and she recognised that they had to
stop soon whether they found somewhere suitable or not.

What she had not expected was to find a villa nestling
amongst groves of olive trees, its white marble walls
gleaming in the last of the day's sunlight.

'At last,' sighed Chryseis. 'Somewhere decent to stay.'

'Wait!' snapped Acantha, grabbing the young woman
to prevent her from immediately marching into the
residence and demanding shelter. 'Whoever lives here
may not like travellers visiting them unannounced.'

'We can ask,' insisted Chryseis. 'What would you
have me do? Sit outside, huddled over a meagre fire,
and chew charred rabbit?' She shrugged Acantha's arm
away and for the first time that day managed a turn of
speed as she headed towards the building.

'She's right,' said Eucrates over his shoulder as he
followed. 'There's nothing to be lost by asking.'

Acantha hung back a moment, furious at being ignored, then reluctantly followed the others through the
open gateway.

Inside, the courtyard was beautiful. A shaded cloister
formed a continuous walkway around the perimeter, so
that even at midday the villa's occupants would be able
to stroll around at ease and enjoy the sight and smell of
the central gardens. The air was heavy with scents from
the shrubs and flowers that grew in carefully tended
geometric patterns of colour, separated from one another by narrow gravel paths. The paths themselves
linked small open spaces in the profusion of plants, and
in the centre of each space stood a sculpture of pristine
marble.

Acantha went over to examine the nearest carving. It was of a man and woman, joined together at the peak of their passion. The woman was on her hands and knees, her head thrown back and her mouth open in an endless cry of ecstasy. The man knelt behind her, his muscles knotted with the force of his lust as he drove himself into her. From the shape of the woman's hanging breasts to the arch of the man's back, the detail was immaculate. Acantha stroked the cold flesh, needing to feel the subtle texturing left by the stonemason's chisel to reassure her that the figures had been carved from stone.

She looked around at the other sculptures. Each depicted one, two or more figures poised at some moment of sexual passion. She saw a couple, head to tail, pleasuring each other with their mouths; two men penetrating a single woman, her face frozen in surprised gratification; even a lone man stroking his own upright member and laughing as he displayed himself with pride. Chryseis and Eucrates were wandering together from tableau to tableau, pointing out the more lewd poses and standing closer to each other with every step. Acantha stared after them, seeing what was happening between them and feeling left out.

'The sight of the figures often awakens desire,' said a soft voice behind her.

Acantha spun round sharply, her hand instinctively reaching for her sword. A lone woman had approached from the main building and now stood quietly, her hands clasped loosely before her, politely waiting for Acantha to respond.

'I'm sorry. You startled me,' Acantha replied, relaxing. 'We're travellers and seek shelter for the night; even a warm stable would be a comfort.'

The woman laughed. 'I'm not that inhospitable to my guests,' she rebuked gently, dismissing Acantha's suggestion with an airy gesture. As she waved her slender arms, the rows of bracelets on her wrists chimed melodiously and a hint of her perfume wafted to Acantha's nostrils. She felt herself quicken and noted that it was not merely the statues that could awaken desire; the woman's eyes had a tangible presence that made Acantha tingle.

'You are most kind,' said Acantha with a bow.

The woman smiled and clapped her hands sharply, summoning two servants from the shadows. 'These two will show you to my guest rooms and, once you are all refreshed, you will join me for a meal. I am Mellita, by the way.'

Chryseis and Eucrates joined them and, when introduced to Mellita, seemed as quick to respond to her as Acantha had been. The woman was all charm, enquiring after their needs and instructing the servants to make sure they had anything that they desired. Even Chryseis dropped her sullen attitude in favour of a responsiveness that Acantha had not realised the girl possessed.

'How fortunate we are to have stumbled upon such a generous host,' commented Eucrates with a puzzled frown as he watched Mellita return inside.

Acantha looked at him sharply. 'What are you implying?'

Eucrates pursed his lips and shrugged. 'Not a thing. Who am I to deride the charitable instincts of others?'

'Exactly,' interjected Chryseis. 'Don't judge everyone by your own standards; there are honest people in the world.'

Eucrates shook his head but said nothing else as they were shown to their room. The servants did no more than place their meagre baggage in the centre of the floor, then retreat again in total silence. Then he nodded towards the closed door. 'They don't seem very happy here.'

Chryseis snorted with derision. 'I might have known you'd care more about your own class.'

Acantha preferred to keep quiet rather than side with either of them. In any case, she was too busy looking around their accommodation. The room was decorated with elegant simplicity, just three beds down one wall and a pair of sandalwood chests for their belongings against the other. An archway led off to the side and she gave a cry of delight when she realised that it led to a smaller room with a sunken bath in its centre, aromatic steam already curling from the water.

She immediately began to peel off her travel-soiled clothes, but Chryseis was quicker and plunged in, spraying water everywhere. Acantha hurriedly tossed her garments aside and jumped in beside her. The hot water stung her skin, but after a moment she grew used to it and the feeling settled into a steady glow. She relaxed and let it soak through to her bones and muscles, easing the knots and weary tensions of the day. It was amazing how a little comfort could dispel the dreariest mood and make everything seem fine. Even her companions seemed only fractionally as irritating as they had before. 'Come on,' she called to Eucrates. 'There's plenty of room.'

Eucrates eyed them for a moment, then shrugged off his tunic and eased into the water beside them, sighing with pleasure as he did so. 'Now all I need is someone to wash me,' he commented drowsily, at last seeming to throw off his suspicions.

'Mmmm. That could be fun,' murmured Chryseis.

'That's not what you said the last time I asked you,' said Acantha, referring to their argument at the watering hole, though without any rancour. It seemed a long time ago.

Chryseis looked at her sideways. 'Maybe you should ask again,' she said coquettishly, and under the concealing bubbles Acantha felt fingers lightly caress her belly. 'But,' Chryseis added with a giggle as she drew back, 'I think that at the moment I'm hungrier for food than for

91

anything else, so I wouldn't want to get distracted – at least for now.'

The three finished washing themselves separately, but in high spirits and with an expectant air. When they emerged from the bath they found their old clothes had gone and fresh chitons of soft wool laid out for them. There were bottles and jars of oils and lotions, too, as well as phials of delicate floral perfumes. They dried and adorned themselves happily, then went in search of their hostess.

They found her in a chamber of scarlet porphyry and pink-veined marble. Acantha hesitated in the doorway, struck by the room's opulence. A ring of slender pillars supported the roof and formed shielded alcoves, most of which were occupied by further erotic tableaux. A final statue of a lone woman formed the centre piece for the room: the splashing water of a fountain cascaded over the undulations of her body, forming rivulets around her breasts and rippling through her fingers as they pressed fervidly between her thighs.

Mellita languished on a padded couch, trailing her hand in the fountain's cool water. 'Make yourselves comfortable,' she said. 'I hope you will find something to your taste.' She gestured to where further couches crowded within easy reach of a low table laden with jugs of wine and golden dishes of pungent cheeses and bright fruits. The warm, yeasty aroma of fresh bread made Acantha's mouth water.

The travellers settled themselves on their couches, awed into silence by their surroundings. Even Acantha, who considered herself the equal of anybody, felt daunted by their hostess's display of wealth. Mellita smiled smugly, evidently aware of the effect she was having on them, then clapped her hands to summon her servants.

A line of silent men and women with downcast eyes appeared. They carried more platters of food and piled them on to the low table until Acantha wondered how they were supposed to consume even a quarter of the feast. After they had brought in the banquet, the servants remained and knelt or sat beside each of the diners, helping them to lie comfortably on the soft couches, then plying them with food. Acantha had a young man and woman to look after her and was too busy tasting all the morsels they presented to her lips to worry about talking. There were succulent meats, so tender that they dissolved on the tongue. There were vegetables: steamed, baked and roasted. And there was wine the colour of dark blood whose aroma alone induced a heady intoxication. Acantha saw that Chryseis and Eucrates were similarly involved and managed, between mouthfuls, to exchange grins with them. How lucky they had been to find Mellita's villa.

'It's a beautiful place. Do you live here alone?' Acantha asked eventually, when her hunger had evaporated into sleepy satisfaction.

'I used to share it with my sister, Lyria.' Some unknown emotion flickered across Mellita's face. 'But she moved away, to the east, to be with her animals on the other side of the mountain. I live alone now.'

'You're not married then?' Acantha asked in surprise; it was rare for a woman to be a landowner in her own right.

'No. Lyria ...' Mellita stopped and forced a smile, but whether she was hiding pain or anger Acantha couldn't tell. 'Have you tried these?' Mellita asked abruptly, indicating a plate of sweetmeats. 'They are especially nice.'

Acantha sensed dark secrets, but politely accepted the change of conversation. 'I honestly don't know. There is so much ...' She indicated the still laden table. 'I don't know what your servants have been putting in my mouth, I really don't.'

'Then I must be a better host and tend to you

personally,' Mellita said with renewed vigour, waving Acantha's attendants away. She took a golden bowl from the table and sat on the couch so that her warm thigh pressed against Acantha's side. Then she picked a sticky confection from the dish and offered it for the mercenary to taste.

Acantha nibbled on it delicately. The sweetmeat was a mix of fruits, honey and subtle spices; she detected cinnamon and ginger plus others she could not name. Despite the quantity of food she had already consumed that evening, the flavours excited her palate. She opened her mouth wider and Mellita slid the rest of the dainty between her lips. As the woman's fingertips brushed her mouth, Acantha kissed them briefly.

'You like that?' Mellita asked archly, letting her fingers linger.

'It's the way it's served that makes it special,' Acantha murmured. She gripped the woman's hand to stop her drawing back as she kissed the fingers again, sucking them one by one into her mouth, licking each one clean of the sticky sweet.

Mellita chuckled lightly. 'I think you want to eat me, too.'

'Are you on the menu?' Acantha's voice sounded husky, even to her.

Mellita smiled secretively and pulled her hand away. 'No. I'm the cook, not the feast.'

'Oh.' Acantha was disappointed but also intrigued. 'What do you mean by that?'

'I think,' said Mellita as she picked up another of the sweetmeats, 'that your friends would enjoy these, too.' She crushed the confection in her fist, squeezing it back and forth between her hands until it was reduced to a pulp which oozed slowly between her fingers. 'As you said, though, what counts is how it is served,' she whispered, using a single finger to draw a sticky line down Acantha's neck.

Acantha tried to swallow the sudden tightness in her throat. 'It would be a shame to mark such a fine garment, don't you think?' she commented, her voice uneven.

'Then you had better remove it, hadn't you?'

Acantha glanced over to where her companions still lay on their couches. They were watching with avid interest and Acantha's breath quickened under the intensity of their gaze as she stood up to remove her tunic. The chiton was held in place by a clasp at each shoulder. She undid the first one slowly, pulling the pin out until suddenly it came free and the material dropped to expose a single swollen nipple. She stroked it, revelling in her audience's attention, especially delighted by Mellita's intense stare and the hungry way her tongue moistened her lips.

Acantha unfastened the second clasp. It came undone without hindrance, releasing the chiton to cascade into a puddle at her feet. She wore nothing beneath, and did a slow pirouette to show herself off, after which she lay back on the couch again and made herself ready for whatever their hostess had planned.

Mellita took more of the paste and spread it over Acantha's shoulders and chest, then smeared it liberally across her breasts. The confection was cool, causing her nipples to pucker into hard peaks at its touch. Acantha raised one coated breast to her lowered head and tongued the sweetmeat from her own skin. The spiced fruits, warmed by the heat of her body, were already filling her nostrils with their aromatic tang.

'Wouldn't you rather have someone else do that for you?' suggested Eucrates, rising from his seat.

Acantha hesitated, but regardless of how she viewed him personally, he was still a fine physical specimen, and what she felt just now was pure lust. 'I was only waiting for a volunteer,' she said, and slowly tongued another patch of flesh clean. 'But you'd better hurry, while there's still some left.'

Mellita tutted in disapproval. 'I would be a poor host if I didn't provide sufficient fare for all your needs. Let me prepare a proper feast.' She pressed Acantha back into the couch and began arranging her to her own satisfaction. 'You'll ruin everything if you move though,' Mellita warned. 'Do you promise to remain still?'

'Yes, of course,' Acantha replied, her pulse racing.

'Mmmm. You seem very confident. But I think we'd better be safe though, don't you?' Mellita snapped her fingers and one of the silent servants handed her a length of red silken rope. For a moment, worry flickered in Acantha's mind, then she relented, revelling in the sense of trust that allowed her to submit to the woman so completely. She did not resist as Mellita pulled her hands tightly back and bound them together to some unseen fixing above her head, nor did she struggle as her ankles were roped to the legs on opposite sides of the couch, splaying her thighs apart to expose her genitals.

'Now,' said Mellita, as she tightened the last knot and picked up a bowl of fruit, 'I think that maybe some more . . .' Her voice trailed off as she became absorbed in her task. She used slices of soft peach to encircle Acantha's nipples, then crowned them with the pulp scooped from the interior of a pomegranate. The cold juice ran across Acantha's body, pooled in the hollow between her breasts, then trickled down the sides of her ribs in thin, chilly lines. Mellita spooned raspberries into Acantha's navel, forcing her to remain motionless lest their dark red juice spilled out over her pale skin.

Acantha lay back and savoured Mellita's gentle preparation. There was nothing she could do to either aid or prevent Mellita doing whatever she wished, or to shy away from any experience imposed upon her. The situation brought its own frisson of pleasure: the total abdication of any responsibility except submitting to another's whims.

Acantha watched Mellita's face through half-closed eyes. It was taut with suppressed emotion as she concentrated on placing spirals and loops of red, yellow and green fruits across her body, marking lines along her limbs and forming decorative clusters around her most sensitive zones. Eucrates and Chryseis also watched with rapt attention, while the servants formed a silent and impassive ring around them.

Mellita crushed more of the sweetmeats into a paste and smeared the mixture through the copper-brown triangle below Acantha's belly. She spooned dark, wine-soaked cherries on top. The alcohol in which they had been steeped trickled into the narrow cleft concealed beneath the hair, making Acantha catch her breath at the stinging intrusion. Mellita's face lit up with cruel mischief and she poured more of the liquor on top of the confection, easing Acantha's vulva apart with long fingers so that the liquid ran deep within her, causing her to bite her lip as the juice nipped her flesh.

Just as Acantha thought she could endure no more, Mellita relented. 'There. And now, the finishing touch.' She selected another jug from the table and began pouring a thin stream of honey and yoghurt across the outlander's soft skin. The line spiralled her breasts, crossed her belly and puddled amongst the fruit clustered in her navel. Then the rivulet meandered lazily atop the delicacies between her thighs, washing away the last sting of the alcohol and blending with her own copious juices.

Mellita stepped back and walked around Acantha's immobilised form, inspecting her handiwork. Acantha trembled, anticipating the woman would lead the feast which she assumed would follow. Instead, Mellita returned to her own couch and left everyone waiting till she had made herself comfortable. Then, finally, she gestured Eucrates and Chryseis forward. 'Begin,' she instructed them. 'Your banquet awaits you.'

97

Acantha's companions, grinning wildly, hurried to kneel on opposite sides of her supine body. They began their task by licking and sucking the rivulets of juice that trailed down her sides, their warm, wet tongues and pliant lips vivid sources of pleasure on her chilled skin. From there, they worked their way up her sides, probing at her ribs and laughing as she squirmed away. Then, one after the other, they nuzzled the softer flesh of her breasts and nibbled at the toppings of fruit and berries. On one side, Eucrates bit through the peaches ringing her areola while, on the other side, Chryseis sucked the crowning cherry from her breast, then worked her way outwards, lapping at the pomegranate.

'Both of you, suck on her nipples,' Mellita instructed. Her voice trembled. Acantha looked over to where their hostess reclined comfortably on her couch with her dress hoisted around her waist and her hand thrust between her thighs. 'I want to see you enjoy yourselves,' she said. 'I want to see that you miss nothing.'

Acantha's companions obeyed immediately. Eucrates caught one nipple sharply between his teeth while Chryseis' soft lips sucked tenderly on the other. The contrasting feelings radiated from Acantha's breasts to her belly where they merged into a single incandescent blaze. She moaned and closed her eyes, consumed by the sensation.

'You now, Chryseis. Suck harder, engulf her whole breast with your mouth.' Chryseis obeyed as best she could and Acantha's breath grew uneven at the soft ache from her maltreated flesh. 'That's right,' confirmed Mellita. 'Eucrates, move your head lower. Lap the honey from her ribs. Slowly, very slowly, clean it from her skin.' Acantha felt the man's tongue lick the ticklish flesh beneath her ribs, making her twist away. 'Good. Does that make you feel hot? Does your engorged cock long for some attention, too? Yes, I thought so; take it in your hand. Gently, gently. Let me see . . . Oh, yes, you are ready, aren't you? No, Chryseis, I didn't say you could do that; just stroke it. That's enough; you've got to wait for the others.'

Even in the stupor of her arousal, Acantha noted how Mellita's fingers plunged in and out of the dark forest between her legs. Acantha's own sex cried out for similar treatment; it felt hot, on fire, screaming for release and she wished her hands were free to pleasure herself as the others were doing.

'Now clean her belly.' Mellita's voice was insistent. 'Side by side, your cheeks touching, your tongues fighting over the same delicacy. Yes, that's it. Chryseis, move to her navel; probe its depths with your tongue. Acantha! Stay still. And Eucrates, make sure no part of her has been left uncleaned; I like my guests well washed.'

The soft fluttering against Acantha's skin moved lower as she strained against the securing ties. She wanted to grab her companions and force them to satisfy her but, instead, the silken ropes held her firm, unable to do more than wriggle. She groaned with frustration and impatience, and wondered at the apparent indifference of the watching servants. Didn't they feel any urge to participate in the proceedings?

'I think Acantha has waited long enough,' Mellita commented with an indulgent smile. 'You may ease her desire a little, Eucrates. No,' she laughed. 'Not like that.' Acantha moaned as Eucrates removed his finger and wondered how much longer she would have to endure this torment. 'Some more of that honey I think. Smear it along your cock; more, more. And some on those lovely tight balls. Now rub it in so that the sweetness will blend with your skin, but not too hard; we don't want you to add your own cream to the mix. Fine. Now kneel over Acantha and let her taste it.'

Eucrates faced Acantha as he straddled her chest. His thighs brushed her breasts, his knees jammed tightly into her armpits. She could smell his body, the tang of his excitement a bright note against the dark, warm scent of his masculinity. She strained up to meet his sweetened member as he offered it to her mouth and brushed it with her lips, and she extended her tongue to lap the cream from his glans. Eucrates pushed his hips forward, making himself more readily available to her. Acantha craned her neck round to suck on his balls, drawing them one by one into her mouth, increasing the suction till he groaned with pleasure. Then, bit by bit, she licked the sticky honey from his genitals, her hunger increasing with every mouthful.

'Enough, enough. You must not rush your food,' Mellita instructed sharply. Acantha met Eucrates' eyes. She could read the urgency of his desire and for a moment she thought he would ignore Mellita and continue. She sucked harder, encouraging him, eager to taste the bitterness of his come mixed with the sweet honey she lapped from his skin. 'Now, I say,' Mellita snapped, meaning it. A small part of Acantha's mind ridiculed her own subservience as she released her grip and let Eucrates slowly, reluctantly, withdraw from her mouth.

'Just a little patience,' Mellita soothed. 'I think you are almost ready.'

Acantha was more than ready, but still she said nothing, only waited for instructions.

'Chryseis, you may eat the rest of the sweetmeats now.'

At last Acantha felt Chryseis' cool breath ruffle the sensitive hairs between her legs and graze the tender flesh within. The girl's touch was light but insistent as she nuzzled against the wet opening of Acantha's desire and sought out the tastiest morsels from the crevices of her body. The battle-hardened mercenary arched her back in an irresistible paroxysm at the sensation. She bucked and heaved, fighting to rub herself harder against Chryseis' willing mouth, but was held back by both the restraining ropes and Eucrates' weight across her chest. The small, wet point of Chryseis' tongue slithered into her slick chasm and lapped tenderly at her sweet bud till she cried out in frustration and excitement.

'Now,' instructed Mellita imperiously, 'I want Chryseis to climb on top of Acantha; Eucrates will make room. Chryseis, let Acantha scent your own sweet fig, but without tasting it; not yet.'

Chryseis immediately obeyed. Keeping her mouth fixed on Acantha's sex, she pivoted around to present the bodyguard with a view of her dark pubic hair and the swollen lips that pouted so invitingly from its centre. Acantha could see the distended labia glisten with Chryseis' desire, making them shine like glazed fruits. She could smell them, too, a heady aroma of musk and jasmine and sweet flesh, crying out to be devoured. Even Chryseis' pink, puckered anus appeared like a tightly folded flower, and Acantha wished her long fingers were free to prise open its blossom. She craned upwards, stretching her tongue to within a fraction of her goal, then dropped back in defeat.

'Eucrates, you may take Chryseis,' Mellita conceded and the man hurried to obey. He knelt over Acantha's face once more, but this time facing round so that his cock, still gleaming with Acantha's saliva, could plunge within Chryseis' ready quim a hand's span above the bodyguard's fascinated gaze. Chryseis gasped and burrowed deeper into Acantha's sex, driving her tongue and teeth hard against the precious pearl concealed within. The mercenary groaned as she watched, in minute detail, the man and woman thrusting against each other before her face. They slid together like a sword plunging deep within its scabbard, being drawn almost free, then being sheathed again with a snap. Acantha could see Chryseis' vagina stretch around Eucrates' girth, her labia pushing in and out with the ebb and flow of his lust. She craned upwards once more and achieved a fleeting kiss on the underside of Eucrates' cock. It was slick with Chryseis' own juices, sweeter by far then mere honey and a double pleasure to her ready tongue. Acantha tugged harder at her bindings, straining them enough so that she could at last raise herself up to nuzzle at the juncture between her two companions, tasting and lapping at both cock and cunt simultaneously. If she could, she would have slid her tongue right into Chryseis' slippery orifice alongside Eucrates' hard member. Instead, she had to content herself with flickering her tongue against Chryseis' clitoris while Eucrates' balls brushed her cheek.

'Now,' urged Mellita, her voice no more than a tremulous gasp. 'Now.'

The pounding rhythm increased. Eucrates' breath grew shorter. Then he thrust himself to the hilt within Chryseis and gave a long slow cry. Acantha felt his erection twitch and pulse against her lips, detected each spurt of his seed as it shot within Chryseis' womb.

He withdrew slowly, his erection already subsiding, and Acantha pulled herself up to drink the juices that seeped from Chryseis' sodden quim. The musky smell filled her nose as she savoured each drop of the heady mix. In response, Chryseis buried her head between the bodyguard's legs, the young woman's soft hair brushing the sensitive skin of Acantha's inner thighs as she nuzzled the tender sex. The two women worked with fevered urgency: sucking, lapping and drinking each other's juices as the pressure built up. Acantha felt her body tighten, her nerves and senses focused solely upon the closed loop of their mutual lust. The tension increased, gaining in energy, till ultimately the little death of orgasm swept through her.

Eucrates awoke in the pallid light of dawn feeling chilled and stiff. He stretched uncomfortably, knocking a spilled goblet over the edge of the couch to clatter on the floor. It rolled noisily across the marble then stopped against the discarded remnants of the feast.

He looked around and found himself alone; the others must have returned to their room. His mouth tasted sour and his head ached from too much wine. The world lurched uncomfortably as he sat up; there must have been more than mere alcohol in last night's drink.

There was a rustle by the doorway; he looked up and saw Mellita approaching. 'You certainly know how to entertain,' he said, clutching at his stomach. 'I really enjoyed myself.'

Mellita said nothing but advanced towards him, her manner cold and aloof.

'Hey, I didn't make a fool of myself, did I?' asked Eucrates, with sinking apprehension. 'I really didn't mean to give offence, whatever it was. You've –'

Mellita cut in, her voice hard. 'You remember that last night we talked about my sister?'

'Er . . . yes.' Eucrates was confused. He remembered her being mentioned. Lira? No, Lyria, that was it. Had he said something about her?

Mellita's eyes were black pits, as expressionless as a viper's. 'You will kill her for me.'

He seemed unable to concentrate properly and it took a moment for the meaning to sink in. 'Kill her?' Had he missed something? 'Now look here –'

'No. You look.' Mellita pointed to the side, to one of the alcoves which had been empty the night before. Now it held a statue of two women, curved around each other in mutual fulfilment.

'What are you saying?' asked Eucrates, his thoughts still fragmented.

'Listen! Pay attention!' Mellita snapped. 'I'm saying that those are your friends. Do you understand?'

'Oh, someone's done a statue of them? That was

quick.' Now he looked, he could see the likeness. Yes, it was definitely them; Mellita had said so, hadn't she? His mind meandered uncontrollably on to investigating the patterns in the marble. What had she asked him to do a moment ago?

Mellita stepped into his line of view, forcing herself back into his awareness, her eyes boring into his with a strange intensity. 'No, not mere sculpture,' she said, her voice seeming to come from far away. 'It is really them.'

Eucrates was puzzled. 'But that's stone.'

Mellita smiled slowly. 'It is now, but it was flesh before. Are you beginning to comprehend? I used the force of their passion to transform them from flesh to stone. It is one of my many talents; I am a sorceress.'

Eucrates studied her in alarm. Now she pointed it out, he could see the gleam of ancient knowledge in her eyes, could feel the power emanating from her. He stepped away from her.

'Stay where you are!' Mellita commanded, her voice lashing like a whip. He stopped dead. 'You want to see your friends alive again, don't you? You want to rescue them from their fate?'

Eucrates nodded obediently, mesmerised.

'Then bring me Lyria's head, and I will restore them to life.

Seven

Eucrates tore his eyes away from the solidified forms of Acantha and Chryseis, trapped forever in motionless lust and looked around at all the other statues in the room. He had admired them the night before while enjoying the feast, but had not understood their significance. He remembered the statues in the villa's courtyard, too; even more figures frozen in timeless instants of passion.

When he looked back at Mellita, she was standing with her hands on her hips, her mouth twisted in an evil smirk. 'That's right,' she said, as if reading his thoughts. 'All of them.'

Witchcraft made Eucrates' skin crawl. He liked consistency; the notion that reality could be as malleable as a dream frightened him. It was bad enough that the gods themselves had such capabilities, but when it was wielded by his enemies he felt as powerless and vulnerable as a child.

'Who were they?' he dared to ask, awed by the number of lives she had destroyed.

Mellita threw back her head and whooped with laughter. 'What does it matter, little man? You have only two choices: bring me Lyria's head and save your friends, or abandon them to my collection.'

Eucrates believed her implicitly. Only one tiny portion of his mind wondered whether she spoke the truth, but it was small and easily ignored.

He listened obediently while Mellita instructed him on how to find her sister, so under her sway that he didn't even consider killing her with his sword when she returned his weapons. Her authority was beyond question.

Finally, before Eucrates departed, Mellita gave him a small flask. 'This is a magic potion,' she explained. 'Lyria is a witch, too, though not as powerful as me. The potion will protect you against her powers. Drink one mouthful every morning and one at night, until you return, no more and no less. Do you understand?'

Eucrates nodded dumbly and tied the flask to his belt, before allowing the silent servants to escort him from the villa.

For the rest of the day he obeyed Mellita's directions, trudging through the steep hills which rose to the east. By sunset he had covered at least twenty stades, and the green, fertile valleys on the other side of the rugged peaks were spread out before him. It was too late to continue, so Eucrates settled himself for the night. He found a small stream to supply him with water and built a low fire for comfort, then ate the bread and cheese provided for his journey. Finally, before curling up beneath a shallow overhang of rock, he took a mouthful of Mellita's potion, then carefully replaced the stopper so none would be lost. If he were to confront a second witch tomorrow, he needed all the protection he could get.

He slept fitfully, his dreams crowded with nightmare figures who changed shape and billowed through dark skies like storm clouds. He dreamt of deathless statues, unable to move while lascivious maidens danced around them and used the rock-hard bodies for their own gratification. He saw himself there, immobilised as one girl after another pleasured herself on his permanent and insensible erection, and he foresaw eternal desire tormenting him till the stones dissolved into dust.

He dreamt, too, of unyielding women, of bruising himself as he thrust vainly against impenetrable rock and of bloodying his lips against cold marble breasts. And he dreamt of clutching their rigid bodies to him so desperately that they disintegrated in his arms, leaving only gravel and their severed heads rolling across the ground to Mellita's feet.

He awoke trembling and chilled with rank sweat. The eastern sky barely hinted at the next dawn, but he dared not sleep again. Mellita had warned him against too much of the potion, but it was the only defence he had against the terrors of the night. He forced his shaking fingers to uncork the flask then gulped down an extra dose of the witch's elixir.

It didn't help; every mouse rustle, every leaf stirring in the breeze, fuelled his imagination till he was convinced that a robber, wild beast or supernatural monster lurked behind every boulder and tree. He cowered back under the small overhang and drank yet again from the flask in a desperate attempt to dispel his demons.

By dawn, he was so frightened of every noise, every flicker of light, that it took all his courage to stand up and continue his quest. Only the certainty that Mellita would pursue him to the grave prevented him from remaining where he was till he quietly died of starvation. He had never been so petrified in his life, and when he finally crawled from his crude shelter, he kept his sword clutched in his fist the whole time.

He advanced with painstaking care, peering about him at every step, and took most of the morning to descend to the lightly wooded slopes below. Here, his progress became even slower as the trees grew more substantial and the undergrowth between them thickened into layers of concealing screens. A layer of leaf mould covered the ground, muffling his footsteps. It would also silence the sound of any approaching attack and he strained to hear the slightest movement.

He barely dared breathe, and stopped often to wipe the sweat from his hand before his sword slipped from his grasp. And, when the fear became too much, he would quaff another mouthful of Mellita's potion.

Something snapped: air rushed, his feet were snatched out from under him. The world turned upside-down; he dangled from a supple branch by a rope noosed around one ankle.

His sword lay on the ground just out of reach; no chance of cutting the rope. He squirmed around, trying to climb up his body to free his foot. There wasn't time. He glimpsed a woman wielding a rock just before she struck the side of his skull and the world vanished into darkness.

He dreamt again: this time of cramped caves lit by flickering firelight, of bonds around his arms and legs. He dreamt of racking pains that made his muscles tremble and darker nightmares that made him scream aloud at unknown terrors. And, every so often, he dreamt of a dark-haired peasant girl, dressed in the roughest of rags, who spooned broth and gruel into him and held his head as he vomited it back up.

Finally, he opened his eyes with his mind clear and his thoughts lucid. This time, he was sure that he wasn't dreaming. But he was still in a twisting cave illuminated only by a faint glow from the unseen entrance. He tried to stand, with the intention of taking a look round the first bend of the tunnel, then realised his legs were tied together and his hands bound behind his back. For a moment, fresh panic gripped his chest, but he quelled it and took deep breaths to remain calm.

The line between dreaming and waking seemed more tenuous; if this were still a nightmare, he had lost all track of reality. On the other hand, if this were reality, then his dreams had held the essence of truth; so who was the woman who had cared for him?

As if in answer, footsteps padded on the rock floor of the cave just out of sight; a moving shadow blocked the light. Eucrates tensed, staring at the bend in the tunnel, waiting to see who, or what, was approaching. He saw her in silhouette first, then made out that she was the woman from his troubled dreams. She crouched to avoid striking her head on the low ceiling and was balancing a steaming bowl in one hand, a horn spoon in the other. She looked as savage and unkempt as he remembered her.

When she saw him looking at her, she stopped and eyed him carefully. 'You're feeling better,' she stated; it wasn't a question. She laid the bowl down, then stepped aside for a better view of his bonds. Eucrates suddenly realised that his cautious captor was more afraid of him than he was of her. She was scared that he had freed himself and was planning to pounce on her.

'Did my sister send you?' she asked abruptly.

'You're Lyria, aren't you?' he replied with a sinking feeling, answering her question.

'I am,' she agreed.

'Surely a powerful witch such as yourself has nothing to fear from a mere mortal,' he dared mock, and wondered what Lyria had done with Mellita's potion.

'Is that what Mellita told you?'

He nodded.

'And do you still believe it?' Lyria asked.

He wasn't sure; suddenly Eucrates realised that he had taken everything Mellita had told him without question. Normally, he was more sceptical than that and believed most witches were charlatans.

'She drugged you,' Lyria continued, feeding his doubts. 'She's very skilled with herbs and other wild things. She especially favours the use of mushrooms; the deadliest ones can produce strange delusions in small enough quantities. Then she guides the hallucinations with webs of words. I'm not like her; I only want to live in peace.'

It seemed a plausible enough explanation, but Eucrates shook his head and looked away. How else would it appear? Mellita had said her sister was as powerful as herself, and no doubt she could be as deceitful. Why believe one in preference to the other? 'If you don't mean me harm, then why have you bound me?' he asked. 'How can you expect me to trust you when you hold me captive?'

'Because I know you planned to kill me and probably still would, given the chance. You are not the first Mellita has sent.'

'Well,' he said, rolling over on to his side and presenting his bound wrists to Lyria, 'it must be several days since I enjoyed Mellita's hospitality. Surely I've recovered from the drugs by now. It's perfectly safe to untie me.'

Lyria shook her head. 'Not yet. I don't think you are persuaded that easily. In any case, that flask you were carrying held more of Mellita's brews, no doubt described as a protection against me. How much of that did you drink?'

Eucrates winced at the thought he had been dosing himself on the very cause of his nightmares, then snorted with cynical amusement. Which version of the truth should he believe? But, he reminded himself, it was Mellita who had . . . Then he stopped, puzzled. If Mellita wasn't a witch, then what exactly had she done to Chryseis and Acantha?

'I'm sorry,' repeated Lyria, when he didn't speak. She sounded genuinely contrite. 'But I really must keep you tied a little longer.'

'How long is a little? And how much longer do I have to remain cooped up here?' He was angry with everyone, including himself for being so stupid, and his voice came out harsh and unforgiving. 'Surely you could have found somewhere better than this hole.'

Lyria glared back, her lips tight. 'No. This is the best

I could do,' she said, her voice precise with suppressed anger. She pointed over to a small niche piled with animal skins to form a crude bed. 'I sleep over there and I cook on a fire outside. Mellita is the one with the villa and the servants, not me. She is the one who held on to everything that should have been shared between us, and even took those things that were mine alone.'

She drew a breath and when she spoke again her voice was calmer. 'Now, I have made you some broth; do you want it or not? It's no different to what I've fed you for the last three days, but, if you don't trust me, I'll eat it myself.'

Eucrates' stomach answered for him, growling with hunger. Then he realised what she had said. 'Three days?' he repeated in sudden alarm. 'The others –'

'You had companions?' Lyria asked, settling cross-legged beside him and picking up the bowl to give it a stir. 'You must tell me about them. But first, eat. It'll get cold otherwise.' She presented a spoonful of savoury broth to his lips.

Eucrates ate ravenously, barely chewing the vegetables before swallowing, heedless of the way they burnt his mouth and gullet. And, as he ate, he listened to the story of how the feud had formed between Lyria and her sister.

Even as a child, Lyria explained, Mellita had always resented her. It was, she thought, because Mellita had been jealous of the younger sister who had snatched away half of her love and attention. Maybe, though, that was an excuse. Perhaps Mellita had simply been born evil.

Whatever the reason, Mellita had striven to outdo Lyria in everything, and finally even turned to magic in an attempt to prove her superiority. She had picked up bits and pieces of old hearth-magic from the occasional wandering soothsayer or foreign slave, and had added the knowledge of herbs and plants gained from the local midwife. Mellita had been a capable student, absorbing everything her tutors knew, then going on to greater achievements. Her command of herb-lore alone would have made her a renowned physician had she used her skills for good. But, despite her intelligence, Mellita had not had the subtlety to see that before one could receive, one first had to give. Instead, she had used her craft to try and seize what could only be accepted as a gift, and had grown increasingly bitter the less she had.

Lyria sighed heavily and stopped, her hand poised halfway towards his mouth with a spoonful of stew. When she spoke again, her voice was just a whisper. 'Finally, my parents died after brief illnesses. There's no proof, but sometimes I wonder ... Anyway, Mellita immediately claimed everything for herself and threw me from the villa which had always been my home.' She returned the food, untouched, to the bowl and stirred it absent-mindedly, without having offered him any.

'And so you escaped here, across the mountain?'

'Yes. Always too far from home, yet never far enough. I don't know what I keep hoping for; maybe it's just stubbornness and the knowledge that my presence here is a continual irritation.' She drew herself up, shrugging off dark memories. 'Now, tell me your story.'

Eucrates leant back against the cave wall and made himself as comfortable as he could with his hands tied behind him. Then he recounted how he and the others had been lulled into a false sense of security by Mellita's tricks.

'She can't have really turned them to stone,' said Lyria. 'She's not that powerful. As I said though, she is clever at drugging people and making them see whatever she wants them to.'

Eucrates nodded in agreement; it was the conclusion he had come to as well. 'Will you release me now,' he asked, hopeful that their shared tale had formed a bond between them.

112

Lyria laughed softly. 'Not yet. Trust takes time.'

Eucrates felt his guts tighten but dared to argue. 'It's difficult for me to trust you, when you keep me bound like this.' He did not want to aggravate this woman but if he were to aid Chryseis and her bodyguard, he needed to return to the villa as soon as possible.

Rueful comprehension lit Lyria's face. 'I had meant my trust of you. But I see your point, though I had thought my ministrations over the last few days would count for something. I could have simply killed you, after all.'

'I was unconscious while you cared for me,' commented Eucrates, striving for a reasonable tone of voice.

'Another good point,' said Lyria, her eyes crinkling with amusement as they flickered over Eucrates body. 'Still, maybe we can prove our mutual trustworthiness in some other way. Perhaps I need to show my ministrative skills more explicitly.' She reached out and trailed her fingers down Eucrates' chest, following the contours of his muscles from his shoulders to his belly.

Eucrates' breath caught in surprise, and his body tingled under her touch, even through the material of his tunic. 'That would, I suppose, satisfy me,' he responded. 'But with my hands still bound, how would it display my integrity to you?'

Lyria's mouth flickered in an impish grin. 'Why, I do believe that you are right yet again. I need some free and unrestrained demonstration of your good intentions towards me, and yet, I dare not release your arms and legs till I have it. A paradox, yes?' She didn't wait for an answer though, before proceeding. 'I think that I shall have to find something else to release. What do you say?'

Eucrates' throat felt too tight to say anything in response as Lyria lifted the hem of his tunic to expose his naked genitals. She ran her cool, work-calloused fingers over them, assessing the thickness of his penis and the heaviness of his balls while he could do nothing except lie back and let her.

Not surprisingly, his penis responded to the treatment with a burgeoning display of arousal. 'You see?' Lyria asked, her smile widening. 'Already I know you like me; even if only a little.' She ran her fist gently up and down his shaft till he became rigid and his glans peeked out from beneath his foreskin. Lyria tightened her grip, dragging the concealing hood further back till the pink inner skin was stretched taut, forcing his exposed dome to bow its head in submission. The sensation was sharp, verging on pain; delicate flesh protesting at its treatment, yet exciting because of his complete exposure and vulnerability.

Lyria dipped her head, her lips drawn back to reveal white, sharp teeth. She looked upward, watching his expression intently as she nipped the thin skin of his helmet. She scraped her teeth over the silken surface, sending shivers of anticipation trembling through his groin. Gently, she took the entire glans within her mouth, then pulled back, licking the ridge with her tongue. The pleasure sent excruciating tremors of excitement through his body.

Eucrates knew he was totally at this woman's mercy, unable to defend himself in any way. He had no option except to let the woman use or abuse his body in any way she wanted. He had no more power than a toy, totally vulnerable, freed from any sense of propriety or responsibility.

He tried lifting his hips, to assert himself by thrusting himself deeper into her mouth. She immediately drew back her head and clutched his scrotum in her hand. 'No,' she commanded, closing her fist. 'Do you understand?' She tightened her grip till the ache spread from his testicles to his abdomen and he had to stop himself moaning with pain.

Eucrates grunted assent, too sore and genuinely apprehensive to argue as his interest wilted. Lyria laughed indulgently, amused by her power, but did release him. Then, as he subsided with a sigh of relief, she swiftly bent her head and kissed each testicle in turn, flickering the crumpled skin with the tip of her tongue, mouthing the balls with soft, pouting lips. 'There now, that's better, isn't it?' she murmured as his erection regained its rigidity.

'What are you going to do with me?' Eucrates asked, filled with trepidation at what she would demand of him; he knew he could not, would not, refuse her anything.

Lyria stood up and loosened the crude knot that held her garment over one shoulder. The patched material dropped to her feet, leaving her totally naked. It was obvious from the darkness of her skin that this wild woman usually hid no part of her body from the sun's rays and had probably only donned any garment out of some childhood recollection of modesty.

She stood over him, hands on her forward-thrust hips and let him admire her. She was lean-muscled, but had retained the softer curves of bosom and buttock so that she appeared like a voluptuously curved exaggeration of womanhood. Her nipples were large and erect, jutting from the centres of wide, brown areolae which had been dragged into ovals by the weight of her hanging breasts. Her body hair was untrimmed, and formed a soft, shadowy haze on her arms and legs. It tufted from her armpits, and trailed so thickly from the bushy triangle between her legs that the outline of her sex could not be discerned. She looked feral and barbaric, a true primitive in her little cave; not so much a friend of the animals as one of them.

'Have you any idea how long it has been since I had a man?' she asked, jarring Eucrates from his reverent appreciation of her body.

'Too long,' he replied, and moistened his lips. 'A body like yours should not be neglected for even an hour.'

Lyria laughed outright. 'Cheap flattery won't get you untied,' she mocked, but looked secretly pleased. He could smell her musk from here, and knew she was as aroused as he. 'I need more than that. I need total, unswerving obedience. Are you ready to give it to me?'

Eucrates nodded.

Lyria raised an eyebrow. 'I wonder if you really mean that,' she purred, sidling closer.

Eucrates nodded again, his breath shallow with expectancy as he studied her untamed body.

Lyria stood over Eucrates, one foot on either side of his body, as he lay helplessly on the sand floor of the cave. He had a truncated view of her; the dark, impenetrable hairs at her groin, the mounds of her breasts above, and her face peering down from between them. Gradually, she bent her knees, squatting down over him with supple control until her pubes were a mere finger-length above his face, the heavy aroma of her excitement filling his nostrils. He longed to crane up and bury himself in that luxuriant growth, but he had learnt his lesson; this time he would wait.

Lyria put her hands between her thighs, using her fingers to comb apart the dense hairs till the dark creases of her labia were visible as they nestled at her core. She pulled the lips apart, letting him see the glistening flesh within, so richly lubricated with her desire that a drop of her nectar fell on to his upturned face.

He felt his cock twitch upwards as the muscles in his groin tightened, then twitch again as if it somehow had a life of its own and wanted only to be enveloped within those slippery folds of flesh.

Lyria squatted lower over his face, stretching her vulva apart to afford him an unobstructed view of her inner world. 'Open your mouth,' she commanded, and he obeyed. 'Drink me,' she ordered and then released a gentle stream of urine across his face and into his gaping

116

mouth. Shock rippled through him, but was swamped by a tidal wave of arousal. The world narrowed to the vision just a hand's span above him, the warm, slightly salty liquid dripping from his chin and the sound of blood pounding in his ears. He could no longer restrain himself; had no thought of trying. He lifted his mouth to catch each golden drop and gulped it down as if it were ambrosia, then lapped desperately at her succulent flesh, mouthing it with his lips. Her cunt pressed into his mouth, her scent penetrated his nostrils, the wild tangle of her pubes filled his vision. There was nothing in his universe except Lyria; she dominated every sense, saturated it to capacity as she rocked her hips back and forth across his face.

He flickered his tongue over the hard knot of her clitoris, making her keen with ascending passion. Gradually, her cries changed in pitch, becoming more frantic and desperate with each breath, encouraging him to work even harder with his tongue. Finally she gave a shriek of triumph which reverberated back and forth within the tight little cave, making it resonate with her orgasm as if it were a giant womb.

Eucrates whimpered with hungry need for his own release and Lyria hurried to oblige. She turned to face his feet then, with her back to him, lowered herself directly on to his straining erection. He felt the muscles of her quim tighten around his cock, massaging the length of his member as she ground her hips down on his. He thrust upwards so that their bodies slapped noisily together and with enough force to lift Lyria's weight. Her fingers clutched at his balls while her other hand wedged itself further between his legs till he felt her pushing at his anus. Unable to refuse her entry, he relaxed then cried out as her fingers forced their way into him, hurting him with delicious pain that only brought him closer to the oblivion of orgasm. He had never felt so wanted, so ultimately desired, by this woman who could simply get off and walk away from his unsatiated body. She possessed him, and her only desire was for him to spurt his seed within her. The pressure in his balls grew, reaching an almost unbearable pitch as Lyria's domination of his body continued.

He felt the first jet of semen fire along the length of his erection, seeming to burn its own passage through the core of his member, making him cry out with searing ecstasy. Each subsequent ejaculation brought another tremulous cry to his lips till, finally, he groaned in spent satisfaction as Lyria simultaneously raised her voice in a final shriek of gratification.

Simple, untrammelled pleasure washed through his body. He subsided back to the cave floor, and was only vaguely aware of his abused body slipping away into a dreamless sleep.

When he awoke, Eucrates stretched with languorous pleasure before noticing that his hands and feet were untied. He looked around happily, and saw a beaker of water close by, as well as a crudely carved plate piled high with fresh olives and some of last season's apples. Most welcome, however, was the sight of his sword laid out beside the food, an obvious indication of his changed status in Lyria's eyes.

He postponed further exploration in favour of eating and had almost cleared the plate when he heard someone approaching. He assumed it would be Lyria, but even so he reached for his sword and had it ready when the woman appeared round the corner. She stopped abruptly when she saw the weapon ready in his hand.

'Did I misjudge you?' she asked, her voice cool.

Eucrates casually tossed the sword aside and resumed eating. 'I was just being cautious. Thanks for returning it.' He wiped his mouth with the back of his hand and pointed to the sack she carried in one hand. 'What have you got there?'

Something moved within the sack and Lyria held it away from her body with a grim smile. 'Oh, just my head, which you are going to deliver to Mellita, exactly as she asked.'

For the first time since their imprisonment, Acantha and Chryseis were led up from their squalid cell to the luxurious villa above. Acantha allowed herself to be guided between two burly servants without question, keeping her eyes and face expressionless. She had not eaten or drunk in the two days since she had realised that she and Chryseis were being drugged and, though her thoughts still wandered sometimes and she was weak with hunger and thirst, she felt she was regaining control of her mind. Chryseis, however, had been too far gone to follow Acantha's advice, and there was no acting involved in the way she let herself be bustled along by her guards.

Acantha kept an eye open for an opportunity to make a break for it. But not yet, she thought, as she stumbled over a low step; she wasn't ready for a fight.

They were taken back to the room they had feasted in before, where Mellita lay at her ease on her couch by the fountain. 'Ah, here you are, my pretties,' she purred. 'How are you enjoying my hospitality now?'

Chryseis remained blankly mute, so Acantha followed suit, though she had plenty to say.

Mellita apparently hadn't expected a reply, for she went on without waiting. 'Your stupid friend, Eucrates, has been sighted returning from the east. I thought that with the small parts of your minds that you still own, you would like to witness your hero's return. He thinks I will let you free once he has delivered Lyria's head.' She cackled loudly, and Acantha itched to put her hands round the bitch's throat. The anger seemed to burn through the mental fog that still clung to her, so she fed it with ever more violent images to slough off the last debilitating effects of the drugs.

Footsteps approached along the corridor, then entered the chamber. Acantha longed to turn round and see if it was Eucrates and what state he was in, but had to maintain her pretence. Taking her lead from Chryseis, she continued to stare blankly ahead, even allowing a faint line of spittle to trail down her chin from her slack mouth.

The footfalls neared and Eucrates stepped into her field of view. He looked tired and drawn, and in one hand he clutched a crude sack with something heavy in it. His face seemed as expressionless as everyone else's, and Acantha's last vestige of hope died away. As Mellita claimed, he too had been drugged, though presumably with a different potion if he were fit enough to fight. It didn't matter; his valiant effort had failed and the responsibility devolved on her now. She was the only one who could get them out of this mess, though she hardly felt capable.

'I have done as you asked, Mellita,' Eucrates said, his voice flat. 'I have brought you Lyria's head. Will you release my friends now?'

Mellita's face almost glowed with eagerness. 'Give it to me,' she ordered, gesturing to the sack with bony fingers, beckoning him to bring it closer.

Instead, Eucrates held the sack away from her. 'My friends first,' he argued.

Mellita's eyes narrowed suspiciously. 'How dare you challenge me? Where's the flask I gave you?' she demanded. 'Did you drink the potion as I told you?'

'Certainly, mistress,' said Eucrates, indicating the flask tied to his belt. 'It served me well; Lyria's lies would have defeated me were it not for the potion's protection.'

Mellita grunted, her suspicion only partly assuaged. 'Well, since you ask, your friends are over there.' She flicked her hand towards the women and Eucrates turned his head to look at them. Acantha could do nothing to indicate her awareness to Eucrates, because Mellita was looking straight at her; and he, in turn, showed no expression either. 'Now,' continued the witch eagerly, 'give me my sister's head.'

Obediently, Eucrates held out the sack, Mellita snatching it from him in her haste to inspect the contents. Her fingers trembled with eagerness as she untied the neck of the bag and thrust her hand inside.

Her shriek of horror tore at Acantha's ears.

Mellita jerked her arm from the bag, drawing out with it the twisted, dun-coloured body of a sand viper clamped to her hand. The heavy snake was half as long as her body, and its distinctive, horned snout worked rhythmically as it pumped deadly venom into her bloodstream. Mellita gibbered incoherently, dancing backward as she frantically tried to shake the reptile off her. Finally, she dislodged it and it fell with a thump to the floor, forming a coil of hissing fury.

The witch's face was a contorted mask of rage as she looked around for Eucrates. Her expression changed to fear a split second before he thrust his sword through her heart, and she crumpled down beside the snake.

Without instructions, Mellita's servants milled about uncertainly, getting in each other's way and generating more confusion. Only a couple acted with any purpose, and moved around to attack Eucrates from opposite sides. The first, Eucrates tripped and knocked senseless with the hilt of his sword; the second, Acantha clubbed down from behind with her clenched fists.

Eucrates glanced at the second body, then grinned at her in thanks. 'I wondered if you'd really succumbed to the drugs,' he commented, then tossed over a spare knife from his belt, adding, 'Just in case, though I doubt there'll be much opposition now.'

'Good,' Acantha responded, hiding her relief under a display of bravado. 'Then we can get on with this damn journey. I still have a lot of back pay to collect.'

Eight

'When are we going to stop for a rest?' whined Chryseis.

Acantha shook her head in frustration; the more the stupid girl had recovered from Mellita's potions, the more she had returned to her old, spoilt self. At least, when they had said goodbye to Lyria two days earlier, Chryseis had been biddable and easy to control. Now, she wanted everything done for her, complaining that she still felt weak from her ordeal.

To make matters worse, Eucrates indulged her at every turn. Acantha had come to trust him a bit more since he had rescued them from Mellita, but the way he fawned over Chryseis maddened her.

Now, she turned back and spoke to Chryseis with weary contempt. 'I don't know. We could stop right now if you want, just here.' She gestured around at what little could be seen of the bare, scrubby landscape through the persistent drizzle. 'Of course, we ate the last of the food at breakfast, and there's nothing here to shelter us from the rain, but we'll stop right now if that's what you want. Is it?'

Chryseis tightened her lips and glared back. 'Well, since you seem to consider yourself in charge, what are you going to do about it? It's nearly sunset, or it would be if we could see the bloody thing through all these clouds. Are you just going to force us to trudge on through the night until we drop, or are you going to find us somewhere to rest?'

'What?' Acantha flung her hands up. 'What in Hades' name do you think I can do? Magic up some food out of thin air? Anyway,' she added with malicious spite, 'you could do with losing a little of that fat.'

'Better than being a scrawny old hen,' screeched Chryseis.

'Ladies! Ladies,' soothed Eucrates, stepping between them. 'There's no need for this bickering.'

His unctuous tone was the last straw. 'Keep out of it,' snapped Acantha, as Chryseis turned on him with equal venom and hissed.

'Who asked you, slave?'

'I was just trying to help,' Eucrates said, holding his palms up and backtracking quickly. 'You both seemed a bit overwrought.'

Chryseis stamped her foot in frustration, then turned on her heel and resumed walking, striding ahead at a furious pace.

Acantha, equally angry, brushed past Eucrates without apology and followed the young woman's tightly clenched backside with grim determination. Eucrates could follow or not, as he liked. She didn't care one way or the other.

They continued in hostile silence, strung out across the landscape, for another hour or so. The waning light would soon force them to stop, but Chryseis' fury had given her a new burst of energy. Acantha saw no point in wasting it and had decided to let Chryseis stride on for as long as she wanted to.

The young woman was therefore in the lead and the first one to crest the latest rise they were struggling up. 'A village,' she cried back to the others, her voice triumphant. 'There, I told you we'd find somewhere to stay tonight.' And before Acantha could remind her of what had happened the last time they stopped somewhere unannounced, Chryseis had darted on ahead.

'Come on,' Acantha called to Eucrates who trailed

behind. 'Let's see what mischief she's got herself into this time.'

Eucrates gave her a knowing nod and they hurried forward, united in their concern.

On the other side of the hill, the ground fell away gently towards a road about half a dozen stades away, where it joined another track that curved around from the west. At the junction stood a small cluster of buildings. Chryseis' pale figure darted down the slope towards them without any sign of caution.

'The stupid bitch has no bloody sense,' gritted Acantha.

'She's still young and innocent,' Eucrates commented. 'She's not found out how hard the world is yet. I think such trust is very . . .' He groped for a word.

'Stupid,' said Acantha.

'Endearing,' Eucrates corrected, though with a shrug.

Acantha snorted. 'Either way, we'd better go and see what she's doing.'

They followed at their own pace. If there was going to be trouble, there was no point in running into it, or arriving too breathless to do anything about it. As it was, when they finally arrived amongst the scattered buildings, they realised that, by luck, they had stumbled on to a small taverna, serving the trade that came by the crossroads, and with a farm to fill in between times. Yellow light and the smell of cooking led them to the largest building, a whitewashed rectangle of uneven stone with a sloping tiled roof.

They pushed open the door and found themselves in the taverna's main room. It was low and dim with smoke from a poorly laid fire and the flicker of terracotta lamps burning rancid oil. Rough couches were grouped around the walls and silent men were sprawled out on them, supping wine and picking at the simple fare laid out on the three-legged tables beside them. They looked like a group of travelling merchants and they eyed the newcomers with suspicious curiosity.

Chryseis had already sunk on to one of the couches and a heavy, bearded man in a stained chiton stood beside her with his hands on his hips. Chryseis was ordering wine and food and the man was nodding with sharp-eyed distrust.

'And do you have money to pay for this?' he asked, his voice a low rumble.

A flash of panic flitted across Chryseis' face, but disappeared when she saw Acantha and Eucrates. 'My servants have the money,' she said haughtily. 'They will pay you.'

The man's eyebrows lifted in exaggerated scepticism. It was easy to see why; although Chryseis had taken some of Mellita's clothes to replace her own, they were now travel-stained and filthy. Her hair, too, was lank and matted from the wind and rain. She hardly looked as if she were wealthy enough to have servants.

Acantha sighed. Chryseis was creating problems again. 'We don't have any money,' she explained to the taverner, who didn't look even slightly surprised. 'We are travellers, heading to Chalcis, and we seek lodgings and food.'

'Charity, you mean,' the man grunted. 'Well, I don't like vagabonds who try to cheat me. Be off with you.' He gestured with his thumb towards the door.

Eucrates protested sharply. 'We didn't –'

'Your friend here did, giving herself airs above her station.' The taverner crossed his arms and stood splay-legged, blocking their way into the room.

'We're willing to work for it,' offered Acantha. 'We could serve at the tables and clean for you?'

The large man laughed with cynical amusement. 'And steal me blind while you do it? Find yourselves a temple where the priests care for beggars. Maybe they'll pamper you; I won't.' He stepped forward, his bulk pressing them back towards the door.

Anger simmered in Acantha's belly, but the man had

the right of it. Anyway, he was too big to knock down easily and the other patrons of the taverna seemed ready to take his side. She hadn't the heart for a protracted fight, so she told herself that he was a lucky man and turned for the door, not caring if Chryseis and Eucrates followed.

At least the damp night air tasted clean and sweet after the heavy smoky atmosphere in the taverna, and she drew it gratefully down into her lungs, snorting the last remnants of the odours from her nostrils.

'If we'd eaten there, we'd probably have ended up with stomach cramps,' said Eucrates, making light of it. 'Just think of the fate we've been saved.'

Chryseis followed last, tumbling outside as the door slammed behind her. 'Why didn't you do something?' she screeched, turning on Acantha.

'Because you had already done enough.' Acantha couldn't even be bothered to look at the girl.

'And what's that supposed to mean? I was trying to get us some food. If you'd told him you had money he would have fed us. Afterwards would have been too late. What would he have done? Taken the food back after we'd eaten it?'

'Maybe.' Now Acantha turned, her eyes boring into Chryseis' as she spoke with quiet assurance. 'I've seen it happen, when someone has been knifed in the belly.' Chryseis' sudden pallor was gratifying. 'If we had asked the taverner honestly, to start with, he might have helped. But because you tried to cheat him, he wouldn't, even if we begged. Don't you understand anything?'

Chryseis glared defiantly back, but her lower lip quivered slightly before she brought it under control. 'So what do you suggest we do? Just run off into the night and hide? I'm hungry,' she wailed.

Acantha shook her head in despair; when was the child ever going to grow up? 'Come on,' she said. 'I saw a small grove of trees down the road a bit. We can shelter there.'

Chryseis turned to Eucrates for support. 'Are you just going to do as she says? What do you think we should do?'

For a moment Acantha thought he would side with the younger woman, but he had more sense. 'We'll do as Acantha suggests. She knows what she's doing,' he said, to the bodyguard's surprised pleasure.

They were about to leave when a covered ox cart rumbled up the road towards them. The weary beast's head hung low and it snorted dejectedly as the heavy wooden wheels trundled unevenly over the road. Two figures, indistinct in the twilight, sat side by side on the driver's bench.

'Hello,' called one, a man. 'Is this the taverna?'

'Yes,' chirped Chryseis, stepping forward with a seductive smile. 'Are you going in? Could you spare a few copper pieces for some hungry travellers?'

Acantha's face burned with embarrassment; had the girl no shame?

'I'm sorry. We have nothing,' said the other figure on the cart, a woman, probably young. 'We would share with you if we had.'

'In that case,' said Acantha, 'I hope you fare better here than we did. They're not keen on giving out charity.'

'Oh.' The cart was close enough now for her to see the sudden crestfallen look on the man's face. The woman beside him clutched tighter on to his arm and looked anxiously into his face with kohl-darkened eyes. 'Pelex, what are we going to do?'

'I take it you are also short of money?' asked Acantha.

The man drew the ox cart to a halt beside them and leant over from his seat to speak. 'Yes, I'm afraid so. We haven't a single obol between us.'

Chryseis snorted and turned away, no longer interested in what the couple had to say now that she realised that there would be no handouts from them.

'At least you have the cart to shelter in,' said Acantha.

The man laughed nervously. 'Yes, there is that. But it won't fill our stomachs.' He hesitated for a moment, then asked, 'I don't suppose you can play any musical instruments?'

Acantha was too surprised by the question to dissemble. 'Hardly. Why?'

'Well, we used to travel with some minstrels, and carried their equipment with us on the cart. We, ah, got separated from them, but we still have their instruments. I'm sure they wouldn't mind us borrowing them, and we were planning on playing for our supper. Perhaps you could join us.'

Acantha didn't know what to say. She had never learnt any instrument properly, although she had occasionally beaten a drum during campfire songs while on campaigns. Then, of course, everyone had been drunk and singing off-key, and the main criteria had simply been to make as much noise as possible; harmony and rhythm were superfluous niceties. She had certainly never performed for an audience; it required a different sort of courage than that needed to go into battle. 'That's kind of you to offer . . .' she began, but Chryseis interrupted.

'I can play the lyre, and sing, too,' she boasted. 'I'll join you.'

'And I can play the syrinx a bit, even if not very well,' added Eucrates. 'Come on, Acantha. We can give it a try. There were a lot of travellers in the taverna tonight. If we entertain them, they'll be bound to give us a few coins. What have we got to lose?'

Acantha hesitated, then laughed. 'If they really hate us, they can always throw us out.' She gestured up to the dark sky. 'In which case we'll be back where we started.'

The couple introduced themselves as Pelex and

128

Nipha, and then they went round to the back of the cart and unloaded the instruments. They found a syrinx made of hollow reeds for Eucrates to blow on and a lyre for Chryseis. Acantha picked up a tambourine with trailing red ribbons and rattled it experimentally; surely it wouldn't take much skill to play. Pelex picked up a long double flute and Nipha was left with a cithara, looking like a lyre with a flattened sounding box, which she strummed awkwardly.

When they returned inside the taverna, the owner advanced on them immediately. 'I thought I told you lot to clear off,' he growled. 'And take your friends with you.'

'Excuse me, sir,' smiled Nipha sweetly, with a slight bow, 'but we are wandering minstrels and would like to play for your guests.'

'I can't afford frivolous crap like that,' growled the man, his beefy fists resting on his hips.

'We don't expect you to pay us yourself,' Nipha explained, her dark eyes seductive. 'We'll take a cup round your guests when we have finished. They can pay us what they think we're worth.'

The man scratched his beard, considering. 'And do I get a share?'

'You get our custom when we have a few coins,' interjected Acantha, determined not to give their earnings away. 'And if your guests enjoy themselves, they may feel tempted to buy a little more of your wine themselves. We can all profit.'

The inn-keeper grunted assent and gestured them towards a vacant corner next to the fire. 'Let's see how good you are,' he said.

Nervously, the group threaded their way through the tables and spent an inordinate amount of time making themselves comfortable.

'What shall we play?' asked Eucrates finally.

'How about "Apollo's Dream"?' suggested Nipha.

'I don't know that,' said Chryseis. 'Do you know "Sunlight"?'

'Is that the one that goes . . .' Nipha hummed a few flat notes, and when Chryseis shook her head, turned to Acantha. 'Have you any suggestions?' she asked.

'The only songs I know are campaign ballads. You know, like "The Priest and the Whore" or "The Blood of Virgins".'

Nipha sighed. 'Hardly appropriate.'

'No.'

Behind them, the customers were beginning to grow restive. Someone muttered something and there was laughter. Acantha felt her ears redden.

'How about "Sweet Dreams"?' suggested Eucrates.

'A child's song?' scorned Chryseis.

'We all know it though. Yes?'

Reluctantly, they looked at each other and nodded, then hesitated, each waiting for someone else to start.

'Get on with it,' someone in the audience heckled, and the rest laughed.

Pelex blew a fractured note on the flutes, and the rest followed raggedly behind. Acantha tried to keep the rhythm going on her tambourine, but the tempo was so slow as everyone groped for the right notes that she lost the beat. She ended up chaotically banging and rattling in a counter-rhythm to the rest of the players, making things worse. Even so, they might have pulled it together if Nipha hadn't started singing. Acantha reckoned a cat with a mangled tail would have made a better soloist, and the audience agreed. Someone slung a bit of bread past her ear while others hissed and jeered.

Acantha increased the vigour of her beat, pulsing out a steady rhythm for the others to follow. Nipha abandoned all pretence of playing the cithara, and using her voice alone was able to follow the tempo, if not the tune. The others struggled to keep up.

A half-chewed olive struck Chryseis on the leg and the audience laughed cruelly. Acantha realised things could only get worse; a big merchant at the front seemed to be taking particular pleasure in goading the others on.

Nipha tried to dance, but the floor space was too restricted and she bumped into Chryseis, triggering another howl of laughter. With nowhere to move, she was confined to more or less shuffling around in one spot and wriggling her hips. Someone whistled in appreciation, and this time the laughter sounded different.

Nipha gave a smile of relief and danced on. She exaggerated the motion of her hips to the pulse of Acantha's tambourine, then turned round so the audience could get a better view of her buttocks as she gyrated them from side to side. Acantha saw the big merchant lick his lips and dig a few copper coins from the pouch at his belt and throw them to the floor at Nipha's feet.

Pelex, Eucrates and Chryseis were making crude music to the beat of Acantha's tambourine, but the performance was going nowhere. Nipha danced her best, but the audience began to grow restive again. The few coins they had received would hardly pay for a single drink. Acantha and Nipha exchanged a glance. What should they do next?

Nipha seemed to know. She moved forward amongst the diners, twitching her hips close to their faces, stroking their hair and cheeks with her long fingers so that each thought he was the one she desired. Some tried to reach up and touch her, but she spun away, dancing out of reach, twisting among the tables. The audience followed her with their eyes, an air of expectation beginning to simmer in the low room.

The big merchant held up a coin, the metal gleaming in the flickering light of the terracotta lamps. Nipha sidled over and tried to pluck it from his fist, but he whisked his hand away, enticing her nearer. She reached for the coin again, leaning over him towards his arm extended out the other side of his body. Her breasts in their soft fabric brushed his face, and he slid his free hand up her thigh, cupping the roundness of her buttock.

Nipha took the coin and bestowed a kiss on the man's balding pate then twisted away as the audience cheered.

Now two more men held up coins. Nipha turned her head from one to the other, choosing. She danced nearer to the one that Acantha would have picked, a young man, muscular and clean-shaven. As Nipha stood before him, flicking her hips back and forth to the pulse of the music, the man held the coin just out of her reach, luring her nearer and nearer till she stood directly before him, between his knees.

The man put the coin between his teeth and held his head up. Nipha danced closer, bending forward till she could accept the offering with her mouth, her lips lingering on the man's before she danced on.

Acantha glanced over at Pelex, wondering how he was taking the sight of his woman kissing another man, but he was grinning widely, enjoying the heady atmosphere as much as any.

Chryseis joined in now, dancing forward amongst the tables to renewed laughter and calls. Acantha wasn't surprised; the girl would do anything for a bit of attention. The big merchant was holding up another coin and Chryseis went straight to him, rotating her hips while strumming discordantly on the lyre. He repeated the trick he had used on Nipha, holding the coin just out of reach so that Chryseis would have to lean across him to get it. With a grin, Chryseis leant forward, rubbing her breasts across the merchant's face, then murmured something in his ear. The man rubbed his hand up the inside of Chryseis' thigh, but she slapped him away and shook her head, turning to leave. Hurriedly, the man offered her more money, and Chryseis returned to him.

This time, she let his hands slide further up her thighs and under her tunic, arching her back as they contacted her more sensitive flesh. The merchant's face became intent as he groped away under her clothes, and Acantha could see the bulge at his groin growing with his excitement. Chryseis discarded the lyre, dropping it carelessly to the floor. She undid the girdle at her waist and allowed the folded material to part down one side, exposing her right breast and hip, just inches from the merchant's face. He leant forward and caught the nipple in his mouth, sucking the pliant mound between his lips till Chryseis threw her head back, her lower lip gripped between her teeth.

The merchant impatiently tore the rest of the garment from her, revealing Chryseis' young body for all to see and provoking a cheer of approval. Chryseis shuffled forward, straddling the merchant's big knees and spreading her legs so that his hands and fingers could slip unhindered in and out of the glistening wetness between her thighs. She clasped his head to her bosom and let herself go, bucking and heaving over his busy hands.

The handsome youth gestured Nipha over to him again, obviously suggesting that she favour him in a like manner, but she shook her head. Not to be refused, the youth took another coin from his pouch and held it up for her to see. Acantha watched as Nipha played the game again, making a snatch for the coin, only to have it again drawn out of reach. She bent forward, obviously anticipating that once again he would want her to take it from between his teeth, but he didn't. He lifted the hem of his chiton to reveal his swollen penis beginning to lift its head from between his legs. Slowly, watching her closely, he drew back on the head to expose the dark, shining helmet below. Then he tucked the coin beneath the foreskin and rolled it back, so that the disk formed a bulge under the soft flesh.

The music stuttered to a stop.

Nipha grinned, her teeth white and sharp, and knelt down between his legs. The only sound was the rasping of the men's breath as they all craned forward to watch. Nipha used two fingers to hold the base of the man's cock, lifting it up to meet the pouting redness of her lips. She kissed the tip gently and the fleshy rod twitched in response. Nipha's pointed tongue probed at the neck of the opening, burrowing under the concealing flesh for the coin. The man drew in a long shuddering breath, his eyes locked on Nipha's mouth as it quested over the head of his straining erection.

Nipha's lips tightened over the tip of the penis and she slowly engulfed it, forcing herself further and further down its length until it seemed she would leave no part of it exposed. Then she retreated, the shaft glistening with the wetness of her saliva. Again and again she bobbed up and down the man's length, the motions increasing with vigour with each pulse.

Acantha took the rhythm of Nipha's bobbing head and struck the tambourine in time to it, one beat to each downward thrust. Someone began clapping in time, then someone else, catching the upward motion to make a double beat. The tempo quickened, stroke by stroke, as the audience clapped and stamped in time to the most ancient dance of all. The man arched back on his couch, his eyes closed, his fists clenched. The beat increased, louder and faster, until with a cry that was echoed from every throat in the room, the man jerked his hips up to meet Nipha's mouth, his balls visibly twitching as he emptied himself into her.

Nipha sucked on him, draining him of every drop so that when she finally released him, his penis was left clean and shining with her saliva. The coin was gone, but Nipha opened her mouth and extended her tongue so everyone could see the silver token resting on it, still covered in thick, white jissom. She plucked the coin from her mouth and held it between her fingertips, slowly licking the last drop of spunk from it before slipping it into her pouch and standing up.

It was like a signal permitting the audience to start breathing again with a collective sigh of stifled passion.

'Here, me next,' called someone.

'No, me. Here's five drachmas.'

'I've got ten.'

Nipha turned, looking around her, glowing triumphantly but confused by the clamour for her attentions.

'Here,' the big merchant urged, holding up a coin of gleaming gold with one hand, while the other still moved restlessly between Chryseis' thighs. The audience fell silent, waiting to see what he had in mind, and Nipha stepped towards him.

The merchant grinned, and slipped the coin between Chryseis' legs. She thrust her pelvis forward to meet his big fingers as they pushed the token deep inside her. Then he encouraged Chryseis to turn and sit beside him on the low couch. At his whispered suggestion, she lifted her knees up to her chest and put her hands beneath her, drawing her buttocks and thighs apart to reveal the shining lips of her swollen sex and the tight puckered ring of her anus. She put one finger in her mouth, wetting it, then used its tip to slowly circle the smaller entrance, rubbing it until it relaxed enough to draw her in to plunge tightly in and out of herself. With the other hand she stretched apart the lips of her cunt, splaying it open as wide as she could go so that the gold coin could be seen gleaming at the heart of her pink petalled flower.

Acantha felt herself turn to liquid at the sight. As much as Chryseis was an irritation, she was endowed with a beautiful body and Acantha yearned for the touch of the soft smooth flesh. Before Nipha could get there, Acantha cast the tambourine aside and stepped forward to kneel between Chryseis legs. She looked up into the young woman's face, and was angered by the sight of the triumph she could see there. Chryseis seemed to be gloating at her, and for a moment Acantha was ready to stand up and walk away.

'Eat me,' Chryseis ordered, holding herself further apart. 'Do it, slave.'

The audience seemed to hold its breath in anticipation as, ashamed but hungry for release, Acantha did as she was bid. She leant closer, inhaling the gut wrenching aroma of Chryseis' fresh moistness. The heat rose from Chryseis' sex like the yeasty aroma of freshly baked bread from an open oven, carrying with it the promise of wholesome fulfilment and nourishment. Acantha closed her eyes, savouring its low warmth like a ravenous man relishing tender meat, or a connoisseur appreciating the heady bouquet of rich wine. She moved closer, extending her tongue till it just caressed the soft, swollen flesh of Chryseis' labia. The woman groaned, bucking upwards with her hips to force herself upon the visiting mouth, but Acantha moved back, refusing to be hurried, playing her own game of power with the young woman. An appreciative murmur of amusement ran through the crowd as they watched the interplay.

Only when it suited her, did Acantha run her tongue gently over the rippled flesh, tracing the convoluted folds that nestled within their concealing fold. She lapped delicately at the juice-filled crevices, adding her own saliva to the brimming lubrication, supping on the essence of woman as her nose nudged the pillowed flesh of the swollen labia.

Chryseis' clitoris was like a hard knot against the forward curve of her pubis, angled forward as if drawing attention to itself. Acantha skirted it, deliberately tormenting the young woman, driving her crazy with desire, though she too ached to caress it with her tongue and lips.

Each time Chryseis lifted her pelvis, seeking to position the engorged bud beneath Acantha's mouth, Acantha moved on, always staying just out of reach. In the end, Chryseis could endure the torment no more. 'Eat me properly,' she commanded, digging her fingers into the mercenary's hair and dragging her down on to her waiting sex.

Now Acantha gorged herself on the copious fluids running from Chryseis open cleft, lapping and sucking on the delicate flesh as if barely restraining herself from biting, chewing and swallowing it. Her tongue probed ravenously at the pleated flesh, focusing on the hard peak that marked the core of Chryseis' passion. She nipped it with her teeth, teasing the woman till she squirmed uncontrollably. She'd show her who was boss; who was enslaved to whom.

Acantha drew back, withholding her services, resisting the fingers that still clutched at her hair. Chryseis tugged harder but, meeting only refusal, her face crumpled in despair. 'Please,' she begged, the word almost torn from her. 'Don't stop now. Please.'

Acantha smiled with cruel satisfaction, and dipped her head once more. Now it was she who forced the young woman's thighs further apart, pulling the opening as wide as it would go so that she could bury her face into the soft envelope, suffocating in pleasure as she probed deeper for the elusive coin. There, she could feel its edge now, could just manage to flick it with her tongue, to entice it out.

She had forgotten the audience, forgotten that she was being watched, that there was anyone else in the entire universe, until she felt feather-light caresses over her own back and buttocks. Unknown hands, male or female, tugged at the straps holding her leather skirt in place and, within moments, cool air played across her exposed genitals. She thrust them up higher, putting them on display for whoever was in a position to look, and lowered her face deeper into Chryseis' sweet cunt.

Her shift was the next to go, leaving her naked apart from her jewellery and ever-present amulet. Ghostly fingers explored her flesh, gripped her buttocks, squeezed her breasts, delving within her, rubbing her swollen clit as she lapped, cat-like, at the cream of Chryseis' desire. More than one pair of hands travelled across her skin, and the thought of so many strangers touching her in search of their own gratification increased her excitement even more.

She sucked hard at Chryseis' sopping quim, finally being rewarded by the coin slipping into her mouth. Now she could finish the real task. She drew her head back enough to gulp down a lungful of air, then reapplied the tip of her tongue to the bead of Chryseis' clitoris, vibrating over it with frenzied speed.

Something warm and wet, another tongue, slipped between her own vulva. Gentle breath rippled the hairs of her crotch. She wondered who it was and hoped it was Nipha. In her mind, the image of the three women, with herself in the middle, stoked her passion to a new blaze of intensity. She flickered over Chryseis' clitoris with new urgency and was rewarded with the young woman's scream of release as she ground her sopping pubes over Acantha's face. The pressure forced the mercenary back on to the unknown mouth below, increasing the intensity of her own stimulation. Her passion continued to mount, building in pressure till she was no longer sure she could contain it. It erupted from her with a force of its own, feeling as if it were bursting out of every orifice in her body simultaneously, driving a cry from her that was like the birth of the universe.

Acantha regained her senses to feel warm moisture splash across her skin. She looked up and saw an encircling crowd of men ejaculating over her and the other women. A shower of sweet semen rained down upon her naked flesh as the men rubbed themselves to climax. She opened her mouth, catching what she could on her tongue. The remainder trickled down over her face and neck, and formed sluggish rivulets across her breasts which she rubbed in till her skin absorbed the life energy of the fluid.

Finally, the shower subsided to the last few drops, and she laughed aloud with quiet pleasure. Then she put her fingers in her mouth and hooked the coin out from under her tongue where she had secreted it. As she held it up, there was a cheer of approval from the onlookers, and many added their own donations to the fund. Soon, the impromptu minstrels had a small mound of money, more than enough to pay for a meal and a bed for the night, had anyone permitted them to spend it. Instead, they were fêted all evening and plied with as much food and drink as they could consume.

And in return there was only one condition: that they never sang in public again.

Nine

It seemed like the first time in ages that Chryseis woke up feeling fully refreshed. She stretched languorously, enjoying the touch of the soft woollen blanket against her skin, delaying the moment when she would actually open her eyes. Beside her, someone else stirred in the bed. Chryseis grinned to herself at the realisation that she had no idea who it was, not even whether they were male or female. What did it matter anyway? She had discovered so many lovers the night before, all giving her such unimagined pleasure, that she would be happy to wake up beside any of them.

A hand stole quietly across her belly, tracing the lines of her ribs, stroking the soft flesh of her stomach. The fingers followed the lines of muscles, circling the indentation of her navel, then spiralling within it, tickling the tightly whorled flesh with a fingernail, a sensation which sent spears of pleasure to her groin. She twisted slightly, uncontrollably, but hid the smile that pulled at her lips, pretending to be still asleep.

The hand drifted lower, following the thin line of hairs down from Chryseis' navel to where they thickened into the luxuriant forest of her pubic hair. Nimble fingers made occasional forays into the dense, wiry undergrowth, but always retreated swiftly, as if nervous of what they might encounter within the mysterious depths. Instead, they traced the silken skin on either side of her secret triangle, following its crease round and down to where her thighs pressed tight together, sealing off all further progress. Only then did the hand return to her tangled bush, at first skimming across it so that its passage barely disturbed any but the longest growth. Very gradually it settled deeper, like a bird alighting in the tree tops, then worked its way to her gentle mound and the secret glade within.

Chryseis lay back and enjoyed the delicious sensation. There was no urgency yet, no need to hurry, just the gratifying pleasure of being touched and admired by another human being. It was an end in itself, and one she would happily spend the entire day pursuing.

Warm, moist breath caressed her breast; a slick tongue rotated around her nipple, then flickered across its peak. Soft lips nuzzled her tender flesh, exploring the heavy roundness of her breast as it rested sideways against the curve of her ribs. Teeth, hard and sharp, scraped the surface of her skin, a contrasting thrill that added spice to her perceptions of the varied caresses.

The hand at her groin insinuated itself irresistibly between her thighs. Chryseis stirred, as if in pursuit of some elusive dream, and let her legs shift apart so that the exploring fingers could find their way to her hidden bower. There, they stroked the tender petals of her labia, swollen and blossoming outward from the split bud of her sex. The fingers probed deeper, sliding easily within her lubricated bloom, travelling directly to the engorged seed-case of her pleasure.

Chryseis bit her lip to stop herself crying out and heard a low chuckle, her deception had been revealed.

'You can stop pretending now,' said Nipha's voice, warm and honeyed.

Chryseis screwed her eyes tightly closed and began to snore.

'Oh, dear,' sighed Nipha. 'Well, if I haven't woken you yet, then I never will. I suppose I'd better just give up.'

141

The hand between Chryseis' legs began to recede. With a giggle, Chryseis grabbed the wrist and clamped it between her thighs to prevent it escaping. She opened her eyes and looked into Nipha's face, hovering just above her own.

'Ah, good. I thought that might get a response,' the woman grinned as she leant over her. 'Now, how about returning the favour?'

Chryseis ran her hands up Nipha's warm skin, as soft as velvet. She slid her hands round to cup the weight of the young woman's breasts, feeling the hard nipples press into her palms as they hung like ripe fruit over her. She twisted round, so that her own nipple and Nipha's could rub together, watching in delight as both hardened and elongated, as if kissing each other.

Nipha rolled further on top of her, until she lay like a man between Chryseis' legs, pubis to pubis, breast to breast. Slowly, gently, she slid back and forth over Chryseis' body, thigh against thigh, lip on lip: the maximum contact possible between two bodies. Chryseis let her mouth open beneath the woman's questing tongue, playing with the slick, lithe intruder as it ran over her teeth, tasting the shared flavour of saliva and breath. Skin on skin was the whole sensation, and the rest of the world faded into insignificance.

Chryseis lifted her legs, drawing her knees up towards her shoulders, exposing herself more completely to Nipha's imitation thrustings. She could feel the scratching pressure of Nipha's mound on her clitoris; could hear her own breath rasping in time to Nipha's urgent pant. Their tongues met and flickered round each other more furiously, drawn first into one mouth, then another as if fighting over who should have the privilege of devouring the other, and who should have the sweeter privilege of being eaten.

Nipha thrust harder, the mounting pressure on Chryseis' vulva squeezing her clitoris till it felt as if it would burst into flame and ignite the whole of her body. Flickering warmth spread up from her groin, filling her belly with electric excitement, making her breasts ache with the need for release. The heat spread up to her chest and throat, inflaming her skin as it made its way up her neck and kindling a black roaring fire in her skull that escaped from her mouth in a timeless cry of achievement and loss that was echoed back from the figure on top of her.

Slowly, the beating pulse in her ears faded as she clutched Nipha's trembling body, sharing the palsied aftermath of their orgasms, stroking the quivering flesh, soothing it as Nipha soothed her own flesh in return.

Gradually, the heat faded and their cooling flesh shivered in the light morning air. Nipha reached behind her for the blanket, pulled it up to cover them both before sliding off Chryseis' body, though leaving one arm and a leg draped possessively across it. 'Come with us,' she whispered as her fingers brushed stray hairs from Chryseis' brow. 'We could do this every night and every morning. I would make you happier than you have ever imagined.'

Chryseis smiled with satiated pleasure. It seemed that there was no need for anything else from life; this was the only gratification one ever truly needed and even food and drink were only incidentals, to fortify the body for further loving. 'Of course,' she said. 'I'll follow you anywhere.'

Except, later, when she had told Acantha that she was abandoning all plans to marry Timon and was going to take to the life of a wandering minstrel, the barbarian had other ideas. First, she had chuckled offhandedly, as if Chryseis had made a joke. Then, when Chryseis had repeated her intention, Acantha had told her not to be such a romantic little idiot and get her things together because they were leaving immediately. Even when Chryseis had turned to Eucrates for help, the man had let her down, siding with the coarse, load-mouthed mercenary. Chryseis was sure he was only doing so in order to keep her close to him for a while longer. Well, he could dream as much as he liked, but she wasn't interested.

Finally, when Chryseis had tried to sneak away with Nipha and Pelex, Acantha and Eucrates had drawn the minstrels aside and spoken quietly to them with much shaking of heads and sidelong glances. The couple had left swiftly after that, without a backward glance.

'See?' said Acantha. 'They obviously weren't real friends, were they?'

'Bitch,' Chryseis muttered as she turned away, and for the rest of the morning she led the way, never looking back or acknowledging the presence of her travelling companions in any way. At midday, when they stopped beside a gentle stream, she ignored them and followed the waters upstream, seeking solitude in which to bathe.

'Will she be all right?' Eucrates asked, as he watched Chryseis' retreating back.

'I pity the man or animal that tries to tangle with her,' grunted Acantha sourly.

'It's not much of a fate for her, is it?' Eucrates pressed. 'Being forced to marry someone she has never met, someone who she knows is old. It must seem that anything is preferable.'

'Except you, apparently,' said Acantha as she stretched out with her back against a tree and rummaged through the sack of provisions they had purchased at the taverna. 'I notice she still avoids you like the plague.'

Eucrates pursed his lips and busied himself with gathering up some kindling to start a fire. Acantha said nothing, and after a while he voiced his feelings. 'She doesn't trust me,' he said. 'Not after you pointed out that I'd been a slave.'

'Do you blame me? I knew nothing
except that brand on your shoulder.' ?
fig, using the back of her hand to wipe
from her chin. She held another of th'
Eucrates.

'No. You did the right thing,' Eucrates conceded,
accepting the fruit. 'Anyway, she was bound to notice
the brand herself, sooner or later.' The fig was tart and
juicy, and he rapidly sucked the seed-filled flesh into his
mouth rather than let it spill away. Once he had
swallowed he continued, feeling the need to explain. 'I
really am the son of a merchant, from Corinth. I was
travelling throughout Euboea, setting up new contacts,
when I landed in debt.'

Acantha leant forward intently, her head to one side.
'And how did you manage that?' she asked.

Eucrates scratched his ear, embarrassed, but he had
said too much to hold back now. 'I gambled on anything anyone would accept a wager on. In the end, I lost
nearly all the money my father had given me. I was
desperate; he wouldn't have understood. So I made one
last wager, gambling everything I had and some I didn't
have on one bet, a fight between two quail.'

'Quail?' repeated Acantha, her eyebrows lifting.

'Haven't you seen any quail fights?' Eucrates asked,
and when Acantha shook her head, he went on. 'I know
they're small birds, but they are surprisingly vicious,
especially when they're forced into a wicker cage together.' He shrugged and returned to the thread of his
story with a sigh. 'Anyway, the bird I backed lost, and
I had nothing to cover my debts except my own body.'

'You said your father was a merchant. Wouldn't he
help?'

'No. I was the youngest son, and in any case, he had
sent me on this journey to learn some sense after I'd run
up debts at home. He didn't even reply to my captors'
request for a ransom.' The memory was still painful and

...red his head, concentrating on eating the rest of
...ng.

'So, if your father didn't pay for your release, how did
you get free?'

Eucrates snorted mirthlessly. 'There, I'm afraid, your
original guess was correct. I ran away. If they ever catch
me, I'll be put to the sword.' He threw the fig stalk aside
and scratched idly at the dust by his feet, then looked
up to meet Acantha's clear green eyes. 'I've learnt my
lesson now, you know. I'll never gamble again. All I
want is a chance to start over.'

The mercenary nodded briefly. 'Why not? It sounds
like you've paid your dues. In any case, who am I to
judge?' She busied herself with the bag of provisions for
a moment. 'Now, do you want some cheese? I'm sure
there was some in here somewhere.'

The day was hot and still. As Chryseis followed the
meandering stream amongst the trees, her tunic adhered
unpleasantly to her body, and her skin prickled with
drying sweat. When at last she came upon a spot where
the crystal water chuckled over smooth stones before
widening into a small pool, she immediately decided to
bathe. She cast her chiton aside, then gingerly lowered
herself into the chilly water, shivering as it leeched the
heat from her skin.

Still, it was a relief to sluice the grime and stale
perspiration from her body, and the cold ache which
sank deeper into her bones with each passing moment
was a small price to pay. She finished quickly, then
hurried from the water to stand in a beam of sunlight
that speared down through a gap in the foliage. She
squeezed the water from her hair, then wiped the excess
from her skin, swiftly running her hands down her arms
and across her belly, over her breasts and between her
thighs, so that the sparkling droplets cascaded to the
ground. When most of the water had been removed, she

inhaled deeply and turned slowly in the sun's rays, letting the warmth revive her damp, goose-pimpled skin.

For a moment, Chryseis forgot her quarrels and frustrations. The here and now was pleasure enough after the morning's journey. There was no point in hurrying back into aggravation and tension, so she lay out on the soft turf to dry slowly in the dappled sunlight. She stretched and closed her eyes, inhaling the sweet scent of the grass and the delicate tang of wild thyme. The stream whispered secrets as it tumbled over the rocks and, from the branches above her, a golden oriole fluted prettily in reply.

The world drifted away from her as she felt herself cocooned in drowsy sleep, at peace and untroubled.

A twig snapped in the undergrowth.

Foliage rustled.

Chryseis' heart tripped within her chest and she almost sat up in alarm. Then she realised that it had to be Eucrates, spying on her as he had done when they had first met. Damn him, she cursed, but though she was annoyed she was feeling too lazy to get up and confront him. Let him look. She knew he wanted her; let him look and know he'd never have her again.

She twisted indolently, as if turning unaware in her dreams, repeating the game she had played only this morning with Nipha. Her thighs opened and she could feel the sunlight warm the cleft of her sex. She twisted further, imagining the rays of heat came directly from Eucrates' eyes, and turned herself so that they fell deeper within her, piercing upwards to her womb.

With absent-minded languor, she let the fingertips of one hand trail down her body, dragging them over the gentle slope of one breast, casually circling the dimpled skin of her areola, spiralling in to the peak at its centre. She wriggled suggestively, letting her thighs close over her exposed pudenda, concealing her smile at the thought of Eucrates' imagined disappointment. Still, she didn't want him to lose interest completely, and after a moment she stirred once more to stretch and lay herself open to his bright gaze.

She continued to twirl a finger around her hardened nipple; such a small, delicate sensation but one which created echoing shivers in her belly and loins. She imagined that it was Eucrates' mouth playing with her, imagined his hard hands as they caressed her fragile flesh. Making love with him by the pool when they first met had been pure delight, and she had entertained a momentary hope for their futures together. It had been a blow to discover that he was no more than a slave: a suitable plaything but hardly a fitting consort. Maybe she could allow herself the pleasure of his body again. But, if she did, he would be harder to give up a second time. Better to keep him at a distance and let him pine for her like a faithful puppy.

She let her fingers wander further down her body, feeling the firmness where her skin stretched taut over the curved arch of her lower ribs. She had lost weight, she realised. The flesh was falling from her with all this walking. Was that good or bad? Certainly, she didn't want to lose her curves, but from looking at Acantha, she could see the merits in the lean and hungry look.

She checked for loose flesh across her belly and found surprisingly little. She examined her thighs too, pinching them between her finger and thumb. With a giggle she realised that she must be presenting an odd sight to her audience. Still, what did it matter?

She sat up and bent over, inspecting herself. The skin of her legs was silky and smooth, and she examined it carefully, noting the way in which it formed a crease between her thigh and the rounded flesh of her mound. The black hairs formed an untidy line, and she stroked them as if combing them out, brushing them this way and that with her fingers. As she groomed herself she kept her body angled so that the movements of her hand first revealed, then concealed, her secret garden to the unseen watcher.

She glanced over to the other side of the stream and detected a faint quivering amongst the dark, glossy leaves of the bushes. He was still there, though she couldn't see him. She felt a rush of warmth spread from her loins at the thought that there might be a reason for that particular motion.

'Shouldn't Chryseis be back by now?' Eucrates asked, looking around.

Acantha opened her eyes and sat up, a frown creasing her brow. 'You're right. She's probably only sulking, but we'd better check.' She rose to her feet in a single, lithe movement, and looped her sword belt over her shoulder. 'We'll leave the provisions,' she said, hooking the bag over a low branch, out of reach of hungry animals. 'We should be back soon, and if there is any reason for alarm, they'll only hinder us.'

Eucrates picked up his javelins, carrying two in his left hand, the third balanced in his right. 'She went upstream, that way. I can't imagine she'd have gone far. She's probably just fallen asleep.'

'Or met a bear,' muttered Acantha dryly. 'In which case my sympathies lie with the bear.'

'Talking of which . . .' whispered Eucrates with a nod to where the sound of something could be heard approaching. 'That's not the way she went.'

Acantha moved a few steps aside and unsheathed her sword, while Eucrates took a throwing stance and readied the first of his spears. The sound came slowly closer: snorts and rasping breath plus the crackle of twigs and foliage forced aside. Whatever it was, it was a big, clumsy creature, and Eucrates was ready for anything except the bent peasant woman, dressed in black, who puffed into view with a bundle of wood as big as herself on her back.

'Mercy,' gasped the woman when she saw them, dropping her load and raising gaunt hands to her trembling lips. 'Oh, mercy, please. I'm nothing but an old widow. I have no money for you, please, please . . .'

'Hush, woman,' ordered Acantha gruffly, putting her sword away and holding up her empty palms. 'We mean you no harm. Eucrates, put your weapon down.'

Eucrates did as he was bid, the tension easing from his muscles. 'Have you seen a young woman?' he asked. 'Pretty, but dressed poorly.'

The woman's brown, weathered face showed alarm, the creased eyes opening wider. 'A young woman? No, I haven't. You said pretty. How pretty?'

'Very,' Eucrates repeated, and ignored Acantha's snort of derision. 'Some would say beautiful. Why do you ask?'

'Oh, the poor dear,' the crone muttered. 'It's a bad time. A bad time indeed for a girl to be out alone.'

'What are you babbling about, woman?' snapped Acantha. 'What is there to be afraid of?'

The woman paused in her mumbling and looked sharply at the mercenary. 'You are not the only ones looking.'

'Not the only ones? What do you mean?'

'You must hurry, and pray you are not too late.'

Chryseis plucked a long stem of grass from the ground beside her. At its tip was a fluffy ear of minute seeds, like a soft and delicate feather. She stroked the improvised brush against her skin, its touch the merest whisper on the surface of her flesh. It was a sensation as far removed from the insistent exploration of a heavy hand as possible, and yet its delicacy in no way made it less pleasing.

She continued to play with herself, her mind drifting off into calm peace as she soaked up the sun's rays and inhaled the rich scents of earth and forest. The tinkling water formed a drowsy background to the scratching of insects and the occasional warble of birds.

Chryseis trailed the grass stem down her leg, from hip to calf, noting the change in sensitivity from one part of her limb to another. She bent her leg so that she could reach the soft spot at the back of her knee, where it sheltered between the two tendons. Here, the skin was fragile and easy to stimulate. She stroked it lightly, until the shivering sensation lost its edge.

The other end of the broken stalk was hard and prickly. It produced a different impression, sharper and even more localised than before. It seemed to activate each nerve individually, so that she became aware of each pore, each separate hair, each indentation and crease. She followed the underside of her thigh back up her leg, nerve by nerve, until the splintered tip of the stem traced the folded junction between thigh and buttock. Here, the minute touch was crisp and clear, a single gleaming spark in the overall awareness of her body. She traced the point along the crease, first outwards and then inwards, to where the fold joined the deeper cleft between the cheeks of her behind. There, the tiny sensation became sharper, more insistent, and she moved the grass stalk till it ran up and down the hidden cleft and tickled the puckered ring of her anus. Back and forth she trailed the stem over that receptive hollow, her breath becoming deeper, her urgency increasing.

She shifted the focus of her attention, so that now the stem walked amongst the hairs of her groin, lightly tickling each follicle in turn, a barely perceived touch. It was a deliciously lazy way to indulge her own body, to make love to herself, but she wondered how long she could endure so much, yet so little, feeling.

The need for something more gratifying was growing within her belly. The slow prelude was almost at an end, and her body's demands for the finalé was becoming more pronounced.

She used her fingertip to trace the delicate flesh of her swollen labia. It was still the lightest of touches, but after the infinitesimal caress of the grass, it was like an explosion of sensation. With urgent passion she homed in on the nub of her clitoris, so responsive and aware that she imagined she could discern every whorl and ridge of her fingerprint.

Warm pleasure radiated outwards from that pivotal point, a gentle flow of incipient delight, mounting, ever mounting, as her breath grew ragged and gurgled in the back of her throat. Then, ever so gently, she tipped over the edge of arousal and down the other side in the cascade-like release of orgasm. Awash with warm contentment, she let her finger slow and stop, returning once more to the world around her. She noticed again the scent of grass, the sun on her body, and the oriole, still whistling in the trees above her head and undisturbed by her cries.

She also remembered Eucrates watching her from the bushes on the other side of the stream and hoped he had enjoyed the show, because that was all he was going to get. Her self-gratification had been far too satisfying for her to spoil it by sharing it with anyone else.

She angled her head to one side, so that she could see past her upraised knees, and called out, 'Okay. You can come out now. I know you're in there.'

There was a sudden hush as the whole glade seemed to listen for a reply.

'Oh, come on, Eucrates. I know it's you. Did you like watching me? Come out and show me what you've been doing to yourself.'

The silence continued, and Chryseis began to wonder whether she had been mistaken after all. Then the bushes rustled and she glimpsed a flash of white cloth. But the mocking laugh with which she would have greeted Eucrates turned to a gasp of fear as two men, whom she had never seen before, emerged from the undergrowth and stood studying her.

152

Chryseis scrambled to her feet and scooped up her tunic, which she held in front of her in alarm and unthinking embarrassment.

'Don't be frightened,' said one. He was the older of the two, a lean, grey-haired man wearing a white, toga-like, himation.

'We mean you no harm,' said the other. He was barely older than herself, with black hair and liquid brown eyes.

'Who are you?' she demanded, her heartbeat returning to normal as she realised that they weren't going to immediately pounce on her. In fact, looking at the younger of the two, she could almost regret that they weren't. He was so good-looking, if she had known he was there she would have invited him to join her earlier. She let her grasp on her concealing garment slip a little, and was rewarded by the sight of him swallowing hungrily.

'We are priests from the temple at Dirphos. We are on a quest.'

'A quest? For what?'

'For perfection,' said the older priest smoothly. With a slight inclination of his head towards her, he added, 'And we seem to have found it.'

'Oh?' Chryseis affected disinterest, but inside she laughed with delight at the compliment. She abandoned any effort to conceal herself and let her hands drop by her side so the men could admire her further. 'And tell me, what have you found?' she asked, fishing for further flattery.

'We have discovered the goddess Hera, Lady Protectress and wife of Zeus, walking amongst us in the guise of a young woman,' said the older priest. 'We beseech her to come to our temple and be our High Priestess.' He prostrated himself on the ground till his forehead touched the soil. The younger priest hurried to follow his example and the two of them remained like that, awaiting her pleasure.

Chryseis' mind seemed to be buzzing with different thoughts and it was hard for her to maintain her pose of insouciant indifference. Had she heard right? Were they really offering her the position of High Priestess based simply on her supposed resemblance to Hera? If so, it would give her the power to do what she wanted with her life. She would no longer have to obey her guardian, Pythias, nor would she have to let herself be bullied by that overbearing barbarian, Acantha. And, most of all, she would not have to marry Timon.

The younger priest glanced up. 'Please, Lady. Say that you will at least visit our temple and let us honour you in the fashion you deserve.' A small flicker of a grin lit his features as he added, 'I am sure there are many ways in which we can please you.'

'You may well be right,' Chryseis conceded with an act of haughty grandeur. 'Very well, I will indulge you, for a while at least. Take me to your temple.'

'What do you mean, old woman?' demanded Eucrates, cold fear gripping his bowels. 'Why should we pray that we're not too late?'

'The priests from the temple at Dirphos seek a new priestess. The temple is dedicated to Dionysus and, each year, the priests seek a woman in the likeness of Hera and punish her for her sins.'

Eucrates groaned in sudden realisation.

'What sins?' interrupted Acantha impatiently. 'I am not from these lands and I haven't the time to learn of your countless gods and goddesses. I know of Dionysus from our encounter with his worshippers back at that village, but what crime did Hera commit?'

'It is said that Dionysus, the god of wine and pleasure, was fathered by Zeus on a mortal woman, Semele,' explained Eucrates. 'On hearing of this, Hera, who was Zeus' wife, became insanely jealous and arranged for Semele and her child to be killed.'

154

'Dionysus was saved, however,' continued the old woman. 'But when she found out, Hera's rage knew no bounds. On her orders, the Titans tore the infant boy to shreds. Only Rhea, his grandmother and the great mother of the gods themselves, was able to restore him to life.' She faltered, seeming unable to continue.

'And just how do Dionysus' followers punish Hera?' insisted Acantha.

'Once a year, at the summer solstice, the priests initiate a young woman as her priestess,' explained the old woman, her voice unsteady. 'Then they tear her apart, as Dionysus himself was torn apart, and offer up her flesh as a sacrifice to him.'

'And the summer solstice?' prompted Acantha, her voice grim.

'Tomorrow.'

Ten

'Are you travelling alone?' asked the older priest, a scrawny man with sharp, bird-like movements, who had introduced himself as Xenophanes.

Chryseis thought of Acantha and Eucrates before replying. No doubt they'd find something wrong with becoming Hera's priestess, and try and prevent her from accepting the offer. 'I'm travelling alone,' she replied without further thought. 'I became separated from my companions when we stopped overnight at a taverna. They fell in with some wandering minstrels and went off with them the following morning.'

'Leaving you alone?' enquired Xenophanes, cocking his head to one side.

'Yes. One of them, my maid Acantha, fell for the minstrel girl called Nipha; and Eucrates, my bodyguard, is so infatuated with Acantha that he followed them both like a puppy.' It was always easier to remember a lie when it was based on truth.

'That's outrageous,' commiserated Xenophanes. 'Still, had it not been for your misfortune, we would not have found you. And we do not like our priestess to have any unfortunate ties to the external world. Once she is within our walls, we do not want her sullied by external influences.'

'Of course, I quite understand,' Chryseis agreed.

'Where were you heading?' asked Eudoxus, a pale, soft-looking man. 'Who is expecting you?'

'I doubt if anyone is,' explained Chryseis. 'We were heading to Chalcis by ship when we were caught in a storm and swept overboard. No one even knows we are alive.'

'Oh dear, how unfortunate. Still, you are with friends now; isn't she, Xenophanes?'

'Absolutely. We shall look after you with all the care possible. Our priestess lives a life of unparalleled luxury,' said Xenophanes with a brief smile. 'Now, I think there is nothing to delay us from returning immediately to the temple.'

The priests waited till Chryseis had dressed herself, then led her away upstream, chattering away about all the things she could expect once she was High Priestess. Late in the afternoon they eventually rounded the shoulder of the mountain. Before them, the land dropped towards lush valleys with fields of vines lining the slopes. The tired sun lay cradled on the horizon between two peaks and tinged the few wisps of cloud a delicate pink. A gap in the blade-like cypress trees revealed a white marble temple and its surrounding buildings built on the summit of a rocky outcrop jutting from the side of the mountain. In the flushed sunlight it shone with a golden nimbus, as if favoured by the gods. It radiated serenity and peace, and Chryseis shivered with excitement at the thought that she would live here for the rest of her life.

'Come on,' she urged. 'I want a closer look.'

'Of course,' agreed Eudoxus, and led the way down the uneven path that wound between the trees. The track ran above a turbulent river which crashed and boiled through a narrow defile cut into the rock of the mountain. They followed the course of the water down the side of the mountain till it widened and slowed, and finally disappeared into a large, lightless cave directly beneath the temple. 'We get our water from this river,' Eudoxus explained, 'It emerges on the other side of the hill and the current carries away our wastes and rubbish.'

'The gods provide,' intoned Xenophanes. 'It would be churlish of us to refuse their bounteous gifts.' He smiled at Chryseis, obviously intending the description to include her, and gestured her forward to where the path curved through the gateway to the temple grounds.

At the entrance, they met another group of travellers arriving from the other direction. Two of them, a man and woman, were dressed like the priests accompanying Chryseis, in white tunics with dark red borders. The final member of the group was a young woman, about Chryseis' age, dressed in a peasant's threadbare chiton. She had been crying. Salty tears had cut through the dust powdering her face and dried to white-edged streaks. Every few steps, she halted and tried to turn away, but the priest and priestess each had a firm grip on one of her wrists and jerked her forward with grim determination. The action had the appearance of weary repetition, as if they had travelled a long way in the same, futile, conflict.

The priest and priestess looked surprised when they saw Chryseis. 'Hey, Xenophanes, where did you find this one?' called the man.

'Chryseis is a traveller through these lands,' replied Xenophanes. 'We were very lucky to find her and persuade her to join us.'

The peasant girl grunted scornfully. 'You mean you haven't told her about the competition,' she mocked.

'What competition?' asked Chryseis, annoyed that there could be a catch to the priests' offer.

'To be Hera's priestess, you idiot,' the girl said, her tone tinged with contempt.

Chryseis turned to Xenophanes in anger. 'You promised me that I would definitely be High Priestess,' she accused. 'Nothing was said about a contest.'

'Promised?' squawked the other girl, her face the

picture of shock. 'You mean you want to be selected? Listen to me, –'

'Enough!' barked the priest holding her, jerking her wrist. 'No conferring with the other candidates. Come with me.' And he and his companion hauled the girl away.

Chryseis put her hands on her hips and watched the departing figures turn the corner of a building and disappear from sight. 'Well,' she said, turning back to Xenophanes and Eudoxus. 'What have you to say for yourselves? What is this competition?'

Xenophanes spread his palms and smiled complacently. 'Well, it is true that there is a contest to find the most suitable candidate,' he said smoothly. 'But we were so certain you would win that there was no point in mentioning it.'

Chryseis knew she was being flattered but, even so, believed there was probably an element of truth in what the priest had said. After all, she was certainly better looking and had more poise than the ragged peasant who had been dragged in ahead of her. 'How many candidates are there?' she demanded. 'And why was that one so reluctant?'

'I don't know how many other candidates there will be. When we are in need of a new priestess, we go out in pairs across the neighbouring land, seeking any who are suitable. Some –' he said, nodding after the peasant and her escort '– are less discerning than others.' He took Chryseis' arm as he talked, lightly urging her forward into the temple grounds. 'On the final day, however, only the most deserving one is selected for the honour.'

'And her reluctance?' Chryseis persisted, though not so suspiciously; she already felt somewhat mollified by Xenophanes' warm reassurances and did not resist as he guided her amongst the imposing buildings.

'I don't know, I truly don't.' The priest shook his

head and sucked air between his teeth, as if such strange behaviour was beyond his comprehension. 'It's a great honour to be chosen, but some girls don't really appreciate it. Perhaps it is because they are forced to compete by their fathers, who stand to make a lot of money if their daughters are chosen. Also, many are upset by the nature of the competition; we are looking for a woman who will please Dionysus, and he is a god of unabashed pleasure. It is not a role for immature virgins; only women who are already experienced in the ways of the world and who are eager to learn even more will appreciate the position.'

'In that case,' said Chryseis with a confident chuckle, 'I am certain that you'll find me more than suitable. I have always prided myself on my desire to acquire new experiences.'

'Good, good,' said Xenophanes, bobbing his head in approval. 'That is what we thought as we watched you by the pool. Well, here we are.' He ushered Chryseis into a small building in a secluded corner of the temple grounds where oil lamps already flickered a yellow welcome in the encroaching dusk. 'This is where you will stay tonight. Make yourself comfortable and a few of our younger neophytes will be along soon to look after you. I suggest you rest well, in preparation for tomorrow.' With that, he saw Chryseis through the door, then withdrew with a low bow, taking Eudoxus with him.

Chryseis examined her room carefully. It was obviously intended as temporary accommodation only, just a single large combined living and sleeping space which opened directly to the outside. A narrow archway led through to a second, smaller, room. It contained a large bath and, in an alcove hung around with sweet-scented herbs, a stone seat with a hole leading somewhere underground. From below, she could hear the sound of running water and presumed it was the river that she had seen earlier.

She stretched out on the bed to wait for Xenophanes' neophytes, and within moments felt herself drifting into sleep.

'Damn the stupid girl,' muttered Acantha as she crawled back from the crest of the hill overlooking the temple, being careful not to silhouette herself against the sky-line. It wouldn't help to be spotted spying out the lie of the land.

'Did you see her?' Eucrates sounded distracted with worry and Acantha hoped he wouldn't be tempted into trying something gloriously heroic but fundamentally stupid.

'No chance. It's like a small village down there; she could be anywhere,' Acantha replied curtly, then turned to the old peasant woman who was still catching her breath after having struggled to lead them to this vantage point. 'Have you no idea where they hold the candidates, Sela?'

The crone shook her head. 'None,' she wheezed. 'I've not been to the temple for a long time; not since they took my niece for their foul sacrifice, and that was 23 years ago.'

'That's a considerable period for them to have been preying on the local populace,' observed Acantha, scratching her chin with the back of her hand. 'I'm surprised they haven't been driven out. Or do they have some hold around here?'

Sela looked up with rheumy eyes and snorted in grim amusement. 'Oh, they're too clever to always take a local girl. Usually they bring in some contenders from outside: a few slaves or cheap harlots whom no one will miss. For the last few years, though, the grape harvest has been especially bad. So, to appease Dionysus, they're planning a special ceremony this year.' She hesitated, her brown skeletal fingers fluttering over her mouth as if to block her next words. 'And for that, they

161

need something better than a few scrawny foreigners; only the prettiest and most nubile sacrifice will do, regardless of where she is found.'

'And everyone just goes along with this?' Eucrates asked, quivering with incredulous anger. 'No one tries to stop them?'

Sela shook her head. 'Around here, everyone lives by the grape. It is natural that they worship the god of wine, and natural, too, that they want to keep him happy. If the harvests fail, it is not just one pretty girl who will die; whole families could be wiped out by starvation. People do what they think they must in order to survive.'

She sighed. 'In any case, as is the way with such things, the most powerful local figures are also members of the cult and defend its interests. Of course,' she added cynically, 'they are also free to enjoy the rituals in the knowledge that it will never be their daughters who are chosen.'

'There must be something we can do,' said Eucrates stepping forward and frowning down at the temple.

Acantha yanked him back, her nerves taught with anger. 'There may,' she hissed. 'But if so, we'll stand a far better chance of success if we aren't seen making our plans. Now keep down and out of sight.'

Eucrates glared back, and half-raised a clenched fist. Then he lowered his eyes and nodded ruefully. 'Sorry. I wasn't thinking,' he admitted.

Acantha gave him a forgiving slap on the shoulder. 'No matter. We all forget ourselves occasionally. Now, though, we need a good plan before we try and rescue our brainless companion.' She turned again to Sela. 'You can't be the only one around here who has had enough of the priests,' she stated. 'Who else is there? Especially anyone who might know their way around inside the temple.'

Sela shook her head again. 'There's no one. Least

ways, the only people who really know anything about the inside of the temple are devotees and would lead you false or betray you.' She raised her head suddenly, her watery eyes widening with realisation. 'But there is someone though,' she said excitedly. 'An old hermit by the name of –' she paused in thought for a moment '– Notos. That's it. He was actually a priest at the temple, till he couldn't stomach the sacrifices any longer. Then he left and went to live alone in a cave up in the mountains. I don't even know if he's still alive. It's years since I saw him.'

'This Notos, does he – did he – live near here?' Eucrates asked while looking at Acantha. The question in his eyes was easy to guess.

Sela shrugged, her palms held up. 'Not so very far, but more than I can manage. I'll tell you the way, but you'd have to make the journey alone, and he might not talk to you once you got there.'

'It sounds like a long shot,' mused Acantha, considering their meagre options. Without help, they would have no choice but to try sneaking into the temple grounds on the off chance of finding either Chryseis herself, or someone who was willing to show them the way. It wasn't much of a choice. She rubbed her hands over her face wearily, as if that would help her make a clear decision. 'All right,' she agreed finally. 'But we'd better hurry if we are to find him in time.'

Chryseis awoke with a start. A young man and woman of about her own age had entered while she slept. Both wore simple chitons made from white wool bordered in green, and Chryseis assumed they were the neophytes whom Xenophanes had told her to expect. They looked nervous, and bowed deeply before speaking.

'I am Zeuxo,' said the woman in a soft voice, barely louder than a whisper. 'And this is Hipparchus.'

The youth bowed again. 'Our pleasure is to serve you,

mistress,' he said with a tremor. 'There will be food ready soon, but we wondered if you would care to bathe first.'

The afternoon's hike over the mountains had left Chryseis feeling grimy again, so she readily agreed. The two servants scuttled away like timid mice to fetch the water and Chryseis grinned to herself. They had actually seemed in awe of her, and she relished the idea of being fawned over. No one had ever taken her seriously before; even the slaves back on Pythias' estate, who had known her since she was a little girl, had treated her with gentle affection rather than respect. Her personal maid, Palmeda, had been the worst of the lot. She had known far too many of Chryseis' intimate secrets to be impressed by their difference in status, although her loyalty had never been in doubt. Chryseis wondered what she was doing now and realised, to her surprise, that she missed the slave's easy companionship.

She cast the memory aside; this was not the time to be having second thoughts. Instead, she sat on a low chair to await the return of her new servants. Tonight, she would begin as she meant to continue. From now on, she would command the respect she deserved. A flutter of excitement at her potential power stirred in her belly.

Hipparchus and Zeuxo returned shortly, each struggling with one of the large, three-handled hydria used for carrying water. They emptied them into the bath, half-filling it with hot water. Steam curled from the surface and Hipparchus gathered up the empty urns and was about to head out the doorway when Chryseis stopped him. 'Where are you going?' she demanded.

'To fetch more water, mistress. Zeuxo will remain to help you.'

'Let Zeuxo fetch the water,' Chryseis ordered. 'I want you to attend to me.'

The two neophytes exchanged a glance, then Zeuxo

turned to her and spoke up hesitantly. 'Of course, you may have either of us attend you, mistress,' she said, her eyes uneasy. 'But tomorrow will be a busy day, and we would not wish for your appetite to be blunted before the competition begins.'

'Xenophanes said nothing about it. He said that I would have no trouble,' said Chryseis, toying with them. 'Do you think that I will?' The last question hung like a trap ready to ensnare them.

'Of course not, mistress,' Hipparchus interjected hastily. 'But two other priests have found another contender who is almost as pretty as you, and who is just as eager to win. They are also sure that they have found Hera's next priestess and although we don't agree – how could we after having seen you? – we think it advisable you conserve yourself for tomorrow.'

'What a sweet tongue you have,' purred Chryseis, delighted by the flattery. 'Is it just as nimble in other circumstances?'

'I –' Then Hipparchus caught her meaning and looked down at the floor as his face grew bright pink.

Chryseis laughed aloud; she had not expected such coyness here. 'Well?' she asked Zeuxo. 'Is it? You can tell me.'

Zeuxo's face showed a myriad of emotions; surprise and mischievous delight being the main ones. 'Well, mistress, the honest truth is that none of us have found out. Hipparchus only arrived here two days ago, and so far he has evaded everyone's attentions.'

'Tsk tsk. That's not good enough,' Chryseis said with mock severity. 'Especially for a future priest of Dionysus. I think tonight we had better find out if he is capable of living up to his responsibilities.'

'But, mistress,' Hipparchus protested. 'What about tomorrow?'

'Mmmm. That is true. As Zeuxo so eloquently put it, I don't want my appetite to be blunted ahead of time.

What I really need is for someone to put an edge on it.'
She grinned at the couple standing in front of her. 'So,
I therefore think it best that I bathe myself, while you,
Hipparchus, demonstrate your skills on Zeuxo.'

Hipparchus looked horrified, but Zeuxo was having
difficulty hiding her smile. 'It will be our pleasure,
mistress,' she said formally and nudged Hipparchus
with her elbow.

'Of course, of course,' the youth agreed, his throat
bobbing conspicuously as he swallowed.

Chryseis stood up and undid the clasp holding her
chiton in place, letting it fall in an untidy pool at her
feet. She kicked it into the corner of the room, then
sauntered between the two neophytes, brushing them as
she passed. Hipparchus averted his eyes but Zeuxo
watched her swaying breasts with unabashed interest.
Chryseis stepped into the hot water, then lowered herself into the tub and reclined back as the soothing
warmth seeped into her muscles. Zeuxo continued to
watch, her eyes following Chryseis' brown nipples as
they protruded above the surface of the water. Hipparchus, on the other hand, continued to stare at the floor.

'Now,' Chryseis commanded, curious to see how he
would react, 'I want you both to take off your clothes.'

As she had expected, Zeuxo obeyed instantly, undo-
ing her tunic and letting it drop without the slightest
hesitation. The neophyte had a small, delicate body,
that looked light enough to be picked up in one hand.
There was no surplus fat anywhere, and even her breasts
were economical cones with swollen areolae that gave
the greatest effect for the least bulk. Her legs were
slender enough not to press tightly together, allowing
the soft light of a lamp on the far side of the room to
glitter between them. The glow silhouetted the deep cleft
of her ripe vulva and the small patch of black hairs that
blurred the outline. The young woman stared back
throughout Chryseis' inspection, her eyes shining with

166

pride as she drank in the admiration. Chryseis exchanged a knowing look with her, the mutual recognition of a kindred spirit and the promise of future pleasures. It made her wonder why Zeuxo herself did not compete for the role of Hera's priestess. Neophyte or not, she had more experience in temple affairs than Chryseis, and certainly seemed adequately qualified in other respects. Before she could voice her curiosity, however, she became distracted by the fuss that Hipparchus was making over getting undressed.

The youth was fumbling with the simple clasp, his face burning and his eyes resting anywhere except on the two naked women. Zeuxo put on an incredulous expression and gave an exaggerated shrug that made Chryseis chuckle. 'Help him out, Zeuxo,' she said. 'I'm sure you know how.'

Zeuxo slapped impatiently at Hipparchus' clumsy fingers, making him let go of the pin. Then she carefully undid it herself. Her tongue protruded slightly from the corner of her mouth as she concentrated on freeing the clasp from the tangle of wool that Hipparchus had managed to knot around it. Even so, it took only moments before the garment slipped down Hipparchus' body. The youth snatched the material to his chest before it reached the floor, and both women laughed at his shyness.

'Give it here,' ordered Zeuxo, gently tugging at a corner. 'You wouldn't want our candidate to fail, would you.'

Hipparchus shook his head dumbly.

'Then we had better entertain her; don't you agree?' She tugged the garment again, gently, and Hipparchus let it slip from between his fingers, drawing a shuddering breath as he was finally revealed in full. He was lean and well muscled, and even if he didn't consciously know what was going to happen next, his penis was already semi-erect, raising its head in instinctive anticipation of the forthcoming action.

'There, that wasn't so bad, was it?' asked Zeuxo as she consigned his garment to the same pile as the others, and delicately cupped his balls in one hand, causing his member to twitch in response. Hipparchus looked embarrassed, as if the display was something shameful, rather than an honest compliment to the woman, and she had to hold on to his hands to prevent him from covering himself.

Chryseis watched with amused interest as Zeuxo continued to caress the young man's genitals. She had a sure touch and coaxed them into life with the same subtlety and patience as a farrier cajoling an unbroken foal to come within his reach.

As Hipparchus' erection elevated itself above the horizontal, Zeuxo sank to her knees and kissed the mauve, glistening tip as tenderly as if it were a new-born child. Hipparchus groaned, the sound a low rumble in his throat as his eyelids fluttered half-closed, revealing nothing but the whites of his eyes.

Chryseis watched Zeuxo's style with appreciation as she encouraged Hipparchus' erection to full rigidity. First, the neophyte covered the whole organ with feather-light kisses, starting at the tip then working back to where his balls hung loose in their sack. She kissed and licked his scrotum, nudging the hanging testicles with her nose, as if scenting at his maleness, then drawing them, one by one, into her mouth and rolling them between her lips. Judging by the raggedness of his breath, Hipparchus found the sensation highly pleasurable and when Zeuxo drew back, Chryseis could see that his balls were drawn up tight to his body, ready to fire. Zeuxo, too, smiled in pleasure at the sight, like a craftsman taking pride in her work. She returned her attentions to the shining purple head of his weapon, slipping her lips over it, engulfing as much of his turgid flesh as she could. Then she insinuated a free hand through his legs and around between his buttocks.

Hipparchus jerked abruptly, his eyes opening wide; then his eyelids drooped shut again and he began to gasp loudly as his hips rocked back and forth. His heavy breaths became a series of short, rasping pants, increasing in urgency till they culminated in a long groan of pleasure. He thrust forward, as if trying to plunge deep within Zeuxo's throat. She drew back hurriedly, evidently surprised by the swiftness of his orgasm, and his thick, white semen spurted over her face, dribbled down her neck and trailed across the dark shelf of her breasts in long, stringy strands.

On seeing Zeuxo's disappointed face, Hipparchus' look of satisfaction faded into guilt. He evidently lacked the experience to know how to hold back, or to know what to do next, and Chryseis decided it was time to come to their aid. 'It's not over yet,' she reassured them. 'Hipparchus, lick her clean.'

The lad looked startled for a moment, his eyes flickering uncertainly to where his seed clung to Zeuxo's olive skin, dripping down the sides of her breasts and across the subtle corrugation of her lower ribs.

'Do it,' Chryseis instructed sharply. 'Or you will have to be punished.'

Slowly, almost reluctantly, the lad knelt opposite Zeuxo then bent his head and tentatively tongued the milky line that trailed across her right nipple. He seemed apprehensive of how his sperm would taste, as if he had never before had the curiosity to sample his own seed. He licked the line slowly, pausing to savour the flavour, unsure whether he would like it. Chryseis felt her mouth and her vagina watering as she watched him, remembering the first time she had tasted fresh semen and imagining the salty, pungent flavour in her own mouth and lingering at the back of her throat.

Zeuxo dipped a finger into the rich cream, lifted it for her own tongue to taste, then held it to Hipparchus' lips for him to suck clean. Then she cupped a breast in one hand, lifting its pointed snout up to meet Hipparchus' mouth, while with her other hand she caressed his neck and guided him down to meet her.

Slowly, as if still uncertain about what was permitted or, absurdly, whether he would give offence, Hipparchus placed his hands on Zeuxo's waist and drew her to him. Tentatively, he rubbed his cheeks across her flesh, smearing the sperm into his own skin as well as hers, slowly being consumed by a welling appreciation of his own primitive sexuality. Still kneeling before him, Zeuxo now arched backward till her buttocks rested on her heels and her head touched the floor behind her. Her body formed a graceful curve, with her belly and the dark tuft of her pubic hair marking its crest.

Hipparchus could no longer reach as far as Zeuxo's breasts. Instead, he circled the hollow of her navel with his tongue, lapping at the white semen that had accumulated there like a cat lapping a bowl of cream. Zeuxo sighed and shifted her weight, so that her knees spread further apart, but Hipparchus didn't take the hint.

Chryseis rose from the bath, still dripping with water and strode over to the young man. Her own sex screamed out for release and she fully understood Zeuxo's need for satisfaction. She took the youth by his hair, forcibly pushing him down so that his mouth covered Zeuxo's sweet mound. 'Drink from her,' Chryseis ordered, pushing his face forward between Zeuxo's legs.

The youth resisted only a moment, then obediently bowed his head.

The young woman juddered as Hipparchus's tongue flickered hesitantly across the cleft of her sex. 'More,' Chryseis ordered, her fingers slipping into her own nook with an irresistible determination to satisfy her personal needs.

Hipparchus lapped again at Zeuxo's spread vulva. Chryseis watched closely to make sure he did it proper-

170

ly. She loved to see the way he ran his tongue between the folds of Zeuxo's labia and swallowed her sweet syrup with the abandoned delight of the newly converted. He gave a long, slow groan, heavy with lust, and inhaled deeply with his nose buried in the dark hairs of the young woman's pubic hair. He opened his mouth, pressing it against the open vagina, straining forward, as if trying to drink from Zeuxo's very core. The neophyte juddered, and made small, high-pitched whining sounds in the back of her throat as Chryseis guided the lad's head back and forth, encouraging him not to miss any part of the feast spread out before him. Zeuxo's breath came sharper and swifter, and Chryseis could see the warm red flush spread up from her chest and suffuse her neck. 'Now, lad,' Chryseis urged. 'Find the little nub of pleasure there between her lips ... Got it? Flick your tongue over it, first light and swift, then slow and firm, see which she prefers ...' Zeuxo's breathing sounded like a whimper now, growing more urgent as Hipparchus explored the range of sensations he could impart to his lover. 'That's it lad, she likes it slow, now don't stop, just keep it like that ... yes ... yes, yes!' Chryseis' urging rose to a peak as Zeuxo bucked and twisted violently, as if to get away from Hipparchus' insistent mouth. But when he tried to draw back, Zeuxo clutched him firmly between her thighs, her fingers knotted in his hair, grinding her pubes into his face with fierce determination as her cries reached a long, lingering crescendo.

Finally, Zeuxo subsided, her skin damp and steaming with sweat. She eased her legs free from under her body, stretching them high and wide as Hipparchus, his face glistening with her juices, bestowed tender, butterfly kisses to the pouting lips of her vagina. Gradually, the tempo of Zeuxo's breathing increased again, and she lightly rocked her hips back and forth against Hipparchus' tongue. This time, the lad needed no encouragement to home in on the pinnacle of her pleasure, lifting her swiftly and smoothly to her climax. When Zeuxo came, it was with a gentle explosion of delight that left her chuckling contentedly as she pulled Hipparchus up to kiss his mouth in thanks.

Using all her will-power, Chryseis turned her back on the scene and withdrew her fingers from the slippery folds of her own sex. She refused to let herself have the relief of an orgasm. Instead, she was going to bank down the desire that burnt within her, letting it smoulder overnight so that tomorrow it would be ready to explode into a raging inferno.

Eleven

Chryseis' thwarted libido spun sensual dreams to disturb her night. She awoke twice to find herself caressing her own body, and reluctantly stopped before her lust was gratified. When, finally, the grey light of dawn seeped into her quarters and cockerels sounded from distant farms, Chryseis was glad to give up the struggle for sleep and rouse herself from her bed.

By the time Hipparchus and Zeuxo arrived with platters of bread and fruit for her breakfast, Chryseis was already up and waiting for them. She greeted them warmly, but they seemed subdued today, and barely mumbled a reply.

'What have I done?' asked Chryseis. 'Or are you two just tired after a night of getting to know one another?'

Hipparchus and Zeuxo exchanged glances which Chryseis took to mean that her comment wasn't far from the truth. However, they still kept their eyes downcast, refusing to meet her gaze. 'Come on,' Chryseis urged. 'Tell me what's going on.'

'Well, mistress,' began Zeuxo, 'today is the day of choosing and for now, regardless of who finally wins, all the competitors are sacred.'

'Yes, mistress. We should not have done what we did last night,' said Hipparchus. 'If Theophilus, the High Priest, hears of it, he will be very angry with us.'

Chryseis laughed indulgently, remembering that these were, after all, her servants and as such deserved her

173

protection. 'Of course I'll say nothing,' she agreed. 'Now, where's breakfast?'

However, though she knew she would require all her energy, Chryseis could not face more than a corner of bread and a handful of grapes. Her mouth was dry, and she had difficulty in swallowing even the tiniest of morsels; they felt like pieces of splintered wood scraping down her gullet. In any case, her stomach felt too tight and knotted to digest anything, and she eventually gave up the attempt.

She suffered a mild panic attack at the thought that nervousness might quell her appetite for sex, too. Any doubts on that score, however, were put to rest as she let Zeuxo and Hipparchus bathe her yet again. The couple had filled her bath once more, but this time the water was scented with exotic, smoky aromas containing a hint of musk. The fragrances alone were enough to arouse her, even before the two servants began washing her gently, all over, with their bare hands. They ensured that she was cleansed in every crack and crevice of her body, and by the time they invited her to step from the bath, Chryseis felt hornier than ever.

Once they had dried Chryseis with soft woollen towels, Zeuxo and Hipparchus produced several small flasks with long necks, each containing a differently scented oil. They rubbed the perfumes into her water-softened skin, so that the heat of her flesh awakened the aromatic essences, filling the air with the musk of sandalwood and myrrh entwined with the sweeter scent of saffron. The fragrances were surely sufficient to excite any man, but Zeuxo augmented it with Chryseis' own special scent. She dipped two fingers into Chryseis' vagina, working them gently till Chryseis generated some of her own special nectar. For a moment, she thought the neophyte was going to bring her off there and then, but she didn't. Instead, the girl took her dripping fingers and delicately dabbed the redolent fluid behind Chryseis' ears and between her breasts, so that the vapours would subconsciously arouse anyone, male or female, who came close enough to inhale them.

Zeuxo and Hipparchus polished Chryseis' nails and brushed her hair till it shone like silk, then set it with many plaits and curls. Hipparchus even trimmed the nest of hair that lay between her thighs, then brushed it so that it formed a symmetrical triangle, neatly shaped to follow the line of her groin. Zeuxo, meanwhile, accentuated the almond shape of her eyes with lines of khol, and used powdered henna leaves to give a rosy blush to her cheeks, breasts, and even her buttocks.

Chryseis' servants then adorned her with jewellery made from finely wrought gold and silver: long earrings which jingled prettily when she turned her head, snake-shaped bracelets to twine around her upper arms and a heavy necklace of amber beads linked by golden rings.

Finally, they dressed her in a simple chiton of white linen with a pale yellow border, held over her shoulders by gold clasps in the shape of swooping birds. Chryseis fiddled with it for a moment, trying to ensure that the folds draped evenly over the embroidered belt girdling her waist.

Zeuxo laughed. 'Don't worry, mistress. You won't be wearing it for long.'

At last, they were finished and Zeuxo produced a mirror of burnished silver so that Chryseis could admire herself. She felt a lump in her throat when she saw how they had transformed her, for she had never looked so beautiful. 'You've done well,' she said, moved to unaccustomed thanks.

'It is our pleasure, mistress,' said Zeuxo, then cocked her head to listen to the sound of a large gong reverberating across the temple grounds. 'Just in time, too. The contest is about to begin.'

Acantha dragged herself up the last stretch of almost vertical rock and gave a sigh of relief. Before her lay the hermit's cave, with a small patch of level ground in front of it. The remains of a fire formed a charred circle before the opening, and smoke had blackened the rockface above it. 'This is it,' she shouted down to Eucrates, who was clambering up behind her, his face red and beaded with sweat.

'Is Notos there?' Eucrates puffed.

Acantha stepped up to the cave entrance and peered inside, keeping her hand cautiously on her sword hilt as she did so. 'I can't see him,' she called back. 'I'm going to take a look inside.' She ducked under the low opening and blinked to accustom her eyes to the gloom, before taking stock of the shelter. A low bed, made from bundles of ferns and twigs covered with a layer of goatskins, formed a cosy pallet against the rear wall. A smoked haunch of goat hung from a hook in the ceiling and a miscellaneous array of pots and urns were stacked carefully down one side. A small clay lamp rested in a high niche. Acantha reached the lamp down; it was full of oil. And when she inspected the bed, she found that the twigs had been recently cut or broken. Whoever lived here had not been gone for long, and was probably just out in the hills tending his goats.

When she told Eucrates, he agreed with her assessment and cursed their luck. 'He could be gone for days,' he said, running his fingers through his hair, making it look wilder than it already did. 'Now what do we do?'

Acantha squatted down and jabbed thoughtfully with a broken stick at the remains of the fire. 'If he doesn't return soon, we'll just have to go back and try to force a way into the temple ourselves,' she said. 'But let's wait a bit first. I have an idea, and we may get lucky.'

'Here, drink this,' instructed Zeuxo. 'It will prepare you for the contest.' She held out a drinking cup, decorated with red figures against a black background, depicting Dionysus himself surrounded by prancing nymphs. It brimmed with wine so dark it was almost purple.

176

Chryseis was about to drink when she detected the heady aroma of myrrh rising from the liquid. The aromatic resin was good, not only for sweetening the breath, but also for bringing a sense of tranquillity and languor to those who consumed it. She returned the cup, untouched. 'Save that for those who need it,' she said. 'I prefer to keep my wits about me.'

Zeuxo laid the drink aside with a look of satisfaction. 'As you wish, mistress. I did not think you would need it.' She bowed low and gestured towards the door. 'However, we had better go now. It is not seemly to keep Theophilus waiting.'

The two neophytes led Chryseis from her quarters and out into the plaza that stretched up to the foot of the temple steps. The walk across the open space seemed to take forever. Nervousness clutched at Chryseis' stomach and the strain of not letting it show, plus the heat from the glaring sun, made her head swim.

They were not the only ones walking towards the temple. Two other groups also marched towards it across the sun-baked plaza. Each consisted of a single candidate dressed, like herself, in a simple white chiton, and escorted by a pair of neophytes. One of the candidates was the girl she had seen at the outer gate to the temple. Her face lacked expression, as if she had drunk much of the myrrh-laced wine. The other candidate's symmetrical features would have been pleasing if they hadn't been set in such a grim mask. She strode ahead of her escorts as if eager to begin the contest, and Chryseis realised this must be the other likely contender.

Within the temple's shaded interior, Chryseis was immediately struck blind by the lack of light, and had to stop to let her eyes readjust. The first thing she noticed, therefore, was the rich tapestry of aromas that hung in the air. Many kinds of incense formed a cloying background but failed to mask the pungent thread of burning laurel leaves. However, unless she inhaled the smoke directly, the laurel would barely affect her. At least she had avoided compounding its trance-inducing properties with the numbing influence of the myrrh.

She was also aware of many people whispering expectantly. The susurration echoed from the space around her, giving the impression that she stood in a vast chamber long before she could confirm it with her eyes.

When, at last, her eyes adapted to the dim light, she found she was standing in the middle of the temple floor. Broad, fluted columns were arranged down each side of the hall, reaching up to the shadowed roof above. Between the pillars, and packed around the periphery of the hall, stood an animated crowd of spectators, peering over each other's shoulders and jostling for position. Most looked like ordinary citizens. They were separated from the body of the temple by a line of priests and priestesses, easily identifiable by their tunics bordered in crimson or green. All the temple officiants also carried a thyrsus, sometimes called the wand of Dionysus, which was a staff entwined with ivy and tipped with a pine cone.

At the far end of the temple, just in front of the altar mounted on its raised dais, stood two further contenders. They waited with no sign of interest or fear, their expressions stony. At least, thought Chryseis, it would be easy enough to outshine them all in enthusiasm, if nothing else.

A hush fell over the crowd, and Chryseis turned in time to see a new figure emerge from the far recesses of the temple and stand beside the altar. He was an elderly man, dressed like the others in a simple white chiton and, like the others, carrying a thyrsus, though his appeared to be made from gold and inlaid with turquoise. This, presumably, was the High Priest, Theophilus. His lined face was pallid, almost the same shabby grey as his beard and lank hair. He paused

178

dramatically, with his arms outstretched, then cracked the butt of his staff three times on the marble floor. The final whispers from the crowd died away, and in the sudden silence the collective sigh of their breathing echoed around the great chamber like the sound of some sleeping monster.

Theophilus stepped forward with his hands raised. 'Today, we honour the great god Dionysus, and thank him for the many pleasures he has bestowed upon us. We appease him with our gifts so that he, in his turn, may favour us with many more of his. We honour him with our presence, and with the selection of a priestess for Hera, the jealous wife of his father. Now, let the contest begin.'

He banged his staff on the floor again and gestured towards the five contestants who stood huddled together in an uncertain group. 'First, show us who you really are; reveal your true selves. Remove your garments so we may see you truly, as Dionysus intended you, as physical shells for the attainment of delight.'

Well, thought Chryseis, we got straight to the point there.

The other girls hung back, but she sneered at their modesty. They might be frightened of putting their bodies on display, but she had not spent most of the morning beautifying herself in order to remain hidden. In any case, eagerness was always the greatest asset a girl could display. She thrust her way forward, stepped up on to the dais, boldly undid the clasp at her shoulder and let the garment drop. The cool air inside the temple caressed her naked skin as she stood, with her hands on her hips, and let the audience admire her.

'This is Chryseis,' Theophilus informed the spectators. 'I have heard she is a stranger to these parts, but she is obviously willing and keen to please.' The audience murmured in appreciation, but their attention turned swiftly to the next candidate who had to be

179

pushed on to the dais by a couple of neophytes. Theophilus introduced her as Sida, from the neighbouring village of Kambia.

Sida undressed with obvious reluctance. Her body had the lush freshness of youth and would, in better circumstances, have been quite pleasing. However, her posture was hunched with embarrassment, and her hands fluttered across her torso with a nervous life of their own, not knowing which part of herself to conceal first. The crowd sounded vaguely appreciative, but unexcited. Chryseis felt smugly confident.

The following two candidates, introduced as Valonia and Parthenia, acted with similar reluctance. Valonia was nothing special, though Parthenia did raise a ripple of interest; she was undoubtedly stunning and had barely attained the first blossoming of her womanhood.

That left only the woman with the sad face and determined set to her mouth whom Chryseis had noticed earlier. Theophilus identified her as Neysa, and gestured for a couple of neophytes to lead her on to the dais, obviously expecting her to be as reluctant as the others.

Instead, Neysa brushed aside any assistance and stepped up by herself. Then she stood, arms crossed, till the first ripple of impatience ran through the crowd. Only then did she slowly undo the clasp which held her chiton over her left shoulder. The material sagged downwards on that side, almost to her waist, exposing just her breast and its alert nipple. She turned slowly, allowing everyone a good look at the single orb, letting her audience's anticipation grow. The speculative murmur increased and, just as it peaked, Neysa undid the second clasp and let the tunic fall to her feet.

She stepped daintily clear of the discarded clothing, then lifted her arms and performed a slow pirouette. A soft sigh of admiration echoed around the huge temple. Chryseis could see the hunger in the audience's faces, and could understand why. Neysa's body was lithe and sinuous, yet it had not sacrificed any fullness to the curves that mattered. Her breasts were rich and heavy, with large brown nipples that jutted forward with an arrogant demand to be noticed. Her waist was slender, with a deeply carved navel, and her pudenda were shaved clear of any hairs, leaving the inturned folds of her cleft like the shells of a half-closed clam, concealing the pearl within.

Neysa turned and smiled with acidic sweetness at Chryseis, while Chryseis glared back, knowing full well that she had been thoroughly upstaged. She just hoped that she would have a chance to get her own back before any judging was done.

Instead, the High Priest cracked the butt of his staff on the floor again, bringing silence to the crowded temple. When he had everyone's attention, he started talking again. 'Today, we are lucky to have five candidates for the position of High Priestess. However, only one can go forward to fulfil that role; only one can achieve the ultimate honour. We must, therefore, eliminate from the contest those who fail to meet our standards. In time-honoured fashion, each citizen assembled here today will therefore mark a fragment of pottery with the name of the one that most displeases him. The two candidates with the most votes shall be rejected. The remainder shall proceed to the next stage of the selection.'

Young neophytes passed among the crowd, gathering up the shards of pottery that formed the ballot. Then the pieces were heaped in front of the High Priest and sorted into five large urns. Two of the urns remained empty. The other three filled steadily.

Finally, all the shards were sorted and the High Priest stepped forward to announce the losers of the first stage. Chryseis felt her stomach clench as Theophilus called for silence. Surely she had not been eliminated so soon?

But she was not positive and that small, lingering doubt gnawed restlessly away at her.

The chattering crowd fell silent, and Theophilus made his announcement. 'Those who have lost the first round are: Valonia and Sida.'

A ripple of emotion ran through the audience. Some people were obviously disappointed, perhaps having made wagers on the outcome. Others seemed fairly pleased. The two losers, however, seemed overjoyed at the decision, and ran from the temple as quickly as possible.

Well, that was their choice, thought Chryseis. She, at least, was relieved to still be in the running and intended to win.

A small spattering of stones, tumbling down the hillside, announced Notos' arrival. Acantha looked up from the fire she was tending and gratefully laid aside the bundle of leaves and grass she had been about to pile on top of it. The smoke from the damp fuel eddied about, catching in her throat and making her eyes water. However, she had thought the column of white smoke might summon the hermit back to his cave, and it looked as if she were right.

Notos slithered down the slope in a cloud of dust and kept his feet as he landed on the flat ground. He stared at the strangers with no sign of fear, and said nothing as he assessed them carefully.

He was dressed in nothing but a simple loincloth made from badly cured goat hide, and his hair was a tangled, dirty-grey nest, stained like old sheep dags. Acantha could smell the stale sweat of his body from five paces away. Despite that, however, his weathered face had all the sharpness of splintered flint and his eyes were clear and alert, and not in the least bit mad, as she had expected.

'You're Notos,' Acantha said, and when the man nodded curtly she added, 'We need your help.'

Notos brushed past her without saying a word and kicked the smouldering fire apart with his bare foot, stamping out the smoking embers with complete disregard for his own skin. 'We don't want anyone else coming up here, wondering what's burning,' he said. His voice was hard and disapproving.

'We had to find you quickly,' Acantha explained with a note of apology though her patience was already stretched thin.

'I have nothing to do with the outside world,' said Notos. 'It is none of my concern. Now, leave.' He turned and started to make his way back up the hill.

Acantha moved after him; if that was his attitude, she'd soon make him talk!

Eucrates restrained her and gave her a sly wink. 'We'll be gone when you return,' he called after the hermit. 'But it will be to tell everyone about you. We'll tell them you are a seer; that you have the gift of prophecy. People will come here like bees around a flower. You'll never have a moment's peace again.'

Notos stopped halfway up the path and looked back at them, but remained silent.

'I will,' Eucrates assured him. 'I'll also warn them that you are an incorrigible old man, but that if they persevere you will be able to tell them the future. You'll never escape. You'll end up with more visitors than the Oracle at Delphi.'

Notos' shoulders slumped in resignation. Then, surprisingly, he snorted in amusement. 'All right, since you have found my weakness, I'd better listen. What do you want?' he asked, with the beginning of a smile.

It was the second round of the contest. Theophilus approached Parthenia, the young, pretty one, first. The girl flinched back, though judging by the glazed look on her face she couldn't have been fully aware of what was going on. Theophilus gripped her arm and dragged her forward to face the audience.

183

'First,' he called, 'we have Parthenia, a fine figure of a woman.' He ran his hand across her back and cupped each buttock in turn. 'Her skin is soft and without blemish; her flesh is delightfully pliant. She would make a wonderful priestess for Dionysus, and would, I am sure, bring him great joy.' Parthenia yelped suddenly, and Theophilus added: 'She is nice and tight, too. A joy for any man –' he paused, then added dryly '– if he can get within her.' The audience laughed and Theophilus left Parthenia standing huddled at the edge of the stage, miserable tears trickling down her face, while he moved on to Neysa.

'This one, now, is very different, as I am sure you have all noticed.' He drew Neysa forward with a light touch on her shoulder and she undulated towards the audience, wriggling her hips. She squirmed seductively as Theophilus ran his hands over her body, and when the old man tried to speak, he first had to clear his throat. 'This young woman has a body that would make Aphrodite herself jealous. It feels as lithe and sinuous as it looks; a pleasure to caress.' He stopped as Neysa twisted around to rub her naked breasts against his chest and run her hands through his hair. The audience were silent, holding their breath in anticipation of what would happen next. Theophilus turned Neysa back to face the audience, then reached around her and lifted her breasts in his hands, as if offering them to the spectators. 'She has a wonderfully shaped physique,' Theophilus intoned, squeezing the soft mounds as if checking the ripeness of some fruit. 'Her breasts are firm and full, and her nipples are as hard as cherry stones.'

A murmur of agreement rippled through the crowd, and Chryseis saw several heads nodding sagely, as if approving the purchase of a fine horse.

Theophilus ran his hands down the woman's ribs, slapped her flanks, then slipped one hand around her waist to cup her shaven mound. 'And I have never

184

before come across such a finely polished chalice, so ready to overflow with ambrosia and nectar. What a vessel this would be to sup from, don't you agree?'

Before Theophilus could move on, however, Neysa clasped his questing hand between her thighs, refusing to let him remove it. She rocked her hips back and forth, flagrantly gratifying herself on Theophilus' long bony fingers as they remained wedged in her dripping cunt. Within moments, her breathing deepened and she threw back her head, gasping for air as her panting became sharper and fiercer till it formed a single cry of release. Then she slumped back into the High Priest's restraining arms with a contented smile.

The audience breathed a collective sigh of pleasure and a rising whisper of acclaim echoed around the temple. Chryseis suspected Neysa's orgasm was faked, but the audience seemed taken in. Some of the faces Chryseis could see appeared so eager that she was sure they had already decided on the winner. She would have to do something special in order to take the lead.

And it was her turn now.

Theophilus approached warily, as if uncertain of her reaction and half-expecting her to run away. As he came closer, Chryseis saw his eyes clearly for the first time; they were grey, with tiny pupils, and left her with the feeling that he could see right through her. She shuddered uneasily under the scrutiny, but it wasn't just him she was trying to win over. Demonstrating her eagerness and willingness to please, she stepped forward to meet him with her eyes half-closed in sleepy seduction. She ran the tip of her wet tongue around her lips, then slowly smiled in invitation.

Theophilus stepped aside and gestured for her to approach the edge of the dais herself. She advanced with a sensuous wriggle, as aware of the interplay of muscle and bone within her body as any athlete. She did not wait for Theophilus to feel her over like a lump of meat

185

either. She stroked her own curves, held her own breasts out as offerings to the audience, catching the eye of as many individual spectators as possible, separately inviting each one to share her treasures.

'As you can tell,' Theophilus said with a catch to his voice, 'Chryseis also hopes to be our new priestess. Her beauty would certainly grace the office, and her spirit would give it some fire.' He reached out to touch her, to assess her and pass judgement as he had already done to the others, but Chryseis wasn't about to lose control of the situation. She grabbed his hand, the one that Neysa had rubbed herself on and which still glistened with the girl's secretions, and brought it to her lips. She sniffed delicately, scenting the other woman's aroma and excitement on his fingers, making sure that everyone understood what she was doing. Then she extended her tongue, flickering its pointed tip over the High Priest's fingers, tasting the sweetness of Neysa's syrup. Chryseis ran her tongue over his knuckles, down to the crotch between the first and second fingers where the other woman's juices had gathered, then back up again, phalanx by phalanx, knuckle by knuckle till she sucked delicately at the very tip of his digit.

Chryseis sucked the finger between her lips, lowering her head over it gradually till she had taken all of it within her mouth and coated it with her saliva, making it slippery and slick. Once it was ready, she looked up into Theophilus' eyes and held them with hers, watching his arousal grow, as she slowly released his long digit. She stopped, poised at his fingertip, then rushed back down again, her lips gripping the slender flesh firmly. She repeated the movement several times, making sure he would not pull away when she released his hand. Finally, she let go of him, leaving his finger solely under the control of her soft, warm mouth.

The heavy necklace of amber beads which Zeuxo had put around her neck was fastened at the back. She

186

fumbled a moment, then the catch came undone with a snick and the solid weight swung free in her hands.

Maintaining the rhythm of her motion on Theophilus' finger, she steered them both round, so that her back was to the audience. Then she bent over with her legs apart and the cheeks of her buttocks spread. She felt the cool air of the temple brush the hairs of her sex and tickle the sensitive skin of her anus. Judging by the exclamations of surprise, the audience were not missing any aspect of her anatomy.

All the while, she maintained the simulated fellation of the priest's digit, never releasing it, enjoying the savoury flavour of his flesh now that she had sucked it clean of Neysa's juices. She rejected the idea of switching her attention to his penis, although the bulge at his groin looked enticing; his lust for her would serve her better if it was not yet gratified.

Taking one end of the necklace in her left hand, she reached behind her back, and let the beads dangle down between her buttocks. Her other hand went through her legs to catch the free end of the necklace and pull it to the front. Now, she could begin to gently saw the jewellery back and forth between the cheeks of her rump, across her anus and along the groove of her vulva. The round beads vibrated over her flesh, stimulating it in a direct line connecting each of the most sensitive spots in her body, making her feel as if she would split in two with delight.

She changed tactics and threaded the first amber bead through the tight sphincter of her anus. She removed her hands, so that the glittering chain dangled there for all to see exactly what was happening. The audience rustled and moved, but no one spoke. She slipped the next bead in, and followed it, one by one, with the remainder.

All the time, she retained her awareness of the finger that she was using to fuck her mouth. The feeling of the stiff digit penetrating between her teeth, the sensation of it batting against the muscle of her tongue excited her imagination. Her saliva escaped freely, ran in rivulets over Theophilus' hand and dripped to the floor of the temple. It was her juice, the proof of her pleasure, and she let it flow copiously where it would.

Bead after bead fitted within the dark recess of her rectum. She felt their weight within her, pressing inwards, rubbing deliciously against the thin wall that separated that orifice from her vagina. She eased the carved amber and golden links in, bit by bit, till the pressure became more than she could bear without seeking some way to relieve it. When only about three beads were left dangling outside her body, she shifted her attention to the sodden gorge of her sex. With one hand she pulled her aching vulva as far apart as she could while using the other, at long last, to lightly caress the desperate bud of her desire.

Even the lightest of touches seemed intolerable, and she groaned in anticipated pleasure as the explosion of feeling speared up from that tiny nub of flesh to ignite the whole of her body. She imagined the eyes of the audience probing her most secret crevices as thoroughly as her own fingers and the necklace. In her imagination each amber bead was a pair of eyes, viewing her from the inside, seeing the dark pulsing of her blood through her veins, pounding in her ears and suffusing her face with a hot, burning glow.

She bobbed her head with increasing urgency, as if really expecting Theophilus' sperm to shoot from its end and fill her mouth. She imagined hot, spunky liquid splashing across her tongue, filling each cavity of her body to capacity. The pressure in her head grew, the heat increased. She felt her legs trembling as everything seemed to reach a point of no return.

Then the first spasms of pleasure rippled upward from her deliciously aching cunt. As they did so, she grabbed the end of the necklace and pulled it from her rectum in one continuous motion. The beads vibrated through the tight opening of her anus in rapid succession, amplifying the waves of pleasure that coruscated throughout her core. The spasms increased, became a cataclysmic paroxysm that shook her entire body as all the pent-up energy of the last day finally discharged at the same moment. In the distance she heard herself scream, but was detached from it, floating on a sea of release. Then she sank without trace.

For a long moment she was not sure where she was; only the feel of cool marble against her cheek and gentle hands supporting her had any meaning. 'Well done,' whispered a voice that she finally identified as Zeuxo's. 'There's no way they can deny you the place now.' And, as she heard the cheers of the audience, Chryseis knew that the final voting was a mere formality.

Twelve

'You were incredible,' Zeuxo exclaimed, as she prepared Chryseis for her initiation that night, refreshing the scented oils and tidying her long black hair.

Chryseis lay back on the low couch and kept her triumphant grin to herself. One could only maintain one's position by a show of strength and that required her to appear totally unphased by the outcome of the competition. It would add to her mystique if the neophytes believed that she had had no personal doubts about the outcome. Inside though, she quivered with delight. She had made it! She was to be priestess to Hera, Queen of the Gods. Her ignorance of what her duties would entail wasn't a problem. Presumably, if she had needed special knowledge, Xenophanes and Eudoxus would have mentioned it when they had first met her.

However, she did now feel faintly puzzled as to why they would require a priestess to Hera in a temple to Dionysus. It was something that Neysa, the sad-looking contender had said over her shoulder as she was led away: 'Three days ago I received word that my lover died in battle against the Persians. I hope your reasons for wanting to serve Hera here, of all places, are as good.'

When Chryseis asked Zeuxo what Neysa had meant, however, the neophyte simply ducked her head and busied herself cleaning Chryseis' toes. 'I have no idea, mistress,' she said, her face averted. Chryseis was not deceived, and decided that she would probe the matter further at a later date; tomorrow, after her inauguration, would be soon enough.

The gong which had announced the beginning of the contest sounded again, its round, sonorous notes echoing across the temple grounds. Five times it tolled, and Zeuxo and Hipparchus hurried to their feet. 'It is time, mistress. They are ready for you,' said Zeuxo with a low bow.

'Then I had better not keep them waiting,' said Chryseis, though secretly she thought that once her position was confirmed, she would set her own pace in such matters. She wondered what her uncle, Pythias, would say if he could see her now. He would probably ask if he could supply the wine to the temple at a favourable rate. Well, he could forget it. She was never going to forgive him for trying to marry her off in order to seal a trade agreement.

She entered the temple with her head held high, acknowledging the excited murmurs with looks of haughty indifference. These priests, neophytes and common worshippers were going to be hers now, and she was determined to set the tone from the very beginning, just as she had been taught to curb any over-familiarity in a new slave.

She could see little beyond the nearest faces as shadows hung like a cloak over the outer reaches of the temple. Only the central aisle and the dais at its end were illuminated by the scarlet light of glowing sconces, made from applewood and cedar, to add fragrance as they burnt.

Other smells filled the air, low and suggestive. Before she had even reached the dais at the far end of the hall, excitement fluttered in Chryseis' heart and left her mouth dry. The aromas awoke her body, and her loins already ached for the release which, she fervently hoped, was not going to be delayed for long.

Music played from a hidden gallery near the roof of the temple. It was a sweet, haunting melody, picked out on the strings of a cithara with the fluid notes of a syrinx weaving between them. In counterpoint to the harmony, a muffled drum and brash cymbals pulsed in brooding anticipation and Chryseis found her feet unconsciously keeping time as she took up the mood of the piece.

The murmur of voices died, leaving just the faint soughing of their breath and the whisper of soft fabrics. Keeping in time to the muffled beat of the drum, Chryseis paced down the central aisle, her bare toes curling against the polished chill of the marble. Zeuxo and Hipparchus flanked her, and from the corners of her eyes she could see admiration on their faces and knew she was making a grand entrance.

On the dais ahead stood Theophilus, the High Priest. In one hand he clutched his staff of office, the golden thyrsus entwined with ivy and tipped with a pine cone. He wore a long himation, bordered in red, which hung over one shoulder and was draped around him till it hung to his feet. His bare arms gleamed in the flickering light as if his skin had been oiled. The sheen complemented the golden scintillation reflected from the rings on his fingers and the circlet around his brow. He looked like a minor deity himself, descended from Olympus.

He bowed to Chryseis as she approached, and she didn't need Zeuxo's hissed prompt to return the gesture, as equal to equal.

Theophilus smiled thinly and held out a hand, welcoming her up on to the dais beside him. 'Join me, Lady. Join me in this celebration of our God, Dionysus, who sits at the right hand of his father, Zeus, King of all Gods and your husband.'

'Thank you for your kind words, and the honour you do me,' Chryseis replied. 'It pleases me to accept your gracious offer.'

192

Evidently no response had been expected because Theophilus' first reaction was to frown in disapproval. However, it seemed she had done well, for his dark look dissolved into a broad smile as he bowed again. Then Theophilus took a wide drinking cup from the table beside him and held it out to her. 'You grace us with your presence, Lady. Will you join in our festivities, our celebrations of Dionysus' fine gifts of wine and pleasure?'

'With great delight,' Chryseis responded, accepting the cup. It was filled with wine so dark it was almost black. Hoping that she was still doing the right thing, she drank it in a single, long draught. It was stronger than the wine she was accustomed to; she had to suppress the urge to cough as the fiery liquid stung her mouth and throat and ignited a fire of its own in her belly.

She held the empty cup up for all to see and a cheer of approving laughter went up from the assembled crowd. Apparently she had done right again, for now Theophilus held his arms out in greeting. 'Come here and join me, Lady,' he said. 'We have a special welcome for you here, a way for each of our god's assembled worshippers to know you personally, before the final part of our ceremony.' He gestured upwards and a bundle of fine ropes and leather straps were lowered from the gallery above. Chryseis could not make out what purpose they served, especially when they hung in a loose, unshaped tangle. They seemed to form a harness of some kind, though not for any beast that she was familiar with.

'Will you divest yourself of your clothes, once more, Lady?' asked Theophilus, inclining his head graciously.

Chryseis allowed herself a small smile; it appeared her desires were to be slaked at last. She shucked her unwanted garment in seconds, and Theophilus gestured her towards the hanging straps. Intrigued, she moved closer and allowed Zeuxo and Hipparchus to begin attaching the harness to her. Straps went round her wrists, others around her upper arms. More straps went around her ankles, her thighs, and even around her waist. Though each part of the harness was firmly attached to her, they did not bind her. She could still move around with complete ease, though the dangling strings made her feel like a puppet with unseen operators in the high gallery.

'Are you comfortable?' Theophilus asked, his smile a thin line in the subdued light of the temple. When Chryseis nodded, he gestured again to the unseen workers above.

The ropes holding Chryseis tightened as they were pulled upward. For a fleeting moment she wondered whether she really was to become a puppet. Then she swung completely clear of the ground, and laughed in delighted realisation; she was in a cat's cradle of ropes, suspended at waist-height above the ground but reclining backward in the air, with her arms and legs spread wide. In this position, her weight was distributed evenly throughout the anchorage points, and though she was virtually immobilised and helpless, she was perfectly comfortable. She relaxed with a glow of anticipation, curious as to what was going to happen next, but confident that it was something she was going to approve of.

'Now where are we?' said Eucrates, coughing as smoke from the fire brand he carried curled off the low roof and caught in his lungs. The flames had shrunk in the cold, damp air of the cavern, and he was scared they would fail completely, leaving them lost in the darkness.

Acantha, in the prow of the crude boat of stitched goatskins stretched over willow, shook her head. 'I don't know,' she replied softly, without turning round. Her voice echoed within the enclosed space, almost drowned out by the wet slaps of the river. 'Notos said there was a way through, but I can't see it. And the ceiling is getting lower.'

'Can we turn back?' he asked, hoping his voice didn't betray his tension.

'Not now,' said Acantha. 'The current is too strong; we could never paddle against it.'

Her voice was steady enough, but Eucrates heard the faint note of fear and swallowed his own rising panic. He had argued against following the river under the temple, half-believing it was a trap, but also knowing how the tight space would press in and threaten to crush him. He had always been frightened of small places, of enclosing walls that would constrict around him, making it harder and harder to breathe. Acantha's warning that the ceiling was getting lower made him sick to his stomach, and he trembled under the onslaught of his imagination.

'Hold that light up, damn you,' cursed Acantha, and with a start Eucrates realised that he had closed his eyes and let his arm droop.

'Sorry,' he muttered, concentrating once more on his surroundings. They had borrowed the boat from a fisherman further upstream, and had allowed the river to carry them into the dark cave under the temple. Here, the rock walls looked like melted beeswax, tinged with russet reds and slime greens as they trickled and dripped to the black rippled surface of the water. It was cold, too. This stone was never warmed by the sun and its perpetual chill seeped into Eucrates' bones as if he were already a corpse. Perhaps he was. Perhaps they had taken a wrong turning and already floated on the Styx into Hades' dark domain without realising it. In either case, there was no turning back now, only the hope of coming through successfully.

The noise of the water bounced back from the walls, hiding the sound of Acantha's cautious paddling as they searched for a way up into the temple above them. Notos had vowed that one existed, but as the clearance between water and ceiling shrank even further, the suspicion grew that they had been tricked. Finally, they were reduced to lying in the bottom of the boat and watching the rough rock pass just above their faces. The flames from the fire brand licked the ceiling and left a blackened trail of soot behind them. The boat scraped against the lowest parts of the roof, then caught firm, unmoving. Water gurgled furiously against the immobile craft, then spun it free of the obstruction in a swirling eddy.

Eucrates heard Acantha's juddering sigh, and realised with surprise that she was just as scared as he was. 'Roof's getting higher again,' she said, and carefully raised her head above the prow of the boat, ready to duck again if another low spot loomed in front of them.

'See anything?'

'Not a thing.'

They continued in bleak silence into the velvet blackness.

Zeuxo came forward and stood between Chryseis' open legs as she hung suspended in her cradle of ropes. The neophyte held a small, long-necked flask, glazed in red with black figures dancing round its spherical body. Carefully, she tipped a little of the contents over Chryseis' pudenda. The amber liquid ran sluggishly, like thick oil, and seeped slowly into the crevices of her sex, chilling her skin. Then, as Zeuxo massaged the lotion into her skin and the oil warmed up, Chryseis felt a tingle spreading from her loins. It was like a fire on the surface of her skin, like an itch that needed to be scratched or like the most desperate need to have her sex fondled, stroked and gratified that she had ever had. She flung her head back, gasping with the fierceness of the sensation, hoping that it was not going to be long before someone did something to assuage her needs.

Zeuxo was the first. Kneeling on the floor so that her mouth was level with Chryseis' dripping vulva, the girl leant forward and kissed her gently on the open mouth of her sex. The feeling of the girl's tongue flickering over her swollen clitoris was exquisite: a warm, sensuous contrast to the sharp heat of the stinging oil. Chryseis felt her body shudder with her first orgasm, soft and gentle, like the sound of distant thunder presaging the storm to come.

No sooner had Zeuxo finished with her than Hipparchus stepped up. He had discarded his clothes and his erect penis advanced before him like a lance held at the ready. The lad had obviously rid himself of his debilitating embarrassment, and it was with evident pride that he slid into her, thrusting so hard that Chryseis swung on the end of her cradle like a gigantic pendulum. Once she was moving, Hipparchus simply stood with his hands on his hips, letting her helplessly swing back and forth on the end of his member. That was their only point of contact, sex reduced to the most fundamental friction between two sets of genitals. The rawness of it, the unadorned primitiveness, ignited Chryseis' imagination and, combined with the effects of the fiery lotion it took only moments before she bucked in another paroxysm of pleasure while Hipparchus simultaneously pulsed within her.

No sooner was he finished, than Hipparchus withdrew from her, his penis still firm, in order to make way for the next worshipper at Chryseis' altar. This was another woman, one Chryseis had not seen before. She knelt and buried her face in the sodden hairs of Chryseis' aching quim, her tongue delving as deeply as possible to draw out every last drop of their passion. Chryseis felt herself overflow with Hipparchus glorious seed and her own juices as they trickled round between the cleft of her buttocks and tickled the ring of her anus. The unknown woman's tongue followed the flow, lapping it up, then twisted its way within her tight little hole, causing Chryseis to groan and laugh simultaneously as another wave of pleasure washed over her.

Theophilus himself stepped up behind her and tilted her backward in the cradle till her head was lower than her hips. He eased the gleaming dome of his knob between her receptive lips and she sucked on it eagerly as, from her inverted position, she watched the High Priest's testicles sway back and forth within their delicate sack. As he filled her mouth, she felt something else, rough and hard, being pushed up within her vagina. It took her a moment to identify the object as a thyrsus, the staff of Dionysus, and realise that she was being symbolically fucked by the god of pleasure himself. The sensations at either end of her body flooded through her and when they combined and mingled in her belly she climaxed again. Moments later, Theophilus withdrew from her mouth to eject his creamy sperm across her inverted body and she felt the warm fluid spurting as far as her right breast.

Within moments, another acolyte was sucking on the semen-smeared nipple, his bristling beard scratching her skin while he mauled her other breast with calloused fingers. Suddenly the man stood back and began pounding his fist up and down along the length of his erection till he spurted over her, mingling his jissom with that already there.

One athletic and naked woman hoisted herself into the web of ropes, holding on to them as she suspended her depilated sex over Chryseis' waiting mouth. Chryseis craned upward to lick the smooth labia and glistening nub of flesh till the woman cried out and released a stream of warm, golden liquid over Chryseis' face.

Two men took her then, swinging her round in her cradle till one could push into her vagina from the front while the other thrust into her anus from the rear. She could feel both their members pumping inside her, could feel them pressing against each other through the thin wall that separated them as they grunted and drove their hips at her, one slapping against her buttocks, the other grinding against her pubis. She did not even notice whether they came, only being vaguely aware of the spasm that ran through her body like shock waves.

Then came a young woman with barely formed breasts and a gigantic wooden phallus strapped to her hips. She pushed her way into Chryseis' rectum, stretching her wide, while her busy fingers stroked the delicate skin of her clitoris, making her scream with intolerable pleasure.

Another penis, another mouth, fingers, tongues and teeth scraped, pummelled and stroked her flesh till she no longer knew or cared where one sensation ended and the next began. Her sides and stomach muscles ached from the repeated contractions of orgasm after orgasm; her vagina, anus and mouth felt swollen and battered by multiple invasions of every kind she had ever imagined, and her skin stung and itched from the drying semen, urine and saliva that smeared it. Never before had she felt so tired, battered, and utterly satisfied.

Finally the parade of lovers, abusers, fornicators and sodomites came to an end, and Chryseis swung gently back and forth on the end of her pendulum, the ropes creaking softly under the gentle motion. She thought of making some joke, of asking whether that was all that they had to offer, but knew she had had enough. They may take her seriously, and she couldn't stand being fucked again within the immediate future. It was going to be days before she stopped aching, but she wouldn't have missed it for the world.

A soft footfall scuffed the floor as someone approached, and Chryseis turned her head to see who was left, or whether the Priest had at last come to release her from her cradle. She saw the audience gathered around, staring at her intently, saw that most were naked and that they had not limited their indulgences to her, but had been entertaining each other as well. They stood with their arms wrapped around each other and with hands still casually exploring each other's bodies, but they were all silent, all watching the one last person approaching Chryseis.

Chryseis couldn't make out who it was at first because the figure was silhouetted against the light. She could only tell that it was a woman, and when she saw the gleam of metal held in one hand, she assumed that it was a knife to cut her free of the harness.

'What's that?' Acantha muttered suddenly as she peered intently ahead. When she spoke again her voice was full of relief, 'Yes, there it is. Light from an opening and what looks like stairs. Douse that torch before someone sees it and keep quiet.'

Obediently, Eucrates plunged the torch into the water, killing the flame with a sharp sizzle. The darkness that followed seemed absolute, and he strangled the whimper growing in his throat. He concentrated instead on the thought that he had to rescue Chryseis, that she needed him. He just hoped that Acantha had not lost sight of the way out, and that they wouldn't be swept past it in the darkness.

He heard Acantha paddling and the rasp of her breath, then gradually became aware of a vague reduction in the relentless darkness. The boat bumped into something solid. 'We're here,' Acantha hissed. The boat rocked violently as she scrambled out, then he felt her hand clutch blindly at his arm. 'This way,' she said, and guided him out of the unsteady craft on to a narrow and slippery rock surface.

As his eyes grew accustomed to the dim light he could make out that they were standing on a tiny quay. A flight of uneven steps, crudely hacked into the rock, led upward to where the light became a diffuse mistiness from a high opening. A rope dangled down from the distant circle of light, and Eucrates saw it was attached to a bucket which hung just above the height of his head. It gave the clue to where they were: this must be where the temple got its water; they were standing at the bottom of the well.

They were going to get more than fresh water from this source, he thought, as he unsheathed his sword and nodded to Acantha, indicating that he was ready to make the ascent.

Within the temple, the figure took another step closer and the light fell across her face. 'Carme!' exclaimed Chryseis through bruised lips as she recognised Seba's queen from the village of satyrs and nymphs. 'What are you doing here?'

'Following my god's will,' the girl said softly, her eyes intent on Chryseis'. 'Did you forget that we also worshipped the great one, the one of wine and laughter?'

'No. I just never thought you'd be here.'

'But of course I am. This is the major celebration of the year, and I begged to be allowed a leading role. You do remember my vow to you, don't you?' She held up the knife and twisted it so that the blade gleamed in the light.

Suddenly, Chryseis felt unsure of herself and, through her sex-befuddled mind, she felt a frisson of alarm. 'You are going to cut me down, aren't you?' she asked, her voice suddenly sounding very small and weak, all pretence of grandeur gone.

'Oh, yes,' agreed Carme, her smile slow and languorous with sleepy evil. 'But not all at once,' she added, and turned the blade once more so that it caught the light, seeming to slice it into all the colours of the rainbow.

Eucrates was only a few steps from the top of the well when he heard the faint scream. 'That was Chryseis,' he said, throwing caution aside and hurling himself up the last few steps of the shaft and over the parapet around the well.

He found himself standing in a small, deserted courtyard. It opened to the cloud-veiled moon above and was enclosed by a two-storey building with a gallery running around the upper floor. Doorways led in all directions, from the upper level as well as the lower. As another distant scream echoed between the walls, he found it impossible to judge its direction and decide which door they should leave by.

Acantha clambered from the well to stand beside him, her sword drawn. 'This way,' she said, gesturing to the right.

Eucrates hesitated, wondering how she could be so sure, but now wasn't the time to argue.

They ran into a narrow corridor, deeply shadowed from even the glimmering stars and made their way along it by touch. Open voids beneath their fingers indicated where doorways led off to the side. Eucrates could see nothing, but had faith that Acantha knew where she was going. All he could do was concentrate on keeping up with her, and keeping his sword pointing down in case she stopped suddenly.

They emerged into a wide plaza, surrounded on all sides by a variety of buildings. In the twilight it was hard to distinguish one from another, and there were few lights to identify them. Eucrates looked around in panic, then saw that one building was grander than the others, with fluted columns across its facade. 'This way,' he called, and would have immediately burst through the wide doors if Acantha hadn't caught him by the shoulder.

'Let's see if there's a back way in,' she hissed. 'There's no point in running straight into the middle of something till we know exactly what it is.' She let go of him, and set off round the corner of the building in an easy loping run, leaving Eucrates to follow as best he could, his sandals slapping loudly on the pavement.

Chryseis screamed and struggled within her cradle of ropes as Carme drew nearer. What had seemed a comfortable harness to conveniently suspend her for the delight of Dionysus' worshippers had become a web to entangle her like some enormous fly. And if she were the fly, then Carme was the spider, approaching for its meal.

Chryseis could see the nymph's eyes now, could see the pinpoint pupils and the unblinking stare. Chryseis shuddered and drew back as best she could within the sling, as frightened by the madness in Carme's eyes as by the threat of violence. There was something particularly terrifying about insanity, as if it could suck others into its own incomprehensible realm of nightmares, as if it were a disease that could infect others with a glance. Chryseis juddered with sudden cold and swallowed the bile that rose in her throat.

Frantically, she looked around at the spectators, hoping that someone would come to her aid. It took only one glance for her to finally realise that this had been planned from the start and that her death was the intended climax to the evening. She kicked and thrashed with her arms and legs, trying to free herself, but all that happened was that she started the cradle swinging. It swung sluggishly back and forth in front of Carme. The nymph giggled maniacally and held aloft the gleaming blade.

Suddenly, the harness jerked upwards out of Carme's reach. Chryseis saw the surprised look on the nymph's face, before she was jerked up again and in moments was rising swiftly upward to the gallery near the temple's ceiling. From below, she heard Carme's shout of fury and the surprised babble of the audience. This was not part of the usual proceedings; it was not some further refinement of the torture.

She looked up to the shadowy ceiling of the temple where the rope went over some kind of wooden framework jutting out from the gallery. One, no, two figures were there, hauling away on the rope like fishermen landing their nets.

From below, Theophilus shouted upward at the workers in the gallery, while everyone else milled about in drunken confusion.

As soon as the cradle came level with the gallery, rough hands hauled her peremptorily over the low parapet. 'Come on,' snapped Eucrates, cutting off the ropes attached to her wrists and ankles, without bothering to remove the straps themselves. 'We've got to get out of here, fast.'

Chryseis wrapped her newly freed arms around him in relief, not yet wondering how he came to be there. 'Oh, gods, it was terrible,' she wailed.

'Save it,' barked Acantha, yanking on her arm. 'Let's get out of here before they sort themselves out.'

Chryseis turned, then stumbled over the body of a young priest with blood-soaked clothes. She stopped and stared, then noticed the red stain along the edge of Acantha's sword. Her stomach turned over, but Acantha didn't give her a chance to brood on it. 'Hurry,' the mercenary ordered. 'There's no time for that.'

Eucrates took Chryseis' other arm and helped bustle her along the gallery towards a narrow doorway in one corner. 'Hurry, before they trap us up here,' hissed Eucrates, urging her down the steep flight of stairs that spiralled downward. Acantha sped ahead of them and soon disappeared around the next bend.

A shout rose from below, mingled with the ringing clash of metal on metal, and the guttural cries of battle. Eucrates pushed past, almost dislodging Chryseis from the thin step, and leapt down the last few steps with a shriek of blood-curdling fury. A flurry of ringing sword strokes followed, then the sound of running feet. By the time Chryseis stumbled into the small room at the foot of the stairs it had been cleared of opposition. It was a store of some kind, with amphorae of wine and flasks of oil stacked along the walls. Acantha and Eucrates were hurriedly barricading the door leading into the interior of the temple. On the opposite side of the room an open doorway led out into the night.

'You take her. I'll hold the door,' yelled Acantha.

'But –'

'Do it, man!'

Eucrates grabbed Chryseis' arm and hustled her outside. She tried to keep up with him, but she ached all over from her exertions of the evening, and had to be dragged behind. She had no idea of their route; it was all one blur of alleys and doorways. Suddenly they were standing by the black opening of a well and Eucrates was insisting she clamber inside. Chryseis balked at the request. 'I'm sorry,' she said. 'I can't.'

Eucrates said nothing, but swung his legs over the wall and dropped down inside the well. Chryseis cut short her gasp of fear as she realised that he was standing on something just out of sight. 'Come on, I'll help you,' he said, holding out his hand.

Trembling, she did as she was bid, and stood nervously on the tiny topmost step while the dark maw of the pit tried to lure her down. 'Hold on to my shoulder and follow me,' Eucrates said, and cautiously, step by step, she followed him into the underworld. They went down a long way, till she could hear the sound of running water from below. The pallid disk of light above grew smaller, then abruptly it was blotted out by someone climbing down after them.

'It's me,' Acantha whispered. 'Are you there?'

'Yes,' Eucrates replied in a low voice. 'Are they still following you?'

'No.' Acantha gave a snort of grim amusement.

'They're running around trying to make sure we don't escape out the gates or over the walls, but they never thought of this.'

She spoke too soon. A shout from above revealed that their escape route had been found. Chryseis panicked and tried to hurry, then stumbled on the uneven steps. She collided with Eucrates who barely managed to hold her.

'It's all right,' he said. 'We're at the bottom. Crouch down and feel for the edge of the quay. Got it? Right, now reach out; there's a boat there, climb in.'

Something rattled and banged down the well from the surface. 'Hurry,' urged Acantha. 'That was a spear they threw down after us.'

Chryseis found the edge of the boat and half climbed, half fell into its bottom, followed by Eucrates. More spears clattered around them, rebounding off the rocks in all directions. Acantha gave a sharp cry of pain, probably as she was caught harmlessly by one of the tumbling hafts. Something heavy tumbled into the boat almost capsizing it, then Chryseis became aware of movement as the grey circle of light began to recede as they drifted away with the current.

She laughed with relief; they'd made it. Then she noticed the hot reek of blood and the warm wetness dripping on to her naked skin.

Thirteen

The underground river was so dark that Chryseis couldn't tell if her eyes were open or closed. She could see nothing except imaginary sparks dancing before her light-starved eyes but, even so, she strained forward, seeking any clue as to where they were.

'Are you all right?' Eucrates whispered.

Still without any clothes, she was very cold as well as scared, but that wasn't what he meant. 'I am,' she replied. 'But I think I've got blood on me. Acantha?'

There was a faint, pain-racked groan in reply.

'Oh, gods! She's hurt.'

'Where? Can you tell?' asked Eucrates. He sounded frightened, too.

'I'll have to feel ...' Chryseis replied. She stretched out a hand, identified a knee, then worked her way up the thigh. She felt the edge of Acantha's brief leather skirt, the curve of her hip. The mercenary wasn't moving, wasn't responding in any way to Chryseis' handling, though her flesh was still warm. Her fingers encountered something sticky at Acantha's waist. She lifted her hand to her face and sniffed; the tang of fresh blood was unmistakable. Scared by what she might find, Chryseis continued her examination by touch. She felt the jagged tear in Acantha's leather tunic, the warm wetness within. Acantha whimpered and tried to twist away from the probing examination.

'It's her left side. There's a gash. Hades! There's blood

207

everywhere.' Chryseis felt her stomach lurch at the thought of sitting in a pool of the mercenary's blood. Worse came the appreciation that it could have been her own. She sniffed in miserable terror, and began to cry.

'Shut up,' Eucrates hissed, with so much venom that Chryseis was taken aback. 'Stop whingeing and feeling sorry for yourself, and do something to help.'

Chryseis smothered the retort which rose to her lips; Eucrates had never spoken to her like that before and his anger disconcerted her.

There was the sound of cloth ripping, then Eucrates spoke again. 'Here, take this and staunch the flow till we have some light.'

In the darkness, she reached out tentatively until she encountered his arm, then fumbled along it to his hand. He was holding a wad of cloth which she took from him. Then she fumbled her way back to the wound in Acantha's side. She touched the material to the gash, too nauseated by the smell of blood to do more than dab it lightly across the open wound. Acantha groaned loudly and thrashed weakly as she tried to get away from the pain. It was no good. 'I can't stop it. She's still bleeding,' Chryseis wailed, her teeth chattering with fear and cold.

'You've got to press harder,' Eucrates ordered roughly. 'Better a little pain than to bleed to death. Now hold the pad of material firmly against the wound.'

Swallowing her revulsion, Chryseis did as she was told and Acantha yelped like an injured puppy at the pressure.

Apart from intermittent moans from Acantha, they continued in silence. Only the whisper of the water and the occasional rasping noise as their craft brushed unseen obstacles marked their progress. Chryseis spent the time wondering what she had done to deserve this. Were the gods really that displeased with her? Eucrates seemed to think it was all her own fault, but was that true?

It seemed that she had a long time to contemplate her mistakes before she eventually detected a faint change in the darkness. The air seemed fresher and the sound of the water no longer echoed back from all sides. When she saw a faint sprinkling of stars decorate the sky above her head, tears of relief stung her eyes.

'How's Acantha?' asked Eucrates.

Chryseis hurriedly returned her attention to the mercenary. 'No change; I think she's unconscious, but she's still breathing.'

Eucrates grunted acknowledgement, but continued staring ahead as if looking for something.

'Where are we going?' she asked.

'We planned for someone to meet us,' Eucrates replied. 'They'll show us where we can get ashore. Then we need to get away as quickly as possible; presumably the temple guards will follow us downstream.'

The thought of being captured and returned to the temple made Chryseis shiver. Looking after Acantha was going to make their escape more difficult as well. One option would be to leave the mercenary behind and escape by themselves, but she dared not suggest it. Anyway, she felt slightly guilty for even thinking it.

'Hush,' Eucrates breathed. 'Get down and keep silent.'

Chryseis' heart thudded in her chest. Ahead she could make out a small ember of light by the edge of the river. 'What is it?' she whispered.

'Our friend I hope, but maybe searchers from the temple. We'll wait and see.'

They huddled together in the bottom of the boat, hoping its low, dark silhouette wouldn't be noticed against the gleam of the water. They had almost drifted past, when a voice came to them over the water: 'Eucrates? Acantha? Is that you?'

'It's Sela,' Eucrates sighed with relief, then picked up the paddle and started to guide the clumsy craft towards the light. For a moment it seemed as if he had left it too late and that the river would carry them off. He grunted with effort as he paddled furiously, eventually managing to get close enough to the bank for the current to lose its grip. Once there, it was easy to ground the craft on the rough shore.

An old peasant woman stepped forward, carefully shielding the flame of a crude oil lamp with her cupped hand, to light their way to land.

Eucrates wormed his hands under Acantha's body, then lifted her in a single fluid motion. The movement must have torn her wound, but Acantha didn't make a sound, just lolled in his arms like a limp rag. Chryseis reached up to support Acantha's head, which rolled helplessly from side to side, and between them they got her safely ashore.

Sela lifted the lamp high to inspect Chryseis, eyeing her up and down her with distaste. 'My, my,' she commented caustically, then unfastened her cloak and handed it over. 'Here, you'd better have this. It's chill at night.' Then she turned away, not bothering to wait for any thanks, or perhaps not expecting any.

Chryseis pulled the ragged garment over her shoulders and huddled within it feeling cold and alone. If even an old peasant felt superior to her ... She shied away from following the thought to its conclusion.

'I've made arrangements,' said the old woman. 'Come on; follow me,' she instructed and, despite her age, set a good pace up the hillside away from the river. Eucrates followed, struggling with Acantha's weight, his breath becoming ever more laboured, though he never complained. Chryseis brought up the rear, cursing the rough rocks that cut at her bare feet.

The sky had lightened with the coming dawn by the time they reached a stand of cypress trees bordering a rutted road, where firelight glinted between the trunks. There was the commotion and bustle of people breaking camp, and donkeys braying in protest as large panniers were strapped across their backs.

'Is this them?' bellowed a large, overbearing man with a jutting grey beard, as he strode forward. The other workers nudged each other and commented on Chryseis' bare flesh visible between the folds of Sela's cloak.

'It is,' responded Sela, then introduced them to him one by one. 'Thales is a merchant,' she said. 'He is going to the market at Chalcis, and I thought it best if you travelled with him. The priests won't be looking for you in a large party like this.'

Thales meanwhile was pulling at his beard and glowering at Acantha's limp body. 'And what's the matter with her?' he demanded. 'I'm not holding up my caravan for a sick woman.'

'It's not catching, Thales,' said Sela tartly. 'She's been wounded.'

Thales studied the dark bloodstain on Acantha's side and grunted. 'Well, so long as it's not disease. I can't afford sickness in my men.' He tugged at his beard. 'In any case, I don't know how we can carry her, regardless of what ails her.'

'How about that ox cart,' suggested Sela, pointing to where it stood at the head of the forming column.

'For my own use,' said Thales. Then, with a sideways look, he added, 'It will cost extra.'

'I've given you everything I have,' Sela protested. 'I don't have any more.'

Thales shrugged, unmoved.

'We'll pay,' said Eucrates. 'But first, let's make her comfortable.'

Thales looked as if he would argue, then squinted at the rising sun. 'All right. Later,' he agreed. 'We've lost enough time already.'

They did as best they could, clearing some space in the back of the cart to make room for Acantha, even

211

though it meant transferring the load on to some of the donkeys. Then they laid Acantha out in the back on some old sacks. Her face was grey and clammy with sweat, and the stain at her side showed the brightness of fresh blood. Someone handed them a skin of fresh water and Eucrates crouched in the cart beside her, wiping her face with a damp rag before feeding a few drops of water between her lips.

'Ready?' demanded Thales brusquely. 'The day's wasting.'

Eucrates nodded and Thales gave the signal for the caravan to move out.

It was a long morning. Eucrates and Chryseis took turns riding in the back of the cart to tend to Acantha, bathing her wound and feeding her small amounts of water. The mercenary didn't seem aware of their presence, and only tossed and turned in response to troubled dreams of enemies whom she cursed in a foreign tongue.

Chryseis didn't know which was worse, walking along on aching feet, or being crunched up in the back of the cart, tossed from side to side as it lurched into every pothole. She did a lot of thinking though, trying to understand how she had ended up in this terrible mess. Had it really been all her own fault? Perhaps. Though her uncle was strict and had no time for foolish diversions, he had never mistreated her. In fact he had looked after her ever since her parents had died and he had always seen to it that she had everything she needed. Up to now. But wasn't she entitled to choose her own husband?

And how about Acantha and Eucrates? They had risked their lives to save her. But Acantha wouldn't get paid until she delivered Chryseis to her uncle. Had the hired bodyguard really cared about her welfare, or had she simply been looking after her own interests?

And what did Eucrates get out of it? He'd already fucked her; what else did he want? Even the old peasant woman, Sela, had to have an angle. What was it? Chryseis didn't know, and her head ached too much from lack of sleep for her to really care.

Thales finally ordered a rest in a grove of trees which would shade them during the hottest part of the day. Eucrates immediately lifted Acantha from the cart and laid her out on a patch of sweet turf, away from the others where she could stretch out properly. The mercenary's face was an unpleasant shade of grey, but after Eucrates had wiped her face again she seemed to subside into a more peaceful sleep. 'That's better,' he said. 'She finally seems to be getting some rest.'

'How long before she recovers?' Chryseis asked.

'I don't know,' he replied. 'She's still got quite a way to go. We can only hope.'

Chryseis stepped back and left him to it. She needed a rest herself, and she sought out the cool shade of a twisted tree, slightly apart from the others. Just as she was making herself comfortable, however, she noticed the lichen growing down one side of the trunk. It reminded her of the old physician at her uncle's estate who had applied something similar to cuts, claiming it helped them heal. She hesitated, almost ignoring the memory, telling herself it probably didn't matter. Then she sighed and wearily began scraping the lichen from the bark, gathering a bundle of it for Eucrates to bind on to Acantha's wound.

Eucrates accepted the lichen enthusiastically, and Chryseis felt absurdly pleased. 'I've seen this before, too,' he said. 'It's supposed to be good. Is there any more? We should collect some extra while we can, to make sure we have sufficient to change her dressings.'

Chryseis wanted nothing more than to sit and rest, but she couldn't bring herself to refuse his request. Wordlessly, she went off and began going from tree to tree, gathering as much of the lichen as she could. She had just used strips torn from the hem of Sela's cloak to tie the lichen into a fair-sized bundle, when Thales called for the caravan to set off again.

Too exhausted to complain, she passed the package to Eucrates, then helped him lift Acantha back into the cart. The mercenary stirred uneasily as she was moved, but didn't waken. Eucrates sat beside her, leaving Chryseis to trudge wearily behind, clutching on to the slow vehicle for support.

'Thales talked to me while you were gathering the lichen,' said Eucrates in a low voice once they were moving. 'He was asking about payment for the use of the cart.'

'Do you have anything to pay him with?' Chryseis asked.

Eucrates snorted. 'I have three obols left over from our display at the taverna. I doubt if that will impress him. What about you?'

'Me? You know exactly what I left the temple with,' she replied, anger flaring. Then she sighed heavily and let the point go. 'What are we going to do? Acantha needs proper care.'

'Well, there's one thing we can trade,' Eucrates said, and pointed at the gold talisman that Acantha wore around her neck. 'That must be worth a bit.'

'No!' Chryseis protested. 'We can't. Not that. It's her good-luck piece; she wouldn't part with it.'

'It won't do her any good in the underworld. Better to sell it than die from lack of care.'

'Even so; no,' Chryseis insisted. 'We'll have to think of something else.'

Eucrates shook his head but didn't say anything else and they subsided into silence. The rest of the afternoon passed in a blur. Chryseis exchanged places with Eucrates a couple of times, and even managed to nod off while cramped into a corner of the cart. But when she did drowse, her dreams were filled with troubled feelings of guilt and images of accusing figures. She never seemed able to make out what they said, but whichever way she turned they were always there, pointing angrily at her and laying the blame at her feet. When night came and they finally camped, she was as exhausted as before.

Chryseis helped Eucrates make Acantha as comfortable as possible, even building a small fire separate from the rest of the caravan so she could have some peace. The mercenary was still unconscious, but her breathing was easier, and when one of Thales' men came over with bowls of thin soup, they were able to force a little of it between her lips.

'She's looking better,' said Eucrates. 'A good night's sleep will help her.'

'Me too,' yawned Chryseis, hoping that tonight, her dreams would be peaceful.

'We still have to work out how we are going to pay Thales,' pointed out Eucrates.

Chryseis shrugged. 'Leave it to me. I'll sort him out.'

'How?' Then Eucrates' expression hardened. 'Oh, I see,' he said and turned away, his lips tight.

'Is there a problem with that?'

Eucrates looked back at her with a crooked smile. 'Hades, no. Why should there be? Another fuck or two won't make much difference to you, will it?'

'How else can we pay him? We can't give away Acantha's talisman; it means a lot to her. And anyway –' she shrugged uncomfortably '– I got us into this; I suppose I owe it to her.'

'I'm glad you're at last accepting some responsibility for what happened,' Eucrates said with dry irony.

'Yes, well . . .' She looked at the ground.

'Here comes Thales now,' Eucrates warned. Then he took her by the arms and looked into her face. 'Last chance; you don't have to go through with this if you don't want to.'

'I think I do,' Chryseis replied, then tried to laugh. 'In

215

any case, he looks a well-built man; he may be interesting.'

'What may be interesting?' asked Thales as he strode up in time to catch the tail-end of the conversation.

Chryseis turned to him and put on her most seductive smile. She had no doubts that the merchant would find her irresistible. 'I was saying that you were,' she said, turning slightly so that Sela's cloak would fall open and reveal more of her body.

Thales grunted and his eyebrows knitted in a fierce glower. 'Let me guess,' he said. 'This is in lieu of any payment, yes?'

'Not in lieu of payment,' Chryseis replied. 'As payment.'

'Really? And how much do you think a tired whore like you is worth?' Thales mocked. 'I've seen better than you putting on exhibitions with donkeys in half the brothels of Greece.'

Chryseis felt her eyes sting at the contempt in the merchant's voice. 'I am not a whore,' she responded hotly. 'I'll have you know that I'm the niece of a respectable merchant –'

'Ha!' Thales bellowed. 'Your uncle may be respectable, but you are not. The only family trait you seem to have inherited seems the inclination for barter. Well, I'm not buying. Do you have anything else to offer me?'

Eucrates drew breath to speak and Chryseis knew he was about to offer the talisman. 'No,' she said to him. 'I told you, we can't.' Before he could protest, she turned back to Thales, and said the only thing that came to mind: 'I'll take your men as well, then.'

Thales snarled, and spat at her feet. 'No, not even my animals.' He stood with his hands on his hips, looking them both up and down. 'If you've nothing better to offer, then our deal is ended. The payment I got from Sela will cover your journey to here. You can make the rest of the way to Chalcis yourselves.' And with that, he turned on his heel and strode back towards the main camp, leaving them alone.

Chryseis drew a long shuddering breath, and slumped down beside their meagre fire. Eucrates said nothing as he checked Acantha's condition. Then he settled himself on the other side of the glowing embers from Chryseis, and prodded them with a stick, refusing to meet her eyes.

'Is that what you think of me, too?' she asked.

He shrugged.

'I'm not a tart,' she protested softly.

Still he said nothing.

'I do what I do for me,' she continued, her voice rising. 'For my own pleasure. I'm not for sale.'

'Maybe that's the problem,' Eucrates said finally. 'You do it only for yourself. So much so that the other person doesn't matter. Thales got it wrong; you aren't a whore, you just treat everyone else like one.'

'I don't,' she objected, shocked by the accusation. 'If I really treated others like that, well ... well ... I wouldn't care whether they enjoyed themselves, too, and I do.'

Eucrates shook his head. 'Not really. You like to demonstrate your skills as a lover; nothing else.'

The words hurt all the more because she believed them. She sat in huddled silence, watching the flames, not sure what she was thinking. 'I cared about you,' she whispered eventually. 'But you deceived me. You were no more than a slave.'

'Even slaves have feelings.'

She nodded in silent agreement, then something in his tone of voice made her look up at him again. 'And you still have feelings for me? Even after the way I've treated you?'

He shrugged and added more sticks to the fire before replying. 'Yes. You're not as bad as some slave-owners I've come across. Many would whip us just for the fun of it. You're not like that.'

217

'No, I suppose not.' She wondered how much more to say, then found the words coming out of their own accord. 'Maybe these other slave-owners are frightened that if they let up then the slaves will take over. Maybe they're scared they're not good enough to be in control and must always demand respect.'

She felt his eyes on her, measuring her. 'Is that what you think?' he asked quietly. 'That people will stop respecting you if you treat them properly?'

She nodded. 'Maybe. I hadn't put it into words before, but it sounds right.'

'That's how Mellita was, remember? Pretending to be a witch and demanding subservience; mistaking fear for respect. She never learnt that you had to give before you could receive, and look how she ended up: bitter and unhappy.'

'Oh gods.' The picture chilled her. 'Is that what I'm like?'

'Not yet. But you could be if you don't learn how to open yourself to people.'

She swallowed nervously. 'Will you teach me?'

Eucrates smiled, then stood up and came around the fire to sit beside her. Then he leant over and touched his lips to hers, while their eyes remained locked together. She felt him smile under her lips, and the caress of his tongue as it traced the shape of her mouth. She met his tongue with her own, danced with it, tip to tip, savouring its sweetness. They slipped over and around each other, passing the taste of their mouths back and forth, then turned their heads, seeking a firmer, deeper contact. Chryseis knotted her fingers in the hair at his neck, forcing him against her open mouth, her tongue darting over his teeth, questing along his gums, mingling her saliva with his in a single, heady brew.

Eucrates slid his hands under her cloak, placing them on her sides, where his calloused skin felt hard and rough against her own. He rubbed his fingers across the ridges of her ribcage, his thumbs caressing the under-side of her breasts. The heat emanating from his body, and the insistence of his breath against her cheek signalled his growing arousal. Her own heart beat quicker in response, and she felt a quiver of excitement in her belly.

Eucrates' arms felt strong and comforting as he enclosed her within his gentle embrace, yet he trembled with an unexpected nervousness and she realised this meant more to him than another fuck. Her body urged her to plunge ahead, to gratify her hunger as swiftly as possible, but instead she chose to let him set the pace. She wanted to please him more than herself; she wanted to mend the rifts between them and, paradoxically, to give more than she gained. The slaking of her immediate lust was only incidental.

Eucrates moved his hands higher, taking the weight of her breasts in his palms. Chryseis felt her pliant flesh shift deliciously as he sought out her nipples with his thumbs. The tiny peaks grew alive under his gentle attention and she delighted in the way they hardened and became more pronounced. The sensations from those delicate nubs radiated out, filling her chest, her stomach and spearing down to excite her groin. She squirmed in exquisite pleasure and pressed herself against him.

While her right hand remained behind his head, she ran the other across his shoulder and down his chest in a flutter of fingertips that barely caressed his skin. He shivered with pleasure and she moved lower, first tick-ling the hard ridges of his stomach muscles, then following the contours of his flanks.

He broke the kiss, buried his head in her hair and nuzzled the side of her neck, his lips traversing the fragile flesh with reverent care. She, in turn, mouthed the heavy muscles of his shoulder, savouring the mascu-line tang of his skin. He tasted of woodsmoke and raw

219

wine, and she closed her eyes to concentrate as she ran her tongue over his body.

Eucrates' questing mouth grew more urgent, and she lifted her head to expose the underside of her jaw. He covered the vulnerable skin in a flurry of dry, tender kisses and she felt her throat vibrate against his lips as she moaned faintly in rapture. He followed the line of her jaw back to her ear, sucked the lobe between his lips and nipped it lightly with his teeth. She groaned again, the tone deepening. Then he began to explore the rest of her ear in minute detail, using his tongue to trace along the curled rim of the outer helix, following it as it spiralled into the central well. He probed the recess with the tip of his tongue, laughing as Chryseis squirmed away, then enfolding her in his arms as she returned to his embrace.

Now she returned her attention to his shoulder and the silver brooch which held the front and back of his chiton together. She paused and drew back slightly so she could see what she was doing, then undid the clasp. As the material slipped down his torso, she continued kissing his body, scattering tiny brushes of her lips over his warm skin. He had few hairs on his chest, only some down the centre of his sternum and around his nipples, which were small and flat. She sucked on a nipple with fierce intensity and was intrigued to discover how much it could grow and harden, just like a woman's.

While she kissed his chest, his hands stroked her back investigating the hard nodes of her vertebrae and the broad planes of her shoulder blades. He explored lower, his strong fingers gripping the soft flesh of her buttocks, taking great handfuls of her rump and squeezing it as if assessing its worth. He pulled her tightly to him, pressing against her so she could feel his growing desire.

Chryseis rubbed her hips across his straining erection, approving of its size. But after a moment she returned again to suck and tongue his nipple. Eucrates caught his breath and arched his back under the onslaught and she persisted till the edge of his sensitivity had gone. Then she nipped playfully at the fleshy peak and moved on, to run her mouth over the ridges of his ribs. She probed between bone with the tip of her small, wet tongue, letting the halo of her hair brush his skin as her head travelled down his torso. He trembled under her touch, his muscles twitching uncontrollably as she mercilessly investigated the ticklish skin of his sides. From there, she moved lower down his abdomen till she was prevented from going any further by the crumpled material of his tunic gathered around his hips. She looked up at him without saying anything, and he raised himself off the ground so she could pull the garment away, leaving him completely naked. Unrestrained, his erection sprang up proudly and she acknowledged its presence by kissing its tip and pausing to relish its sharper flavour. But she was in no hurry to bring this encounter to its promised climax and ignored his straining manhood again in order to lean over and kiss and lick at the smooth skin of his hips and surrounding groin.

Chryseis felt Eucrates' fingers on the exposed skin of her thighs, felt them travel up, under the hem of Sela's cloak till they rested against the lower edge of her buttocks. There they stopped, seeming content to stroke the silken skin on the insides of her legs without progressing any higher. She swivelled her hips, enticing him to continue and he moved up, cupping the curve of her rump in his hand as gently as if holding an egg. The tips of his fingers strayed into the crevice between her thighs, and she felt the first whisper of their touch stir her pubic hairs like a summer breeze.

She brushed the delicate skin of his scrotum with a fleeting kiss. His need for her was like a wave of heat rising from his groin, and she rubbed her cheek across his genitals, enjoying the evidence of his desire in the soft and hard flesh. She kissed his scrotum again, then drew one testicle completely within her mouth, enveloping it with a soft caress. She fondled the fragile gland with her tongue and teeth and lips, bestowing upon it reverential care before shifting her attention to its partner. His balls tightened and his penis twitched under her care and she began the long ascent up the underside of his erection to its tip, meticulously noting every bulging vein along the way.

As she worked on him, Eucrates continued stroking her buttock, but began stretching further round so that his fingers ran along the groove of her sex. It was slippery with her welcome for him, but though he must have sensed her readiness he probed no further. She leant back, hoping to push herself over his fingers, but he moved with her, prolonging her agony. She moaned and gyrated her hips, inviting him to delve between the swollen lips of her vulva. Instead, she felt him take some of her rich lubricant on one fingertip and rotated it around the puckered dimple of her anus, toying with it as he had teased her vagina.

Frustrated now by the protracted love-making, Chryseis stopped what she was doing long enough to place a hand on Eucrates' chest and push him right back on to the rough grass. Then she swung herself around and straddled him, bringing her sex above his face while simultaneously drawing his sensitised glans into her mouth with an enthusiasm that made him whimper with pleasure.

Now Eucrates was unable to ignore Chryseis' urgent need for him. He hooked his arms around her thighs, and used his fingers to draw her buttocks apart, exposing every nook and crevice to the cool night air. She felt his breath against the responsive flesh of her labia, felt him breathe over the delicate star of her anus. She could feel her own moisture trickle down the insides of her thighs as she waited in readiness for his attentions.

Finally, he drew her hips down to his mouth, till she

could just feel the tip of his tongue trace along the channel of her sex. He lapped at her, swallowing the nectar that ran from her while she sucked his cock ever deeper within her mouth. With each bob of her head she pushed her lips further and further along his shaft. Each stroke drew more of him into her hungry mouth before her need to breathe forced her to slowly, reluctantly, retreat. Then she would tease him with her tongue, squirming its tip into the tiny hole surmounting his helmet or twirling it around the rim of his glans till he shuddered and groaned and lifted his pelvis in an attempt to drive himself back into her mouth.

In return, Eucrates ran his tongue further along her crevice, making her shiver as it flickered across the ridge of her perineum and then spiralled into the hollow of her anus. He probed the tight orifice with his tongue, licking it till it was slippery with his saliva while Chryseis thrust her hips back in encouragement. Once the narrow opening was suitably lubricated, she felt his finger circling it before gently insisting on entrance. She released her muscles, welcoming him inside her body, then tightened them again to draw his finger deeper within her. The feeling was primitive and raw, making her whole being quiver with the strength of her passion.

She shifted position, forcing her softly swollen sex over his mouth, demanding that his attentions became more intense. There were no more diversions and he immediately used his tongue to quest for the firm nub of her clitoris, sucking it between his lips like a nipple while his finger pumped in and out of her rectum. In the meantime, Chryseis continued to keep her head rising and falling ever more swiftly over his erection. He lifted his hips in time to her eager mouth, and she urged him on, gripping him as tightly as she could with her lips, pushing herself over him till his glans rubbed the back of her throat. She heard him panting, snatching air whenever he surfaced from the enveloping folds of her quim, while she tried to gulp air past the glorious thickness of his cock.

She saw his testicles tighten, felt his cock grow impossibly hard within her mouth, and knew he was close to coming. Her own head seemed ready to burst with the pressure of her own impending climax, and her whole body thrummed like a taut bowstring ready to snap. She broke free from their embrace, ignoring his momentary cry of dismay as she swung round to face him, then grasped his rigid shaft and guided it within her welcoming vagina.

It felt like he had always belonged there, and the walls of her inner sheath gripped his full length, drawing him in towards her heart as she leant forward to press her body against his. Their mouths met, hungrily sucking the air from each other's lungs as they ground their hips together in ever swifter thrusts. Then he erupted, his hot semen spurting into her in long, powerful pulses. She in turn, gave a deep, satiated groan of pleasure as the heat within her belly exploded outward through her body. The groan grew in strength and volume till, as her blood ignited in orgasm, it became a scream of triumph that resounded among the trees.

As the echoes of her passion died away, she heard answering braying from the tethered donkeys and applause from the men around the neighbouring fire. It seemed she had provided them with some entertainment after all. Gradually, the trembling aftermath of their orgasms lessened. Chryseis became aware of the fresh sweat that beaded Eucrates' body and the dampness of her own skin. They kissed again, gently, savouring each other's company as they remained locked together, Chryseis feeling warm and safe in Eucrates' embrace.

There was a grunt to one side, and Chryseis turned her head in time to see Acantha struggle into a sitting position, her hand clamped defensively over her wound. 'Well, I'm glad you two are getting on so well,' she said sourly, 'but do you have to be so noisy about it?'

Fourteen

'You don't have to marry Timon, you know. You could come away with me; I'd make you happy.'

Chryseis shook her head and looked away. In the two days since they had parted company with Thales' caravan, Eucrates must have made the same offer a dozen times in a dozen different ways. Each time, regardless of how much it pained her, she had refused. Her appreciation of him had unfortunately coincided with a growing sense of responsibility.

'Please try to understand,' she begged. 'Pythias is my guardian. I'm sure he loves me, too, and has arranged the best marriage for me that he can. I owe it to him to return and marry Timon.'

Eucrates threw his hands up and turned for support to Acantha. She stood to one side, contemplating the view over Chalcis, which lay at the foot of the hill. Her arm was still in a sling to prevent it pulling on the fragile wound in her side, but otherwise she had almost fully recovered. 'Don't ask me,' she said when she realised with a start that they were waiting for her comment. 'I told Pythias I'd do a job, and I have an obligation to finish it.' She obviously meant what she said, but Chryseis sensed the bodyguard was a bit uncomfortable, as if she were having second thoughts. Chryseis wondered whether, if she tried running away with Eucrates, Acantha would still stop her.

Still, the question was irrelevant; Chryseis had made

up her mind to return to Pythias and marry Timon like a good and obedient ward should, and that was the end of the matter. 'Come on,' she said. 'No good's going to come of standing here talking about it. We'd better get it over with.'

They walked in companionable silence down the dusty track to the city gates. A pair of soldiers, armed with spears and round, painted shields, lazed by the entrance, guarding the way. Their crested helmets were tilted back so that the broad cheek guards and nose-piece covered the top of their heads, leaving their faces exposed. They talked and laughed quietly while lolling in the shade, and offered the dusty travellers no more than a passing glance.

Once inside the gate, the trio stopped and looked around. 'Which way?' Acantha asked, gesturing with her free hand to the well laid-out streets which ran ahead and to either side.

'I know my uncle has a house here he uses when on his travels,' Chryseis replied, 'but I don't know where.'

'In that case, let's go and ask in the market-place. Someone is bound to know of him or of Timon.'

They followed the wide, central avenue which led into the agora in the centre of the city, and looked around. The market was busy today. Covered stalls with brightly coloured awnings filled the plaza, while around the perimeter where the cloisters provided some shade, various traders, vendors and merchants had set out their wares on blankets spread over the ground. They even saw Thales there, sitting amongst a wonderful spread of rugs and woven cloths but he turned away, refusing to acknowledge their presence. Everything imaginable was on sale. Tradesmen made pots or leather goods to order; peasants from outlying farms sold vegetables and fruit of every kind; fishermen sold their catches of fresh fish and squid, while other vendors sold roast meats, ready to eat.

Smells and sounds filled the air. Chickens and quails in tight wicker cages screeched in competition with the braying of donkeys and the bleating of goats. And, interwoven through it all, was the hubbub of people talking, shouting, arguing and playing.

Acantha caught the attention of a young boy of perhaps ten or so, who was walking by with a wax tablet and scroll of papyrus under one arm. 'Hey!' she called. 'Do you know the whereabouts of the house of Pythias? From Ephesus?'

The boy had large, solemn eyes and he gazed in awe at the fierce-looking redhead before gesturing, with a jerk of his head, to the right. 'Down there, on the corner. The big house with the fancy portico.'

'Thanks,' said Acantha, and Chryseis saw her give the lad a wink. 'Meet me for a drink later, OK?'

The boy blushed and darted away, causing Acantha to laugh in amusement. She seemed in a buoyant mood now that their journey was nearly over, and even whistled jauntily as they made their way down the street.

At the entrance to Pythias' house, however, her good humour swiftly evaporated in the face of the door-keeper's stubborn refusal to listen to what she said.

'What do you mean, you have no time for beggars?' she bellowed, thrusting her chin forward aggressively then explained, again, who they were.

The burly slave crossed his arms and frowned heavily as he thought over what she said. 'My master said his niece died at sea,' he said slowly. 'How can I trust you?'

'Obviously your muscles aren't only in your arms, you idiot,' yelled Acantha, her face reddening. 'If she isn't Pythias' niece, I'm sure he will be able to recognise the fact in a mere blink of an eye, so what good would come of us trying to deceive him? Eh? Answer me that?'

The slave's mouth twitched as he tried to follow the reasoning. 'But if I disturb him . . .' he said, uncertainly.

Chryseis came to his aid. 'Look, is my maid, Palmeda, there? Did she survive the journey?'

The slave nodded reluctantly.

'Well, why don't you ask her to identify me? That would be all right, surely. Then if she says I'm who I say I am, you've done your duty.'

The slave looked carefully at them again one more time, as if memorising their faces, then returned inside the house and shut the door.

'Trusting, isn't he?' commented Eucrates dryly.

'Well, he's never seen me before; I've always lived in Ephesus. And we do look pretty uncouth.'

'Oh, well. Let's sit in the cool for a moment. No doubt he'll take his time finding this maid of yours,' Eucrates said and eased himself to the ground with his back to the wall and only his toes extending into the bright sunlight beyond the portico's shadow.

The others joined him, sitting quietly in a row with Chryseis in the middle. She realised, with surprise, that she had grown fond of her companions and would miss them. She was just about to say so when Eucrates interrupted her thoughts.

'You could still run away with me,' he said, though she was sure he was now simply making the suggestion out of habit.

'No, she can't,' Acantha responded, without opening her eyes. 'I've still to get paid.'

'I'll offer you double,' said Eucrates.

Acantha leant forward to give him a sideways look, then slumped back again with a sigh. 'You couldn't afford a sixth, never mind double.' She pulled off her sling and flexed her arm experimentally.

'How is it?' Chryseis asked.

'It'll do.'

Chryseis took Acantha's hand in hers, and squeezed it in affection, then did the same with Eucrates. They sat like that, holding on to each other in silence, as they waited for the door to open again.

'Mistress? Oh, mistress! How did you get here?' Palmeda's familiar voice cried in joy as she came over and almost threw herself into Chryseis' arms. 'But look at you!' she continued, her words tripping over themselves in excitement. 'What a state you're in. How did you get like this?' She turned to Acantha. 'Why haven't you looked after her?' she accused, then gave Eucrates a very sharp look. 'And who are you?'

'Palmeda, do be quiet,' said Chryseis with a laugh. 'Acantha has looked after me very well; my appearance is not her fault. And this is Eucrates. He has helped us on our journey. Now, show us in to my uncle.'

Palmeda quelled her enthusiasm and bobbed her head obediently. 'Of course, mistress. He is inside.' She hesitated, obviously with something on her mind.

'What is it?' Chryseis asked. 'Come on, you know you can speak to me.'

Palmeda nodded, but still looked uncertain. 'It's your uncle, mistress. He's taken your loss very badly. No, I don't mean that,' she said, gesticulating as she fumbled for words. 'He's not grieving; he's angry. He found out what happened aboard the ship. I've never seen him so furious.'

Chryseis swallowed nervously. It was only to be expected, she supposed, but that was the end of any hope for a happy reunion. Pythias' rages were terrifying to witness, let alone endure.

Her resolve was crumbling fast when Acantha took her gently by the arm. 'Come on, girl,' she said. 'Think of all the things you've done since we were washed overboard. Is Pythias really as terrible as Mellita or Carme? You can do it.'

As always, the brusque mercenary put everything into perspective. Chryseis gestured Palmeda ahead, then followed behind with Acantha and Eucrates taking up the rear.

The external door opened into a short corridor which led through the building and into a small open court-yard surrounded by a square of columns. From there, a doorway led to a comfortable room on the far side of the building. Pythias was reclining on one elbow at a low table, idly picking at some grapes while reading a scroll. He looked up at their entrance.

'Uncle!' Chryseis greeted him, then faltered under the force of his glare. She had expected anger, yes; but she had also expected some small flicker of pleasure at seeing her alive. Instead, there was nothing but fury.

Pythias swung himself upright and stood up, the scroll falling, forgotten, to the floor. 'So,' he said softly, looking her up and down, from toes to hair.

She became very aware of just how ragged her ap-pearance was. Oh, why hadn't she thought to stop somewhere and tidy herself first? But she had been in a hurry to return to what she had thought of as the comfort and safety of her family.

'So,' Pythias repeated, with his hands clenched into fists. 'You've deigned to return. Well, if you're hoping to proceed with your marriage, you'd better think again. When Timon heard the sailors' gossip of how you'd almost scuppered a good ship, he accused me of trying to barter off a cheap whore to form an alliance with him.'

As he spoke, a dark flush seeped up his neck and suffused his face. 'I've lost one of the most important trading agreements I've ever had in this region, and a lot of my other contacts have shied away from me on the basis of it. Have you any idea what your frivolous amusement has cost me? Everything! Everything in Chalcis and its neighbours. I'll be lucky not to be ostracised.

'And you have the gall, the arrogant, out-and-out gall, to turn up again!'

He fell silent, the cords in his neck standing out thick

and knotted, seemingly choking on his contempt for her.

Chryseis felt a great, empty chasm of loneliness and isolation open up in her belly, while the blood pounded in her ears and her vision narrowed to the stranger confronting her. She didn't know what to think, what to say, what to do. She felt utterly despised, and wished she could turn to dust and blow away rather than endure another moment of it.

'Nothing to say for yourself?' Pythias mocked. 'I'm not surprised. Well, I'll have to see what you're worth now, before I decide what to do with you.' He turned from her then, excluding her as he addressed her two companions. And that was the worst part, she thought; that her friends should have seen her so humiliated. She stood still, too numb to move.

Pythias spoke to Acantha first. 'I suppose you want paying for bringing this scrap of humanity back to me? Do you think you deserve anything, after letting her perform those filthy acts with nothing but common sailors?'

'Of course,' Acantha replied, her tone unruffled. 'I only promised to deliver her safe, which I have, bar a scratch or two. And in any case, I lost some good equipment trying to fish her out of the sea, and I need paying to replace it. By my reckoning, you owe me for sixteen days, or thereabouts.'

Pythias' mouth curled in contempt. 'Anything for money, eh?' He fumbled with the money bag at his belt, trying to count out the precise amount, then gave up in disgust and threw the whole pouch at Acantha's feet. 'Here. Take it. She's cost me enough already; what do a few more coins matter?'

The mercenary gathered it up without a word and calmly looped it round her own belt.

'And you?' Pythias continued, turning his eyes to Eucrates. 'Who are you?'

'My name is Eucrates, sir,' he began politely, though it sounded forced. 'I met your niece and her bodyguard on the way here, and –'

'And you thought you could have a bit of her, too, I suppose,' snarled Pythias. 'Well, if you're thinking of any reward for helping to bring her back, forget it. Just think yourself lucky I'm not charging you for the use of her body on the way. I'm not paying some money-grubbing little dissolute, like you.'

'He's not!' Chryseis heard herself shout, her eyes burning with tears. 'He's not like that at all. He risked his life to save me, they both did, and not just for your stinking money.' She leant forward, screaming into her guardian's ugly, mean face. 'You're the one who cares only for profit; you're the one who treats me like a whore to be sold like a box of fish or a pot of sour wine; you're the one who –'

His hand cracked across her face, sending her spinning to the floor, where she knelt gasping, watching the blood drip on to Pythias' fine mosaic from her split lip.

'That's enough,' snarled Eucrates, dropping any pretence of civility and stepping protectively between her and her uncle, his hand ready on his sword. He reached down and helped Chryseis to her feet. 'She's coming with me,' he said, daring Pythias to contradict him.

Pythias hesitated, then took a single, reluctant step back, before turning to Acantha. 'You,' he snapped. 'Do your job. Stop him!'

Acantha crossed her arms and remained as unperturbed as before. 'Oh, no. I've made my delivery. My obligation to you is complete.'

'I'll pay double,' Pythias snapped.

Acantha laughed. 'No, thanks. Money doesn't come into it.'

Pythias clenched his fists, his arms rigid by his sides, but he did not move.

'That's it,' ordered Eucrates. 'You just stay there, and we'll leave quietly.'

Chryseis wished she could say goodbye, but nothing seemed appropriate. She left silently, shielded between her two companions, while nervous slaves peered out from doorways and from behind columns.

Pythias followed their exit closely, his eyes tinged yellow with hate.

Later that night, Chryseis lay in Eucrates' arms in a small taverna at the edge of town. It was dark now, but the noises of the city continued. From downstairs came laughter which drowned out the rippling sound of someone playing a lyre. The melody was slow and sweet, a love ballad, and Chryseis thought it fitted her mood perfectly. She ran her fingers possessively across Eucrates' wide chest. 'We could always go down and entertain them for a few more coins,' she suggested, with a giggle.

Eucrates groaned theatrically. 'I couldn't; not again. You'll have to entertain them yourself.'

'Call yourself a man,' she jibed gently, tweaking his nipple. 'Do you think that once is enough?'

'No, no, a thousand times, no. I'm obviously not up to it. You go down and entertain the tavern, and I'll go out and rustle up a dozen or so young men to keep you amused till morning. After that, I suppose we'd better start lining up the old and sick, as well as the women.' He rolled over and studied her face with a concerned frown. 'Just how long do you think the city will last you? Should we start importing men, women and herds of wild beasts from further abroad?'

The laughter leaked out of her, dribbling away like water through crippled hands. She couldn't meet his eyes, and looked down at his chest. 'Am I really that bad?' she asked in a whisper. 'Pythias thought so.'

'Hey, come on,' he said, lifting her chin with his thumb. 'I was joking. I don't think you're bad in this or any other way. The opposite: when I'm with a woman,

233

I like to know she's enjoying herself; I like to know she is fulfilling her own needs, not just gratifying mine. Your uncle, however, never cared for what you wanted, only what honour and prestige you could bring to him. Do you understand?'

'But – well, maybe.'

'Just believe me,' he said, stroking the hair back from her face.

A woman's fierce cry of pleasure filtered through the wall from the adjoining room, breaking the moment of introspection. Chryseis giggled, regaining her humour. 'Acantha seems fully recovered anyway,' she said. 'She had two of those serving lads fawning around her all evening; I wonder which one she picked?'

'I think she came upstairs with both. Do you want to ask her if one's spare?'

'I'd better not risk it. While she was good enough to give us money for our lodging, I think she'd draw the line at sharing her lovers. In any case, she's probably used them both up by now.' She ran her fingers over his scrotum, lifted the flaccid weight of his penis, still damp from their previous love-making, and waggled it playfully. 'Are you sure you can't manage it again?'

Eucrates laughed and pushed her hand away. 'Get off!' he said, rolling on to his opposite side.

Chryseis leant over him so her hair trailed over his shoulder and neck. 'So what are you going to do to satisfy a poor, hungry girl? Surely you don't expect me to gratify myself, do you?' When he didn't reply, she put on a pout. 'Very well, if you won't do it, I'll do it myself.'

She slipped a hand down between her thighs, felt the warmth and heat of her sex as she cupped it in her hand, pressing it gently against the pubic bone. 'Mmmm, that feels good,' she murmured into Eucrates' ear. 'I like the feel of my hand on my mound. I can feel it all hot and wet, just oozing juice.'

'I'm not surprised,' said Eucrates. 'You've drained me for the rest of the night.' He closed his eyes and made a snoring sound.

'Oh, you think you can go to sleep, do you?' She pushed him on to his back and knelt across his chest.

'Let me rest, woman,' he exclaimed, his eyes still closed.

'I am,' she replied. 'I just thought you might like to watch.'

He opened his eyes and looked up at her. She thrust her hip forward, so she peered down on his face between the valley of her breasts, and stroked her hand gently between her thighs. His gaze flickered towards the insistent motion. 'I've seen it,' he said shortly, pretending to fall asleep again. But she could see his eyes gleam from under his lowered lashes as he continued to watch surreptitiously.

She stroked her quim firmly with her right hand, allowing her fingers to part the groove of her sex, though not to penetrate too deeply. It would have been easy to rush; her vagina was so wet and slippery that rubbing herself was like dipping her hand into a velvet purse that opened itself in welcome. Despite Eucrates' claim, the wetness was only fractionally his. She dipped one finger into the warm sheath, then a second, and then a third. Only when all her fingers were inside and she cupped the front of her mound in her palm did she begin to feel stretched and filled. Her hand slid easily in and out of her brimming entrance, the slick moisture spreading out and soaking the hairs of her groin.

She used her free hand to hold open the lips of her vulva and display herself shamelessly to her lover. She knew he was looking, knew he could see deep within her tunnel; she imagined him fucking her with his eyes. Her hand slipped in and out between her legs in time to his visionary ardour, rhythmically lifting her lust to greater heights.

Chryseis let her fingers emerge slightly and used just the first two to rub along the fleshy channel on either side of her clitoris, crushing it and dragging it fore and aft with the motion of her hand. The exquisite sensation spread up from that single point of pleasure like the rays of the sun, infusing her belly with heat and making it tighten in anticipation till it ached.

Now Chryseis abandoned playing with her sex and began, instead, to stroke the rest of her body, soothing the gentle curve of her belly, clutching the malleable flesh of her breast, squeezing it till the nipple jutted out. She bent her head, straining to take the teat in her mouth, to run her tongue over the brown peak and suckle herself. A groan of frustration escaped her lips when she couldn't reach it. What joy it would be to lick herself with all the skill and flexibility she could endow on another while reaping all the benefits. She would kiss and nuzzle her own breasts, delve with her tongue into the depths of her navel. She would, joy of joys, be able to lick and taste her own sex, vibrate her tongue across the pinnacle of flesh that was the centre of her sexual universe. She would drink from her own cup, swallow all the liquor herself, keeping it within her and cycling it around and around in a never-ending circle.

Instead, wastefully, her musky oil ran over her hand and dripped on to Eucrates' chest. Chryseis lifted her hand to her mouth, and drew the fingers between her lips. They tasted of moist earth and humid jungle, the combined flavours of her own secretions and Eucrates' semen. It was a blend which could be formed in no other place than the sacred chalice of her womb. She dipped her fingers into the pot once more to harvest the viscous ichor, then licked and sucked them clean while imagining she had a penis and was fellating herself.

All the while, Eucrates watched her intently from beneath his hooded eyes. He had grown unnaturally still, even for someone pretending to be asleep; tension

236

radiated from him as he held his body taut. Again, she dipped into her chalice then daubed her body with the evidence of her passion, even putting some of the heady perfume behind her ears and into the hollow of her throat. She massaged the lotion into the skin of her breasts and belly, rubbing it in so that she became thoroughly and completely infused with the odour of lust.

Still Eucrates feigned sleep; still he resisted her. His determined refusal to acknowledge her presence needled her and fuelled her determination to rouse him. She slipped her fingers once more into her silken tunnel, lingering to stroke her engorged clitoris before withdrawing them coated with her sacred chrism. Then she smeared the unction across his closed mouth and pushed a slick finger between his lips, daring him to refuse her offering. But he did not ignore her this time. He sucked on the proffered digit, pulling it deep into his mouth, cleansing it with his tongue. She flexed the finger in and out of his mouth, penetrating him, fantasising that she pierced him with a cock of her own. As he gnawed gently on her flesh, savouring the ambrosia she bestowed upon him, she imagined he was kissing and nuzzling at a miniature penis, and that he eagerly awaited the gift of her come.

Something nudged her buttocks as she straddled his chest, something coming alive. She reached round and grasped his penis which lay hard and erect along his belly. It was a sword, ready to plunge within her, and fill her depths. She didn't know which orifice to take him in; she wanted him in her mouth, her anus, her vagina; she wanted his wicked tongue stroking her clitoris, his mouth on hers, his fingers straying into every nook and cranny. She leant forward, pressing herself against him, putting as much of her skin in contact with his as possible. Her lips nuzzled the side of his neck as her breasts squashed against his chest, and she wished she could melt into him, touch him inside and out at the same time.

He reached round to cup her buttocks, then lifted her slightly and adjusted himself so that the wide knob of his glans pressed against the tight ring of her anus. She pushed back, accepting his choice and felt him work his way up inside her rectum, forcing his way deep inside her. She pushed back harder, finding herself so ready for him that there was almost no resistance. Wild, primitive pleasure at his invasion of her body swept through her and she tilted the angle of her hips in order to force herself completely over him, and engulf him within her bowels. She could feel the soft flesh of his testicles brush the cheeks of her rump and reached back to stroke them gently, and to follow his rigid member to where it thrust through her tight sphincter.

She lowered her head, trying to curl round sufficiently to see him penetrating her, but could see nothing beyond the tangled nest where their pubic hairs merged; hers dark, his golden. Eucrates slid his hand between them, reaching for her sex, and she leant further back to allow him access. His fingers sought out her clitoris with familiar dexterity, but pressed it against her pubic bone too hard, making her wince. Concern flickered on his face as he began to withdraw his hand, but she grasped his wrist and gave him a slow grin, wetting her lips with her tongue as she helped him find the pressure she desired.

He moved with her, rubbing the nerve centre with his strong, work-hardened hand, rolling it between his fingertips, making her cry out once more but this time in sharp pleasure. Meanwhile, he slowly rocked his hips up and down in short strokes, sliding his member in and out of her backside, his hand and penis working to the rhythm of her breath. She used her own hands on her breasts, tugging and twisting at her nipples as only she would dare to, knowing exactly how much she could stand. The sensations crackled through her body like lightning, meeting deep within her belly to form a volcano of desire that made the blood roar in her ears. Her vision closed in, growing dim around the edges as Eucrates' strokes grew shorter and his breath became ragged. Suddenly he cried out and spurted hotly within her, his member twitching and juddering within her rectum. She wondered whether she could contain the intensity of so much pleasure and prolong it a little longer, but she couldn't. It started as a quake in the centre of her womb and spread out, a great trembling, shaking wave of release that flooded outward, sweeping everything from its path. Chryseis heard herself cry out, a scream of rapture that hurt her throat with its force.

Gradually, the crashing waves subsided to mere ripples oscillating back and forth along her nerves. She collapsed over him so that they panted together, their bodies seeming to steam with perspiration, and wondered how anything so intense could vanish so completely. She wondered where it all evaporated to; surely so much strength of feeling, of desire and lust could not just disappear, even for a short time. And yet it seemed it had, leaving her so light and unburdened that she could have floated away were it not for Eucrates' tender embrace binding her to him.

After a moment, she leant up on her elbows and looked into his face as she brushed a damp lock of hair from his forehead. His eyes looked clear and untroubled, totally at ease.

He brushed her cheek with the back of his hand. Nothing more needed to be said for the moment.

Gently, as his erection subsided, they eased themselves apart and she rolled on to her side, stretched her legs and made herself comfortable snuggled in the crook of his arm. She could feel the evidence of his ardour trickle between her buttocks; a good feeling though it would itch as it dried. Normality would return, the mundane would come again into their lives, but for the moment she was content to forget everything except the way their bodies –

The door slammed open so hard that it shattered.

Armoured soldiers swarmed into the tiny room, ducking to get their crested helmets under the lintel. 'Stay where you are,' barked one, thrusting his spear forward so that its iron tip rested on Eucrates' bare chest, forcing him to remain flat on the bed. The soldier's eyes were almost hidden behind the broad cheek guards and nose-piece of his helmet, but they glinted menacingly and Chryseis had no doubt he would kill Eucrates on the slightest provocation. The other men formed up around the bed, their round shields up and swords or spears at the ready. There were six in all; six men who had shattered their moment of peace and seemed intent on making it worse.

'Surely there's some mistake,' she stammered, ignoring Eucrates' warning grip on her arm. 'We've done nothing wrong.'

'Oh, no? I think so,' mocked a familiar voice, and Pythias pushed his way to the fore. 'I've come to take you back, and to give this scoundrel the beating he deserves. That will teach him to come seducing the gullible wards of respectable citizens. Maybe next time he . . .'

Pythias ground to a halt, then roared with laughter. 'Oh, gods. Thank you for this tender gift.' He laughed again, and pointed out the slave brand on Eucrates' shoulder to the watching guards. 'A runaway slave, no less. I imagine someone is looking for you,' he said, leaning forward with an unpleasant smirk. 'Or someone else will pay to buy you. Either way, I'll recoup some of my losses out of your miserable carcass. It appears there is justice after all.'

He turned to the soldiers and gestured them forward. 'Take them away,' he ordered. 'Both of them.'

Fifteen

Acantha lay on her back with her eyes closed, and let the two youths she had brought to her room do all the work. Both were young and fit, their smoothly muscled bodies unblemished and clean. Most important, both were in awe of the tawny-haired barbarian and her outlandish ways.

The young men had been serving in the taverna downstairs when Acantha and her companions arrived. Acantha had soon noticed their interest in her, and played her part of uncivilised savage to the full, ripping at her meat with bared teeth and gulping down great goblets of wine.

Chryseis and Eucrates had been shocked by her uncouth behaviour until Acantha had winked and indicated her audience. 'They're fascinated; they think I'm some kind of wild beast,' she confided, wine dripping from her chin. 'They wonder if I'm as primitive when slaking my other hungers. I don't think it'll take much to lure one of them to my room for a demonstration.'

Chryseis had laughed, and clung on to Eucrates. 'I've got my man right here,' she had said, as Eucrates wrapped his arms tightly around her.

The sight had triggered uneasy feelings of loneliness in Acantha's belly. In an effort to obliterate them she had enticed both men upstairs, then ordered them to strip and gratify her every need.

Now, one of the men licked her feet, slithering his

241

tongue like a slippery eel between her toes and across the ticklish skin of her sole, sending shivers of delight up her legs. The other youth, meanwhile, nuzzled enthusiastically at the cleft between her thighs. He explored the sodden crevice with his nose and tongue, showing no inhibitions to restrain him from wantonly revelling in the pleasure of her flesh. He had just targeted the tiny hub round which all her physical delight revolved and begun to knead it with his tongue when she heard Chryseis scream.

At first, she discounted the cry as nothing more than yet another announcement of Chryseis' gratification, and wondered how Eucrates could tolerate the noise. Then she heard men's voices raised in anger and Chryseis screamed again. This time, there was no mistaking the screech of pain for anything else.

'Oh, shit. Here we go again,' she muttered and swung herself out of bed, kicking away the lad at her feet and leaving the other with bruised lips and a mouthful of pubic hair. 'Sorry about this,' she said as she took her sword from beside the bed and unsheathed it. 'You two carry on without me, and I'll be back soon.'

Still naked apart from the ever-present talisman around her neck, she dashed out on to the balcony that ran round the inner courtyard of the taverna. Light spilled from the open door to Chryseis' and Eucrates' room. The back of a large soldier blocked the entrance, preventing her from seeing inside. She must have made some sound, for he abruptly glanced over his shoulder at her approach. She could see, even through the narrow slits in his helmet, that his eyes widened and his mouth stretched in a greedy smile as he insolently inspected her from foot to head. He turned to face her, either so taken by her nudity that he didn't notice her sword, or too contemptuous of her to bother defending himself. He thought she was easy meat, in more senses than one, and simply reached out with one hand for her naked breast.

Acantha had no time for niceties or idiots; she skewered him in the throat and stepped over his corpse before it had finished falling to the floor.

Inside the room, two soldiers gripped Eucrates' arms behind his back, while a third delivered a series of heavy, measured blows to his face and body. Eucrates hung slackly between the guards holding him, blood oozing from his nose. Two other men held Chryseis by the arms and hair, forcing her to watch the beating while, in the far corner, Pythias smirked maliciously as he orchestrated the proceedings.

One of the soldiers holding Chryseis saw Acantha in the doorway. He was quick off the mark, urged to speed by the sight of his dead comrade. He let go of Chryseis, drew his sword and sliced at Acantha's stomach in a single motion. Acantha parried, slipped her blade back along his. He twisted away; she followed, lunged, lunged again and pierced his shoulder. The soldier fell back with a cry, Chryseis shrieked a warning and Acantha swung round in time to deflect a spear thrust from the guard who had been beating Eucrates.

The man jabbed again, the long weapon keeping her at bay. If she could get inside its reach, she would have the advantage, but he was too seasoned for that.

'Get her,' screamed Pythias, pointing with a trembling finger. 'That's the bitch; I want her dead. Five silver drachmas to the man who brings her down.'

'Idiot,' Acantha jeered, while never taking her eyes from the swaying spear-point. 'If you'd offered that much in the first place, I'd have tied Chryseis to me with a leash and none of this would have happened. Now it's costing you a fortune to put it right.'

Perhaps Acantha's opponent saw an opening, perhaps the bounty spurred him on. Either way, he renewed his attack with vigour, making a flurry of short jabs that drove Acantha back to the door. Chryseis screeched and twisted violently in the grip of her captor's huge fist, but couldn't escape. Acantha, however, did not mind leaving the small room where too many things could trip her or snag her sword. She let her adversary think he was forcing her back outside, otherwise he might think twice about where she was going. Then, as soon as she was through the doorway, she stepped slightly sideways. Now, the door jamb shielded the left half of her body, while the spearman had to contend with trying to reach her through the narrow opening.

Suddenly, the soldier fell forward in an uncontrolled sprawl, his spear clattering harmlessly across the floor. Behind him stood Eucrates, unsteadily poised for a second blow. His captors seized him again and threw him viciously back against the wall. Acantha's opponent was clambering back to his feet. There was no time for chivalry. A single upward thrust caught him under the bottom edge of his breastplate, sliding the blade up into his vitals.

Eucrates was on the floor, his head bleeding from where his scalp had been laid open by a blow. One of his guards lunged forward to attack Acantha. She stepped back, using the doorway again, placing herself so that the soldier was standing directly in the opening when he took a swing at her. His sword arced round, the blade caught the remains of the wooden door and stuck. The soldier stared at it in surprise, distracted. Acantha slashed at his exposed neck. He died instantly.

Only two guards remained, the ones holding Chryseis and Eucrates, and they were fresh and wary while Acantha had weakened. Her wound had torn open and it ached horribly. Her sword was heavy and ready to slip from her bloody fingers. Now that the element of surprise was past, she was not in a good position.

The soldiers exchanged a glance. The one holding Eucrates clubbed him on the temple, making sure he couldn't interfere again. The other stunned Chryseis with a slap, then pushed her into Pythias' arms. She cried out and struggled as her uncle gripped her wrists with brutal force, but couldn't break free.

The two men edged towards Acantha in unison.

She stood back on the balcony, hoping they would come at her one by one through the narrow doorway, but they had seen how that trick worked. One picked up a spear and used it to keep her at bay, while his companion used his sword to make sure she couldn't sneak inside the longer weapon's reach.

Acantha was harried back along the balcony, unable to block the two men inside the room. They grinned as they moved towards her in tandem, spear and sword, ensuring she had no chance of penetrating their defence.

The mercenary backed away cautiously, parrying the occasional thrust from the spear, but keeping her distance, moving away as fast as the guards advanced. She passed the doorway to her room; the lads stared out fearfully at the fight, and when she came close they scurried back inside and slammed the door shut. Acantha didn't blame them; they'd agreed to an evening of casual sex, nothing else. They owed her nothing.

Other guests, those on the far side of the courtyard balcony and safely out of harm's way, stood watching in excitement. A fat man with a hurriedly knotted sheet around his waist was taking bets, while a couple of prostitutes leant back against the wall and watched in apparent irritation, probably annoyed by the disruption to business. As the fight circled the balcony, the spectators withdrew into their rooms, then emerged again once it was safely past.

A couple of men began heckling. It was apparent to everyone, not just Acantha and the soldiers, that this was getting nowhere. They could skirmish round and round the narrow balcony all night or until they collapsed with exhaustion. The soldiers apparently decided to bring the fight to a swift conclusion. There were brief whispers, then they split up. The one with the sword dashed back around the balcony, intending to attack Acantha from the rear.

Acantha had only moments left. Her backward retreat was taking her to a doorway where a young catamite and his elderly customer stood applauding the entertainment. Acantha dashed towards them and, before they could slam the door in her face, grabbed the old man by the testicles and yanked him out on to the balcony in front of her. He came swiftly with a terrible screech, but eager not to lose his tackle to Acantha's nails. He stumbled and fell at the soldier's feet. The guard was confused, raised his spear to stab the old man, and Acantha managed to slash his thigh. He fell to the ground, clutching his gaping wound. Acantha stunned him with a kick to the head, though she hurt her bare toes on his helmet.

She heard the last guard rushing at her back and spun swiftly, barely managing to meet his frenzied rush. The man hacked at her furiously, slashing right and left, allowing her no chance for anything except last-minute parries. He used the power of his bulging biceps and broad shoulders to drive her backward, blow by blow. He couldn't maintain an onslaught like that for long, but Acantha was tiring fast. It was trial by strength, and she was losing. Her reopened wound made every move agony, and she could feel the blood dripping down her waist and thighs while her sword got heavier with each blow.

The soldier sensed her weakness. He redoubled the ferocity of his assault, herding her back into a corner of the balcony until she had nowhere left to go. She blocked an overhand blow to the head, but there was so much force behind it that she couldn't stop it completely. All she managed was to turn his sword so that only the flat of the blade cracked against her skull. She collapsed against the wall and slithered down it as her knees gave way. The soldier stepped closer, his sword raised for the final blow. Blindly, desperately, she thrust upward and pierced him under his raised arm. He fell back, clutching himself in shock, his weapon clattering to the floor.

Acantha rolled unsteadily to her feet and brought her sword up in a scything, double-handed action with the last of her strength. It met the soldier's head as he bent to retrieve his weapon, caving in the nose-piece of his helmet and lodging inside with a meaty thud. The man tumbled backward, wrenching the sword from her grasp, leaving her naked and unarmed.

Panting and aching, she leant over with her hands on her knees, gulping down searing lungfuls of air as the watching patrons cheered and whistled, or paid off bets. It seemed that she had run out of opponents.

'Barbarian bitch!' she heard, and looked up to see Pythias standing on the balcony. 'You'll pay for this,' he snarled as he drew a knife from his belt. For one fleeting moment, Acantha thought that, compared to a patrol of fully armed soldiers, an old man with a knife would be easy to deal with. Then she saw Pythias hurl the weapon at her with adept skill. The spinning blade glittered through the air too swiftly for her to avoid. It struck just below her throat and she staggered back, clutching her neck, frantically trying to breathe.

'Bastard! You've killed her, you bastard.' Acantha peered up through a reddened mist in time to see Chryseis fling herself at Pythias' chest with both fists flailing. As if in a dream, she saw Pythias step back under the onslaught, saw him trip over the prone body of the first guard she had killed, and then, with a brief cry, tumble backward down the steps leading to the ground floor.

There was an abrupt silence.

Chryseis stood at the top of the stairs, her hands clenched in horror in front of her mouth.

Curious onlookers peered down to the courtyard below, murmuring quietly to each other in surprise. Eucrates appeared and stood unsteadily beside Chryseis with his arm around her shoulder. 'Dead,' he said succinctly, through bloodied lips. 'Broke his neck.'

Chryseis drew herself up with a shudder, but wasted no time in false remorse. 'Acantha's hurt,' she said, and rushed over to where the mercenary still knelt on the wooden floor, massaging her neck.

'Oh, thank the gods,' Chryseis exclaimed. 'You're still alive. I thought he'd killed you.'

'Not quite,' Acantha responded, 'though he had a good try.' Her voice was hoarse and talking hurt. Silently, she lifted her chin to display the gold phoenix around her neck and pointed to where the knife had gouged into the soft metal before bouncing off.

The ship rose and fell through the waves, heading back toward Ephesus. That was the place that Chryseis considered home and she was eager to take up her responsibilities there, now that she had inherited her uncle's estate. It was going to be a lot of work but, for the moment, the journey was a chance to rest and recuperate. She relaxed under the cabin awning, drowsily listening to the chant the sailors used to keep time on the oars.

Palmeda came under the awning holding a bowl of fresh apples, figs and grapes, plus a large jug of wine. Chryseis gestured for her maid to sit with them. The slave-girl had always been exempt from standing on ceremony, and now social divide seemed even less important. Chryseis pulled up her legs to make room amongst the spread rugs and cushions, but continued to lie back on Eucrates' broad chest. He had his arms protectively wrapped around her, and said he was never going to let her go again.

Acantha raised her head off a plump cushion and

248

waved her goblet in the direction of the jug Palmeda was holding. 'I need another refill,' she slurred. She had been drunk for most of the last week, saying it was the first time she'd been able to afford wine good enough to drink in such quantities. Chryseis didn't mind; as far as she was concerned, Acantha was entitled to remain inebriated for as long as she wanted, though she hoped the mercenary would sober up a bit when they returned to Ephesus. There were several young men, workers at the villa, who Chryseis thought might take an interest in the barbarian. Apart from which, Palmeda seemed drawn to her, too. Certainly the maid responded quickly enough to Acantha's requests, and now poured a good measure of rich, red wine into her cup.

Acantha tried to lift her head enough to drink from the goblet, but sank back with a groan. 'My wound's troubling me,' she murmured. 'It hurts.'

'Oh dear, we can't have that,' said Palmeda. She shuffled across the rugs and positioned herself so that Acantha's head rested on her knees. Then she began patiently feeding the wine to the mercenary, sip by sip. 'Is that better?' the maid asked, stroking Acantha's fine, tawny hair.

'Mmmm. A lot,' Acantha confirmed. 'You have a nice lap to rest in.' She snuggled down, making herself comfortable with her cheek resting against the soft curve of Palmeda's breast.

The slave looked up at Chryseis, her face a picture of mingled desire and frustration. Chryseis guessed what Palmeda was thinking: that Chryseis would be displeased if her maid openly displayed her affections elsewhere.

Chryseis shook her head, denying the unspoken accusation. 'She's my friend,' she said. 'So are you. I've been thinking of this for a while, and now seems the ideal time. Palmeda, from this moment you are no longer my slave; you are free.'

Palmeda looked stunned, even fearful. 'But, mistress, what will I do?' she wailed.

'Well, I hope you'll remain my maid,' Chryseis reassured her hastily. 'I don't want you to go, but you are now free to do as you wish. Apart from that, there will be no real difference, except that you no longer have to address me as "Mistress".' Chryseis grinned and added, 'You will also make love to whom you please, when you please.'

To Chryseis' surprise, Palmeda blushed and looked down at Acantha with a shy smile. 'She is very handsome, mistr –, Chryseis. I've never seen such a strong, independent woman.'

'Neither have I,' said Chryseis with an affectionate look at the drowsing warrior. 'She is quite special.'

Acantha opened one eye and squinted at her. 'I couldn't agree more,' she mumbled but there was no mistaking the smug tone of her voice. 'And I have very special tastes, too.' She looked up at Palmeda's face and Chryseis watched with deep pleasure as the two women shared the unspoken signal that each was ready for the other. Without another word, Acantha put her arm around Palmeda's neck and lifted herself to meet the maid's lips. Their first kiss was a fleeting brush of lip on lip. Then they met again with greater confidence and kissed slowly and sensually, their heads turning as they sought better contact with each other's mouth.

Eucrates' chest was a comfortable presence behind Chryseis' shoulders and his large, bony hands encircled her waist. She wanted more though, and squirmed against him, encouraging him to action. He responded by pulling her more tightly to him and burrowing into the hair cascading around her neck to nuzzle the sensitive spot below her ear.

The entwined women changed position; without breaking their kiss, Acantha lifted her head from Palmeda's lap and let Palmeda stretch her legs backward, so that they lay head to head on the soft rugs but with their bodies extending in opposite directions. They kissed awkwardly, each upside-down to the other, and giggled at the clumsiness. They didn't break their embrace, however, and remained together with their tongues spiralling around each other, passing the taste of their mouths back and forth. Then each moved further down the other's body, first to kiss the other's chin, then the soft flesh of her neck and on to the gentle hollow of her throat.

Acantha rolled completely on to her back while Palmeda rose above her, controlling the speed at which they moved. The mercenary had a contented smile and seemed perfectly happy with the arrangement. Chryseis suspected that the hardened warrior was, in fact, starved of affection and loved being fawned over and pampered.

So did she, if it came down to it. She reached up and ran her fingers through Eucrates' hair, guiding his soft lips along the curve of her shoulder. The clasp of her gown blocked his progress. He caught it in his mouth and worried at it with his teeth till it sprang free. The garment drooped down around her waist on that side, leaving her breast exposed. The cool sea breeze puckered the nipple and a seagull screeched in appreciation.

With a small twinge of self-consciousness, she peeked around to see if any of the crew had noticed. The steersman was her old friend Leonidas, whom she had seduced with such disastrous results on the outward journey. He seemed to be studying the flight of the raucous gull with unnatural intensity, and she detected his eyes flickering repeatedly towards the group on the rugs. She considered lowering the matting walls to the cabin, but decided against it. The air felt good on her bare breasts, its caress like a hundred feather-light hands. It would be a shame to block it off. And, in any case, she was sure Leonidas would like to watch.

She gave him a wink, to let him know she'd noticed him, and he grinned mischievously then turned with an innocent whistle to scan the empty horizon.

Eucrates undid the clasp on her other shoulder, so that the material could fall completely about her waist, then placed his hands on her naked flesh, stroking up and down her torso and across her breasts. He lifted each orb in his hands, hefting the weight as if he were a miser assessing a purse of gold. 'Precious treasures,' he murmured, leaning over her shoulder to watch as he massaged her nipples. 'The only jewellery a woman needs.'

She snorted in amusement and looked down at his disembodied hands encircling her body and teasing the brown nipples into hard peaks. The feeling was gentle and soothing, a delicate glow of contented anticipation, and she relaxed back against him, idly watching her maid and bodyguard as their explorations gradually grew more intense.

Palmeda had moved further down Acantha's body until, like Eucrates, she found the presence of the other's garment an unwanted obstruction. She undid the shoulder clasps with her hands, while Acantha mirrored the action. Then, working in unison, they helped each other push the material around their waists so that now each faced the other's naked breasts. Palmeda, still on top and setting the pace, ran her tongue in exploratory circles over Acantha's right mound, while her own breast swayed enticingly over the mercenary's mouth. Acantha nipped at the hanging fruit with her teeth, seemingly intent to leave her mark on the maid's olive skin.

Palmeda's spiralling motion finally brought her to Acantha's pink nipple. She sucked the tiny peak between her lips, then gradually opened her mouth wider, drawing the surrounding flesh into her mouth as well. Acantha groaned softly, and arched her back, pushing her soft breast further into Palmeda's mouth. The mercenary clasped her hands behind the maid's back and drew her down, biting and nipping at Palmeda's breasts in a flurry of passion. Palmeda giggled and broke away. In moments they returned to each other, kissing and nuzzling the soft flesh of their breasts as if it were a feast to be savoured and lingered over like the choicest of delicacies.

Chryseis wormed back against Eucrates, feeling the soft linen of his tunic against her back. She reached over her shoulder for the clasp that held the garment in place, but could not find it. Instead, she turned her attention to where the lower hem of his tunic was trapped beneath her buttocks as she sat between his legs. She rocked from one hip to the other, tugging the material of both his tunic and her own dress out from under her and up to the level of their waists. The wiry wool of the rug prickled the backs of her thighs, and Eucrates' warm, virile member pressed upright against her coccyx. She squirmed back against it, feeling it twitch with a life of its own while the bush of his pubic hair tickled her skin. Meanwhile, she continued to stroke Eucrates' naked thighs, running her fingernails along the well-formed muscles. He made a low sound in his throat and bit her neck, gripping her breasts harder till they throbbed with mingled pain and desire.

On the other side of the rugs, Acantha and Palmeda still lay head to tail with their garments pushed down around their hips. Now, they overlapped to the point where each could nuzzle the other's belly and their breasts were tip to tip. Palmeda, still on top, rolled her shoulders back and forth so that her swaying teats brushed the mercenary's pink nipples. Chryseis' own breasts tingled in empathy at the sight and she pressed Eucrates' hands against them more firmly, encouraging him to hold her tighter.

Acantha endured the torment for only a few brief

moments before snarling in feral passion and surging up to push Palmeda over on her back. She ripped the remains of the tunic from the maid's body, then plunged her face into the dark triangle between Palmeda's legs. Palmeda mewled in surprise and pleasure, and lifted her splayed knees back towards her shoulders to expose herself fully to the mercenary's ministrations. Acantha pressed further between the spread thighs, running her tongue feverishly along the length of the exposed vulva as Palmeda guided her head to where it would do the most good.

Acantha barely paused in her enthusiastic devouring of Palmeda's sex to help divest herself of the last of her own garments. Chryseis watched as Acantha, now completely naked apart from her talisman, straddled Palmeda's face and lowered her tawny quim on to the eagerly waiting mouth. Palmeda embraced Acantha's hips and drew them down to swiftly burrow her extended tongue between the mercenary's rosy labia.

Chryseis let her fingers stray between her own legs as she watched, remembering from experience how each of the women tasted: Acantha's sharp tang, the sweeter subtlety of Palmeda's nectar. She could smell them both from here and her vagina melted with the desire to join them. Acantha's hips were the closest, so she crawled across the piled cushions to join Palmeda in eating the pink cleft of Acantha's sex. Palmeda saw her approach and hooked her fingers into the crease of Acantha's buttocks, drawing them apart in readiness for Chryseis' ministrations. Chryseis rubbed her face over the graceful curves of Acantha's rump, inhaling the scent of her skin and her redolent juices as they flowed copiously from her slit before bestowing tiny, feather-light kisses to the exquisite flesh.

Behind her, she felt Eucrates grip her waist, felt the round tip of his penis prod at the entrance to her vagina. He thrust forward firmly, parting her lips and pushing himself within her as he held her steady. She broke off her exploration of Acantha's sex long enough to lean back against the thrust and engulf Eucrates' hardness within her. She sighed with appreciation as he filled her, then lowered her head and looked back along the underside of her body. Her swaying breasts framed her dark triangle and Eucrates' balls as he held himself tight against her. His penis pressed at her cervix, leaving no part of her neglected.

Then he steadily withdrew from her till the tip of his penis hovered at the entrance to her slit, barely parting her tender labia. She whimpered, wanting him, needing him inside her. Then he plunged in, thrusting deep until his hips slapped against her buttocks, making her cry out with shock and pleasure. He retreated once more, lingering, prolonging the suspense before spearing inside her again. This time the sensation was less sharp, more mellow, as she accustomed herself to his girth. Gradually, he set up a slow rhythm that made each thrust an individual event, stroking every spot within her silken vagina as if it, alone, were her most precious and tender spot.

Now, with Eucrates gently fucking her from behind, she could again concentrate on the feast of Acantha's swollen vulva which hovered in front of her face. She explored up and down the overflowing crevice with her tongue, extending the motion to circle the dark star of her anus before returning to slip along the scented blossom of her pouting labia. She shared a kiss with Palmeda, passing the taste of Acantha's juice back and forth between their mouths, making it sweeter with the taste of their saliva.

Now it was Palmeda's turn and she fluttered her tongue across Acantha's clitoris while also delving with her long fingers into the mercenary's vagina. Her eyes were drowsy with lust as she watched her fingers pumping in and out of the slippery orifice. Then she held her fingers up to Chryseis' lips, inviting her to taste the juices she was generating. Chryseis sucked the long fingers into her mouth tenderly, gripping them with her lips, lapping them with her tongue, bobbing her head over them as she would a lover's cock.

Eucrates' rhythm increased steadily, his testicles and belly smacking against her as he drove into her with increasing urgency. Chryseis grunted in time to the motion, felt the friction heat spread outward till it suffused her entire belly. She closed her eyes to concentrate on it, ignored everything except the rigid flesh that stimulated the interior of her vagina till the sensation grew so powerful she hardly knew whether she could contain it anymore. The feeling became sharper; sweet pain that screamed for release, yet which she wished could go on for ever. She rocked back and forth on her hands and knees, sliding like a lubricated sheath over the piston of Eucrates' penis. Chryseis bit her lip, and concentrated on the volcano steaming in her belly and knew the eruption could not be denied much longer. Unable to restrain it, she chose instead to drive it on to a grand climax, thrusting back and forth harder than before, pumping up the impending eruption to an explosive orgasm.

Eucrates seemed to swell inside her with each stroke, filling her from side to side and end to end, and she knew his moment was near, too. She reached back between her legs, felt the soft sack of his scrotum drawn tight up to the base of his erection as he moved in and out of her. His breath shortened, became a pant, stopped. For a moment he froze, then with a cry he thrust the full length of his cock into her while simultaneously dragging her hips back as if to force himself further within her. Then he erupted, jetting the white hot lava of his sperm into her.

Unable to hold back any longer, she undulated back and forth on his still turgid member, feeling the slipperiness oozing from her slit as the volatile heat spread through her body, bringing a red haze to her vision. Her excitement peaked, the explosion driving her into a dark oblivion that convulsed her body from end to end.

She was still trembling and recovering her breath when Acantha cried out, and she looked up in time to see Palmeda's feverishly working tongue rub Acantha's clitoris into a second climax. Then Palmeda herself, her face and throat brightly-coloured in arousal, gasped and threw her head back with her eyes screwed shut and her mouth set in a rictus of fierce delight.

Chryseis laughed shakily, elated by their combined orgasms. She felt so euphoric, it seemed as if everyone in the world were cheering them. With a shock she realised that, while it wasn't quite that many, it was certainly most of the crew. All the men stood on deck, peering over each other's shoulder and enthusiastically applauding their performance. Chryseis shared a look with the others, and laughed contentedly. It wasn't everyone who could spread their passion around so many people, and she saw no reason to be ashamed of it. And, if her inheritance ever ran out, she could always go on the road and start giving performances again.

NEW BOOKS

Coming up from Nexus and Black Lace

Emma's Humiliation by Hilary James

May 1997   Price £4.99   ISBN: 0 352 33153 4

When Emma's masterful lover Henry comes back into her life, she is keen to resume their delightful disciplinary dalliances. But they are soon discovered by Emma's Mistress, Ursula, who sends her to a rehabilitation centre to ensure she remains an obedient slave. Under the tutelage of the Headmistress and the Major, Emma soon learns total subservience to her Mistress's strange desires. This is the fifth volume in the highly popular 'Emma' series.

Web of Domination by Yvonne Strickland

May 1997   Price £4.99   ISBN: 0 352 33154 2

The Villa Rafaelo in Tuscany caters for the special tastes of guests keen to make use of their fully equipped dungeon and the other bizarre delights on offer. All goes well until three young travellers lose their way and see things they were never intended to see. The secrets of the villa must be guarded, and the three become pawns in a game of lust and perversion guaranteed to ensure humiliation and silence.

There are three Nexus titles published in June

Citadel of Servitude by Aran Ashe

June 1997   Price £4.99   ISBN: 0352 33155 0

Tormunil: the mysterious citadel of erotic mastery from which there can be no escape. In the Citadel of servitude, every avenue of sexual love must be tested, every strange pleasure explored, and every taboo broken.

Virginia's Quest by Katrina Young

June 1997   Price £4.99   ISBN: 0352 33173 9

Virginia has led a sheltered life until she meets her naughty French cousin Symonne, who teaches her the arts of sensual pleasure. The watchful eye of her cousin ensures that she has remained a virgin: but she now seeks defiantly to lose her virginity and sate her prodigious sexual needs in whichever ways will bring her the greatest pleasure.

Eroticon 2 Forbidden writings from classic texts
June 1997   Price £4.99   ISBN: 0352 31862 7
Like its companion volumes, this unmissable collection of notorious writings from forbidden texts features some of the finest erotic prose ever written. In its variety of people and practices, of settings and sexual behaviours, this exhilarating anthology provides the true connoisseur with the flavour of a dozen controversial works. Don't miss *Eroticon 1*, *3* and *4*, also from Nexus.

There are three Black Lace titles published in May

Avenging Angels by Roxanne Carr
May 1997   Price £4.99   ISBN: 0 352 33147 X
Karen is dismayed by the lack of respect shown to women in the sun
and sex-soaked Tierra del Sol holiday resort, and decides to tackle
the problem by becoming a dominatrix – with surprising results.
There is only one man in the resort who will not succumb to her
charms – and this is the one man she must have, at any price.

The Lion Lover by Mercedes Kelly
May 1997   Price £4.99   ISBN: 0 352 33162 3
When the darkly sensual missionary McKinnon tires of his women,
he sends them to a Sultan's harem. Mathilde Valentine, a medic in
his East African mission post, is warned to be wary of her new em-
ployer, but ignores the advice and soon has to accomodate the lusts
of the demanding Sultan, his sadistic brother and his naive son.
Meanwhile Olensky, her 'lion lover', is plotting her escape. Will he
succeed?

Past Passions: an anthology of erotic fiction by women
May 1997   Price £4.99   ISBN: 0 352 33159 3
This unique anthology features historical fantasies from the female
sexual imagination. Bizarre sexual excesses from days gone by collide
with worlds of secluded passion and scintillating characters delight in
the thrill of total surrender to pleasure and decadent indulgence.

Jasmine Blossoms by Sylvie Ouellette
June 1997   Price £4.99   ISBN: 0352 33157 7
When Joanna is sent on a business trip to Japan, she does not expect
that her sensuality will be put to the test. She is constantly aroused
but never entirely sated by strangers who seem to know her every
desire, and soon finds herself involved in a case of mistaken identity,
erotic intrigue and mysterious seduction.

Pandora's Box 2

June 1997   Price £5.99   ISBN: 0352 33151 8

This is the second of the highly popular Pandora's Box anthologies of erotic writing by women, containing extracts from the best-selling titles of the Black Lace series, as well as four completely new stories. The diversity of the material is a testament to the unashamed nature of the female erotic imagination.

NEXUS BACKLIST

All books are priced £4.99 unless another price is given. If a date is supplied, the book in question will not be available until that month in 1997.

CONTEMPORARY EROTICA

AGONY AUNT	G. C. Scott	Jul
ALLISON'S AWAKENING	John Angus	Jul
BOUND TO SERVE	Amanda Ware	
BOUND TO SUBMIT	Amanda Ware	Sep
CANDIDA'S SECRET MISSION	Virginia LaSalle	
CANDY IN CAPTIVITY	Arabella Knight	
CHALICE OF DELIGHTS	Katrina Young	
THE CHASTE LEGACY	Susanna Hughes	
CHRISTINA WISHED	Gene Craven	
CONDUCT UNBECOMING	Arabella Knight	
DARK DESIRES	Maria del Rey	
DIFFERENT STROKES	Sarah Veitch	
THE DOMINO TATTOO	Cyrian Amberlake	
THE DOMINO ENIGMA	Cyrian Amberlake	
THE DOMINO QUEEN	Cyrian Amberlake	
EDEN UNVEILED	Maria del Rey	
EDUCATING ELLA	Stephen Ferris	Aug
ELAINE	Stephen Ferris	
EMMA'S SECRET WORLD	Hilary James	
EMMA ENSLAVED	Hilary James	
EMMA'S SECRET DIARIES	Hilary James	
EMMA'S SUBMISSION	Hilary James	
EMMA'S HUMILIATION	Hilary James	May
FALLEN ANGELS	Kendal Grahame	

RUE MARQUIS DE SADE	Morgana Baron	
SERVING TIME	Sarah Veitch	
SHERRIE	Evelyn Culber	
STEPHANIE'S CASTLE	Susanna Hughes	
STEPHANIE'S REVENGE	Susanna Hughes	
STEPHANIE'S DOMAIN	Susanna Hughes	
STEPHANIE'S TRIAL	Susanna Hughes	
STEPHANIE'S PLEASURE	Susanna Hughes	
SUSIE IN SERVITUDE	Arabella Knight	Mar
THE TEACHING OF FAITH	Elizabeth Bruce	
FAITH IN THE STABLES	Elizabeth Bruce	
THE TRAINING GROUNDS	Sarah Veitch	
VIRGINIA'S QUEST	Katrina Young	Jun
WEB OF DOMINATION	Yvonne Strickland	May

EROTIC SCIENCE FICTION

ADVENTURES IN THE PLEASUREZONE	Delaney Silver	
RETURN TO THE PLEASUREZONE	Delaney Silver	
FANTASYWORLD	Larry Stern	

ANCIENT & FANTASY SETTINGS

CAPTIVES OF ARGAN	Stephen Ferris	Mar
CITADEL OF SERVITUDE	Aran Ashe	Jun
THE CLOAK OF APHRODITE	Kendal Grahame	
DEMONIA	Kendal Grahame	
NYMPHS OF DIONYSUS	Susan Tinoff	Apr
PYRAMID OF DELIGHTS	Kendal Grahame	
THE SLAVE OF LIDIR	Aran Ashe	
THE DUNGEONS OF LIDIR	Aran Ashe	
THE FOREST OF BONDAGE	Aran Ashe	
PLEASURE ISLAND	Aran Ashe	
WARRIOR WOMEN	Stephen Ferris	
WITCH QUEEN OF VIXANIA	Morgana Baron	
SLAVE-MISTRESS OF VIXANIA	Morgana Baron	

EDWARDIAN, VICTORIAN & OLDER EROTICA

ANNIE AND THE SOCIETY	Evelyn Culber	
ANNIE'S FURTHER EDUCATION	Evelyn Culber	
BEATRICE	Anonymous	
BLUE ANGEL SECRETS	Margarete von Falkensee	
CHOOSING LOVERS FOR JUSTINE	Aran Ashe	
DEAR FANNY	Aran Ashe	
LYDIA IN THE HAREM	Philippa Masters	
LYDIA IN THE BORDELLO	Philippa Masters	
MADAM LYDIA	Philippa Masters	
MAN WITH A MAID 3	Anonymous	
MEMOIRS OF A CORNISH GOVERNESS	Yolanda Celbridge	
THE GOVERNESS ABROAD	Yolanda Celbridge	
PLEASING THEM	William Doughty	
RETURN TO THE MANOR	Barbra Baron	

SAMPLERS & COLLECTIONS

EROTICON 1 – CLASSIC EROTICA		Mar
EROTICON 2 – CLASSIC EROTICA		Jun
EROTICON 3 – CLASSIC EROTICA		Sep
NEW EROTICA 2	ed. Esme Ombreaux	

Please send me the books I have ticked above.

Name   ....

Address   ....

             ....

             ....

             .... Post code ....

Send to: **Cash Sales, Nexus Books, 332 Ladbroke Grove, London W10 5AH**

Please enclose a cheque or postal order, made payable to Virgin Publishing, to the value of the books you have ordered plus postage and packing costs as follows:

UK and BFPO – £1.00 for the first book, 50p for each subsequent book.

Overseas (including Republic of Ireland) – £2.00 for the first book, £1.00 for each subsequent book.

If you would prefer to pay by VISA or ACCESS/MASTER-CARD, please write your card number and expiry date here:

....

Please allow up to 28 days for delivery.

Signature   ....